A HORRIBLE COINCIDENCE

"Terrible tragedy here last night. I don't suppose you've heard."

"No," I said, and something subliminal warned me that this was the reason why Turner was talking to me, that this entire meeting had not been simple chance.

"It happened right down past where you're camping, at the Blackley place. I thought you might have heard something during the night."

He waited until I answered, and I had an instinctive urge not to reveal anything I'd heard or seen. "Not that I remember. What happened?"

"William Blackley, a fine, decent man, apparently had some kind of a breakdown. Took down his shotgun and killed his wife, then himself. The daughter's missing. Either he killed her as well and hid the body, or she ran off in shock. Wouldn't be surprised if she was scared right out of her wits, hallucinating or worse. If you see anything funny out that way, I'd appreciate it if you'd pass word on to myself or the local police. Funeral's tomorrow. Closed casket, of course."

I was shocked but tried, probably without success, to keep my feelings out of my face. I had talked to those people yesterday and now they were dead, and I had the sudden uneasy, unjustifiable feeling that perhaps they were dead exactly because I had talked to them. . . .

SERVANTS
OF CHAOS

DON D'AMMASSA

LEISURE BOOKS NEW YORK CITY

For Sheila,
whose patience with my obsessions
has been phenomenal.

A LEISURE BOOK®

December 2002

Published by

Dorchester Publishing Co., Inc.
276 Fifth Avenue
New York, NY 10001

ISBN 0-8439-5069-2

The name "Leisure Books" and the stylized "L" with design are trademarks of Dorchester Publishing Co., Inc.

Printed in the United States of America.

Visit us on the web at www.dorchesterpub.com.

SERVANTS
OF CHAOS

Chapter One

My first impression of the town of Crayport was that it was trapped in perpetual autumn. Dried leaves blew across the desiccated grass, where it grew in the sandy soil and accumulated in odd corners, forming dark, slowly rotting piles. The unfallen leaves were tinted as well, predominantly green but with the edges already showing signs of yellowing, even though it was only July. I know that sometimes this happens when trees near a major highway are stressed by the constant exhaust fumes from automobiles, but traffic in Crayport was, to say the least, minimal. I assumed the condition was a consequence of high levels of acidity in the soil and let my thoughts and my eyes travel farther ahead, where the road twisted its way through scrub-covered hills to what was surely the least visited town on the seaboard.

Evidence of the blight mounted as I grew closer to my destination. The open spaces were draped with limp, pale grass that seemed to wilt in the sunlight. Wildflowers were scarce and provided no break from the monotonous pale greens and bleached yellows. There were wooded areas, some of them quite thick and extensive, but I saw a disproportionate number that were clearly dead, their twisted limbs denuded of leaves. Those that lived stood in contorted poses, their limbs frequently deformed into bonsai parodies. The only plantlife that grew in profusion everywhere were the vines, thick stemmed and studded with thorns, their enthusiastic, contorted forms strangling trees and lesser bushes, sending feelers across the open meadows, overwhelming the rare stand of fence or other evidence of human activity. For the last half hour before I reached the outskirts of Crayport, I saw only one highway sign, and not a single advertisement. Perhaps so few traveled this road that it was not worth the investment.

Downtown Crayport consisted of one narrow central avenue with five cross streets, only two of which were paved, one at each end. Almost every building along this stretch was a business of some sort—groceries, hardware, two diners, drug store, laundromat, general store, post office, tiny bank, fish and tackle and bait, a locksmith that appeared to have closed permanently, a handful of professionals—lawyer, doctor, dentist. None of the names was familiar. There were no golden arches or any other recognizable chain stores, no hotels, no car rental agencies, no real estate office. I also noticed that there were no churches, and with a population officially hovering just under 600, Crayport should have had at least a couple. The nearest town was forty minutes away in good weather, over bad roads.

The buildings were without exception aging, poorly kept up, and uninviting. Many of the signs had faded to illegibility. I noticed at least one broken window in every block, and it had been so long since fresh paint had been applied that in many cases I could actually see the base wood of the walls. The sidewalks were cobblestone, but wire thin weeds had sprung up in the interstices nearly everywhere, and bone-white beach sand had blown or washed up from the nearby waterfront and formed eddies of lifelessness where it covered the ground. There was a handful of pedestrians walking about when I drove into town that first morning, and they were as drab and colorless as their surroundings, dressed in unseasonably heavy clothing that covered them from head to foot, drab colors and styles long since passed. A few heads turned in my direction, but curiosity seemed as rare as paint in Crayport, and most ignored me as I drove through, my trailer bumping along behind me.

My name is Steven Canfort and I'd been assigned—I'm tempted to say exiled—to Crayport to evaluate it as a possible site for a small marine research station. The town is located on a lonely stretch of coast just north of Plymouth, next to a small but serviceable harbor that has somehow managed to escape being developed along with the rest of the Northeast. Indeed, Crayport was suspended in time in many ways; water samples taken during the spring by a student from the University of Rhode Island had been so atypical that she had dwelt under a cloud of suspicion until her results were confirmed by an independent survey. The water in Crayport Harbor was lower in man-made pollutants than anywhere else in the Northeast, although purely natural biological waste was at unusually high levels.

Jane Lemmon, my boss, had made efforts to find lodging for me for the estimated month I'd be on site, but without success. There was a scattering of cottages in the rolling hills surrounding the town proper, several of them untenanted, but in many cases it was impossible to locate the legal owner, and in those instances where it was, no one was able, or at any event willing, to rent me so much as a shack, let alone an actual room. So Jane twisted arms at the Sheffield Institute and in due course an aging, two-room-and-a-bath mobile home had been placed at my disposal. Fully briefed and with a detailed, but as it turned out not entirely accurate map, I'd set off at 4:00 A.M. on a Monday morning, armed with letters of authorization allowing me to camp along the portion of beach that stretched from the south end of the waterfront to the tip of Sawblade Point.

I cataloged the businesses as I drove through town. I carried enough supplies for a week or two in the trailer, but I'd need fresh milk and other foodstuffs before the end of the week. My refrigerator was tiny and my appetite for fresh vegetables enormous. In due course I would discover that what passed for "fresh" produce in Crayport would have been discarded from the major chain groceries as unsaleable. Even the fish was invariably past its prime, although the town supposedly had an active fishing industry. Certainly I could see the masts of at least half a dozen vessels nestled next to the docks, and not one of them was a pleasure ship, unless the locals enjoyed wading in filthy bilge water, leaning against bulkheads matted with seagull shit, or swimming alongside hulls that had barnacles growing on other barnacles, generation upon generation. The streets bore no signs, but I'd been given directions to Turner House, where I was supposed to check in with Jared Turner, the town manager. It was the last of the unpaved crossroads, but the clearance was so restricted that I pulled over to the curb and parked, preferring to walk the last block or two rather than attempt to negotiate the turn.

When I stepped out of the air-conditioned car, I almost gasped. The pungent air struck me like a physical blow and the next several breaths were quite literally painful. There was salt in it,

of course, but also the reek of fish—rotten fish—
and something else as well, equally rancid but
less identifiable. There was also a hint of ozone,
and I glanced up at the sky, startled to realize that
thunderheads were rolling in from the sea. Half
an hour earlier, there'd been nothing more than
some white streamers of cloud slowly scudding
across the sky, and the radio had forecast clear
skies until late in the week. Now great billowing
masses of dark gray boiled against one another
as though battling for control of the heavens.

I found Turner House with no difficulty since
it had one of the few legible signs in town. It was
a single-story structure with faded cedar shingles
broken by a very few slit windows that couldn't
possibly have let in much light even if it had
stood out in the open. Sandwiched as it was between a commercial block and a much larger
building, the latter boarded up and apparently
abandoned, Turner House dwelt in almost perpetual shadow. The porch steps creaked a protest
under my weight, but the wood held, and a moment later I was knocking on the door. Doorbells,
I was to discover, were a newfangled invention
that Crayport had yet to embrace. There was no
light spilling out from either visible window, and
after a full minute had passed with no response,
I knocked again, with more force if not enthusiasm. More time passed, and I had half turned
away when I heard a sound from within, a faint
scratching at first, then a softer but persistent rustling as though someone was dragging a sack

across the floor. I had raised my hand to knock a third time when there was the click of a disengaging lock, the knob turned, and the door began to open.

Jared Turner was not the most prepossessing man I'd ever seen. He was even shorter than I, probably five foot four if he stood upright, which he seemed disinclined to do. My first sight of him in fact was the top of his head, a speckled bald patch surrounded by a swirl of dirty gray hair that clumped raggedly around each ear. I stepped back instinctively as he thrust through the door. He was fat although not obscenely so, his body massive but obviously soft, covered by a dirty green fisherman's sweater that looked uncomfortably warm and trousers that were perhaps a size or two smaller than they should have been. Turner raised his head to face me and I instinctively disliked him—large, protuberant eyes, a thin nose, his mouth twisted by a faint scar into an expression of permanent distaste.

"Yes?"

"My name's Steven Canfort. I'm looking for Mr. Turner."

"That would be me."

He didn't sound particularly pleased, but I extended my hand anyway. After a momentary hesitation, he took it in his. It took a positive act of will for me not to flinch away from his touch. His fingers were thick and tubular, pale as death, and they felt soft, cool, and clammy. It was as though I were clutching a handful of frog's legs, and I immediately christened them frog fingers in my mind. Concealing my distaste, I shook his hand vigorously, until he withdrew it suddenly. I had the strangest feeling that he found my touch every bit as distasteful as I did his. "I believe Ms. Lemmon has spoken to you about me."

"She did. Waste of time, to my way of thinking. There's nothing here worth the bother of studying. We're just plain people living in a plain town, and we don't need any outsiders stirring things up."

I'd been warned to expect some opposition, but his fierceness put me immediately on the defensive. "Yes, well, it isn't the town we're interested in, you understand. Believe me, once the station is in place, you'll hardly know we're there."

"There's no one here likely to sell you land, though I don't suppose you'll believe me without asking around for yourself."

I had expected to be invited inside, but Turner showed no inclination to extend an invitation. "Jane, Ms. Lemmon, said you'd have some information for me. Names of the local landowners, a map of the town."

"That's what she asked for. I'll get them for you." And he left me standing there while he disappeared back indoors, appearing a few seconds later with a spiral notebook. "It's all in here. You're wasting your time, though."

I ignored his truculent manner as best I could, kept my voice level. "I'll be camping up near

Sawblade Point. Is there anything I need to know?" His attitude was beginning to annoy me and I'm sure some of my irritation was obvious, but it had no discernible impact on Turner.

"I wouldn't go wandering about. There're some sinkholes near the shore. And some people don't take kindly to having strangers poking around on their property without their say-so. Outsiders upset things, make people nervous."

"I'll keep it in mind." There was no warmth remaining in my voice. Turner was clearly as unhappy about having me in his town as I was to be there. Perhaps more so. I'd at least made an effort to be amicable, although I couldn't resist a mild retaliation. "The coastline from Troll Rock to Sawblade Point is all publicly owned, after all. I don't really need anyone's permission to be there."

For the first time Turner's eyes met mine, and there was a hint of something hard there. "That's as may be, but we're a long way from Boston, and Boston's rules don't always take priority here. This is our town, Mr. Canfort. We're not beholden to the outside, which means we don't have much to do with the state government. And as you probably noticed from the condition of the road on your way in, the state doesn't have much to do with us either. We know the laws, but there's always some flexibility in how they're applied."

It was so clearly meant as a threat that I was still floundering for a reply when Turner wished me a gruff "Good day" and disappeared inside without waiting for me to respond.

My stomach was still churning when I reached Sawblade Point and only settled down when I had trouble unhitching the trailer from the back of the car. It took much longer than it should have, I banged my thumb in the process, and when I was finally done, my anger at the inanimate had overcome my frustration with the animate. Fortunately, I managed to dismount the canoe from the roof without too much trouble, which almost restored my good humor, and the small generator started up on the second try, so I had power. I had found a relatively sheltered spot just seaward of a small, rocky hill. A flow of sand dunes separated me from the ocean, which was close enough that I could hear the breaking surf, a sound I've always found relaxing. Less pleasing was the horde of gulls who were hovering about, hoping for a handout or something they could steal, walking stiff-legged around me as I worked, just beyond reach, or perching on the roof of the trailer. I puttered around in my tiny kitchen for a few minutes, unstowing items that I'd secured for the trip, while they walked around over my head, their feet making tiny clicking noises on the metal roof.

By the time I had finished, it was getting to be late in the afternoon, so I decided to take the car and do a small grand tour while there was still light enough to see. Turner's promised map was hand-drawn in sections on various pages of the notebook he'd given me. The different sections were not to the same scale, were arranged in the wrong order, and I suspected that parts of the community had been omitted entirely. The list of local landowners with waterfront property only contained a dozen names, and I suspected that it was similarly incomplete. Turner might not be an active obstruction, but he was clearly not going to do anything more than was absolutely necessary to help me move forward with this project. I'd been warned that Crayport was insular, but if he was a representative sample of the local population, I suspected *xenophobic* would be a more accurate description.

Sawblade Point was near the southern end of the area in which I was interested. Just a bit farther south was a parcel of beachfront property owned by the Blackley family, beyond which the land curved out to enfold the harbor, steepening into ragged hills that discouraged development and that were in any case set aside as a wildlife preserve. The Blackleys were one of my high-priority contacts. After deciphering Turner's cryptic notes, I identified eight more families who had holdings between Sawblade Point and the town pier, four on each side of Saltcrest Road, which wound up into the surrounding hills, where a handful of marginal farms concealed themselves. The bulk of the population lived in clusters around the periphery of the small commercial district. Only three of the shoreline holdings were large enough to house the facility that was planned, the properties owned by the Thornes, the Harfords, and the Jensons. I had made mental notes of each as I drove past, noting that all three had large, deteriorating homes that reflected the general malaise of Crayport. Turner's predictions notwithstanding, I suspected that none of these three families was in a position to reject a generous cash offer out of hand, although I had no idea how generous the institute was willing to be. My job was to evaluate the viability of the sites, make some preliminary contacts, and then report back. Unless I discovered some unanticipated problem, the lawyers would take over from there and negotiate the actual purchase.

I turned south on Shoreline Road and did a quick reconnoiter of the Blackley house, which was large and rambling and set atop a truncated hill overlooking the water. There were no signs of life. Shoreline Road ended just past the house, so I turned around and headed back. The Thorne and Harford holdings were south of Troll Rock, a mildly spectacular pinnacle of convoluted stone jutting up out of the water, and the Jenson house stood slightly beyond to the north. When I reached the town pier I slowed, then continued northward rather than turning left into the shabby downtown. The buildings quickly thinned out to my left as I passed the small town beach, which was completely deserted despite the warm weather. There were a few more homes along the north branch of Shoreline Road, but only one of them was big enough to interest me, the Caspar place. It was no different than the ones I'd seen earlier, except that its architecture was even more chaotic. At least four additions had been made to the main house over the years, each in a different style.

The road continued up into the steep hills that blurred into foreboding cliffs that serrated the northern loop of the harbor. The Crawley family owned most of this area, including a small, undeveloped island within the harbor, but they were not on my list of prime prospects. Their shore holdings were too rugged to be of any use, and the island was exposed and impractical to supply, although it hadn't been entirely ruled out. On my to-do list was a visit to the island, if I could secure the Crawleys' permission, but it was not a particularly high priority. I reversed course before reaching the Crawley home, which is where the road ended, and this time turned into the downtown. It was nearly six o'clock, and I was hungry.

The storm clouds still loomed large overhead, chasing each other across the sky, and a fairly stiff breeze had sprung up, but so far the rain had held off. The few pedestrians I'd seen earlier had disappeared entirely now, and I felt as though I was driving through a Hollywood movie set. There were only a handful of streetlights, and they hadn't been turned on, so shadows filled the streets, only rarely dispersed by lights from inside the buildings.

There were two diners in town, only one of

which was open. It was innovatively named "Diner" and consisted of six booths and twelve counter stools. One booth was occupied by two elderly men who hid behind bushy beards and large cups of coffee. A middle-aged woman was sitting at the counter as I entered, but she left almost immediately. There were no other customers. I took a stool and waited while the waitress, a tall, thin women with thready blond hair, loitered in my direction.

"Coffee, please. Black." She turned without a word and began pouring a cup. I glanced to either side, saw no menus. Several choices were chalked on a blackboard behind the counter, none with prices listed.

The waitress placed the cup in front of me and had half turned away before I stopped her. "What's good today?"

"The chili's pretty good. Fish chowder's a little off, but not too bad." She waited expectantly while I glanced back at the board.

"All right. I'll have a small bowl of fish chowder and an order of chili."

I made a couple more desultory efforts at conversation while she was serving the food, but her responses consisted of shrugs and monosyllables. There didn't seem to be anything specifically unfriendly in her demeanor; she just wasn't interested. Halfway through my meal, the two bearded men left, without a word to the waitress. I assumed they'd already paid since I didn't notice any money in the booth while the waitress was clearing, not even a tip. She thanked me when I paid for my own, and blinked with what appeared to be confusion when I told her to keep the change. By that point I was reconciled to doing most of my own cooking during my stay in Crayport. The chili was mediocre and the fish chowder had been quite a way "off."

Despite the fact that it was still early, I decided to return to my trailer, organize my papers and my thoughts, and call it a day. Although the clouds were starting to thin and let a little of the waning sunlight through, the oppressive atmosphere in Crayport had already enervated me, and I was not looking forward to what my boss had laughingly called a "working vacation." On the way back I counted the fishing vessels in port, eight of them with two empty slips, and wondered why they hadn't gone to sea today. Or perhaps they had already been out and were back, although I saw no evidence of fish on any of the boats or the pier itself. I noticed once again the unusual absence of human activity. No one worked on the boats or the docks, and I passed only two people in the center of town. There was no one at all along Shoreline Road, even though there were several houses along the way. I thought about taking a short detour up Saltcrest, but the road looked to be in very bad condition and I decided to put it off until another day.

The trailer was as I had left it, or almost as I had left it, including the troupe of importunate gulls, who greeted me with squawks, haughty looks, and impatient wing flapping. They hadn't been the only visitors during my absence. There were footprints in the drifting sand that clearly were not mine. Booted feet, considerably larger than my tracks. One set came from the south, somewhere back toward the Blackley holding. Whoever it had been had done an elaborate circumlocution of my trailer, never coming closer than about ten meters, then returned the way they'd come. The second set of tracks were much smaller, possibly a small woman or a child. This person had been bolder, walking directly from the road. His or her tracks were more extensive; they'd checked the trailer from every angle. There were clusters of them under each of the two small windows, although I doubted that anyone could have discerned much through the thick curtains. The smaller of my two visitors had then departed by way of the beach, the tracks disappearing where the water had washed the sand clear and smooth.

There was nothing particularly sinister about it. I was, after all, a stranger in a remote town. My presence was certain to arouse curiosity. But even so, I felt oddly uneasy and didn't get to sleep nearly as easily as I'd expected.

Nor did I sleep through the night undisturbed.

I've never been a very heavy sleeper. Alyson, whom I was already missing very much, could sleep through an earthquake, but I wake up if a car passes on the road below my apartment window. Repetitive sounds don't disturb me—the crying of wind, the pounding of surf, the rumbling of traffic on the nearby interstate. But a vehicle driving down a side street late at night, a neighbor calling to a dog in the early morning, sometimes even a sudden change in the breathing pattern of whoever is sharing my bed—all are sufficient to waken me, at least for a moment. Perhaps this explains why I seem to dream so infrequently; I rarely descend deep enough into sleep for my subconscious to have a fair chance of seizing control.

As is generally the case, I had no idea what specifically had wakened me. I lay in the narrow bed without moving, staring up at the shelf overhead, waiting for whatever it was to recur. A minute or two passed, and I felt myself fading back into unconsciousness. Then it came again, almost the sound of water rolling over a beach. Almost. I was wide awake, straining to hear the sound that was almost but not quite identifiable. After a few seconds it repeated itself, although it seemed fainter now, more distant. It was as if some enormous object were being dragged across the beach below me, a wet rasp. The disturbance lasted only a few seconds, then stopped. I rose onto my elbows, waiting, and after approximately two minutes it came again, more distant yet. In retrospect, I'm tempted to say there was a stealthy quality to the sound, but that was not the case.

Curious but not alarmed, I climbed out of bed,

stretched muscles that complained about the uncomfortable mattress, and walked across the narrow trailer. The sky was clear and cool, the moon a soft glowing light that pressed against the windows. I swept the seaside curtain aside and glanced out, stifling a yawn with the back of my hand. There was sufficient luminescence for me to see the white crests of the incoming waves. Nothing appeared to be moving along the pencil-thin beach, and I turned from side to side to increase my field of view, though with no better results. I had just turned away to return to bed when the sound came again, louder this time and close at hand, from somewhere north of the trailer.

I grabbed my pants from where I'd tossed them across a box of groceries, slipped them on, added a pair of sandals, and went outside. Despite the comparatively cool ocean breeze, it was still hot and muggy, and the air was full of thick, pungent sea smells. Salt, seaweed, and something slightly bitter that stung my nose for a few seconds until I adjusted to it. I skirted around the nearest dune and walked down to the waterline. It was unusually light outside considering the hour, which I later discovered to be just after 3:00 A.M. There was no movement except the steady impact of the waves, and a faint shivering of the scrub growth where it was disturbed by the breeze. For a second I thought I saw something flying low in the sky just off shore, the faintest hint of movement, but it was too large to be a bird, and no matter how closely I peered, I couldn't focus on anything, dismissing it finally as a trick of light. The only thing out of the ordinary that I could find at all was a shallow depression in the sand that extended from beyond the waterline up into the dunes themselves, a trough scooped out by some unknown force, probably a combination of wind and water, since it extended well above the high tide mark.

Or at least that's what I thought at the time.

The night disgorged no further mysteries and, feeling somewhat foolish now, I returned to bed, where I immediately fell asleep once more.

Chapter Two

My second day in Crayport was no less frustrating. I was up shortly after the sun rose, drank two cups of tea with my English muffins and jelly, and took a quick dip in the ocean in lieu of a shower. It was already quite hot, the heat rising visibly from the sand. The sea breeze provided some relief, and the air tasted strongly of salt. I examined the oversized furrow I'd discovered the night before, and it was still there, although part had been washed away and the night breeze had eroded the edges of what remained. By preference I'd have worn shorts and a T-shirt, but I was hoping to make a good impression on at least someone in this town, so I upgraded to a conservative sport shirt and some upscale jeans before

20

setting out to do the job that was responsible for my trip.

My first stop was the Harford homestead. Their house was a three-story, boxlike structure with a fake widow's walk facing the ocean. One of the third-floor windows was broken, and there were shingles missing from the roof. Like every other building in town, it needed a coat of paint, and the porch roof was canted at such an obviously perilous angle that I expected it to fall down at any time. The yard was a mess, rusting equipment scattered through grass that hadn't been cut since at least the previous summer, interspersed with hardier bushes and tangled mats of vines. The driveway was unpaved and the tufts of thick grass that grew there were daunting enough that I left the car near the road and walked the rest of the way. The Harfords owned a wedge of land with its widest side toward the water, their house at the opposite point. Our preliminary survey had indicated that they had the most desirable location, and the property was large enough that we could build our station without forcing them to relocate, so I was making a point of visiting them first.

No doorbell. I used the oversized brass knocker to pound on the door, feeling rather awkward while doing so. The sound seemed to be swallowed up by the interior of the house. I waited a moment or two and knocked again, with the same result. I tried peering in through the front windows, but one was shuttered and the other had the curtains drawn. Stepping off the porch, I walked around the side of the house to see if anyone was outside in the rear, but the back was if anything even more chaotic than the front, and strands of barbed wire scattered through the grass made walking treacherous.

I was halfway back down to the road when I felt that prickling sensation of being watched and turned abruptly, glancing back at the house. As I did so, I saw that the front curtain had now been pulled to one side. As soon as I noticed it, the gap vanished. Whoever had moved it had allowed it to fall back in place. For a moment I considered returning and knocking again, but somehow I knew it would be a wasted effort. A feeble old uncle, a child left alone, or possibly even a family pet. None would be of any use to me. It was a disappointing start, but I would be back.

The Thornes were next on my list, and here at last I had some luck, though hardly the kind I was looking for. Their house was smaller and marginally better maintained, although there was the same overall atmosphere of neglect and disorder. It was situated at the shoreward side of a square lot, just barely large enough to accommodate the facility we planned without infringing too much on the house itself. It was the least desirable of the properties we'd identified, but there remained the possibility of purchasing the entire plot of land and taking over the house as well, so we hadn't completely eliminated it.

The driveway was unpaved and deeply rutted, but I negotiated it with minimal bumping and jolting and parked alongside an aging Volkswagen Minibus whose sides were streaked with rust. There were no signs of life, and when I knocked on the door I halfway expected a repeat of my experience at the Harford house. But this time the door opened after almost no delay at all, revealing a heavily bearded, portly man who might have been a brother of the two I'd seen eating at Diner the previous evening.

"Hi, my name's Steven Canfort. I represent the Sheffield Maritime Institute. We're interested in opening a small monitoring station here in Crayport and I wondered if I could talk to someone about buying or leasing a portion of your land."

The man stared at me with absolutely no expression on his face. The moment stretched so far that I wondered if I should start over. But finally he spoke in what I at first thought was a strong accent but eventually realized was a speech impediment much like a cleft palate. "We're not selling," I interpreted. "Good day to you."

"We'd be willing to consider leasing the property . . ." I found myself speaking to a closed door. Mr. Thorne, if that's whom I'd spoken to, apparently considered the matter closed. I made a mental note to come back only as a last resort and returned to my car, thinking darkly of the consequences of generations of inbreeding.

The Jenson place was just past Saltcrest, facing Troll Rock. The property was shaped like a dumbbell with the family home at one end. The other knob was undeveloped and had the advantage of privacy because of a craggy hill that sat athwart the narrow piece of land in between. It was a bit smallish, but large enough in a pinch, and included quite a bit of actual waterfront. Another unpaved driveway threaded its way through waist-high grass, this one barred by a gate, so I parked, hopped the fence, and made my way to the house, which was, needless to say, in serious need of repair. It was obvious to me that what Crayport needed was an infusion of money, and that made it even more perplexing to me that everyone I'd encountered so far, including the town manager, Jared Turner, seemed genuinely hostile to the prospect of any outside investment.

As I was making my way toward the house, the front door opened and a woman came outside, walking toward a smaller outbuilding that I hadn't been able to see from the road. She clearly hadn't noticed me, so I called out to her as I approached. When she turned in my direction, I was startled by her expression, which seemed frozen in absolute shock. I had time to guess her age at no more than forty, although her hair was unkempt and prematurely gray. She was of medium build, her face was unusually round and full, and her hands, which she clutched to her breasts, seemed disproportionately large. Frog fingers, I thought, and then she was gone, running back toward the house and disappearing through the door she'd left open behind her.

I stopped where I was, uncertain how to proceed. I'd obviously spooked the woman, though I couldn't imagine why. I'd smiled and waved when she turned toward me, and I'm not large or ugly enough to be really intimidating. I had tentatively decided to proceed when two men, one fiftyish, the other about my own age, came out of the house, moving purposefully in my direction. I held my ground without advancing, kept a smile plastered on my face even though their expressions were uniformly grim. When they were close enough, I repeated the same introduction I'd tried at the Thorne house.

"You're on private property," said the older man in an absolutely level voice.

"I realize that, but you don't have a telephone." Almost no one in town had one, I'd discovered. Even some of the businesses had no listings. "I wanted to speak to you about purchasing some of your land."

"That's trespassing, being on someone else's property without their permission." It was the younger man this time, although the voice was indistinguishable from the other. "We could get the law on you."

"I don't mean to intrude, but I didn't know any other way to get hold of you."

"It would be best if you left now." It was the

25

older man again, and I had the uncanny feeling that neither of them had heard a word I'd said. They stopped about six feet away from me, the older man standing with his arms crossed, the younger with hands on hips. I noticed that his fingers were disproportionately thick and much paler than the rest of his skin, and wondered if there was some kind of genetic deformity common in Crayport, or if I was seeing the result of some common experience. It was a fishing community, and I knew the Jensons owned one of the fishing boats. Could this swelling be some kind of reaction to long periods of immersion in the local brine?

"If this is a bad time, I'd be happy to meet with you elsewhere or at another time. If you'd just let me make an appointment, I'd be able to explain our offer."

"My father asked you to leave," said the younger man, and this time there was more than a hint of animosity in his voice. "He doesn't like to have to repeat himself. Nor I don't either."

"Well, I'll be going then." I took a step backward as a gesture of my good intentions. "Can I come again at a better time, then?"

The younger man advanced two quick steps, his arms extended forward, and my eyes were drawn toward his hands, which clenched and unclenched spasmodically. His father caught him by the shoulder, but he never looked away from me.

"Best you be gone, stranger. Lest we help you on your way."

I didn't need an engraved disinvitation.

Obviously things could have gone better. I was too upset to continue to the Caspar house, which was next on my list. Instead I drove by the waterfront, counted eight boats in the ten slips, then turned and drove to Diner in search of coffee. Diner was closed, as was the other, unnamed diner two blocks away. I stopped at the post office and gave my name to a merely mildly surly clerk, telling him that I'd stop by from time to time to pick up any mail that was sent to me by general delivery. "We don't normally do things like that around here," he told me, but apparently couldn't think fast enough to find a justification for refusing. It was clear he would have preferred to do just that.

Frustrated, I drove back to the waterfront, turned left, and parked at the town beach, then walked down to the shore. It wasn't much of a beach, only a hundred meters wide, and even the shallow water was so full of small stones and broken shells that I couldn't imagine wading in it. As before, it was largely deserted, although an elderly man stood off at the far end, staring out over the water. He didn't look around and I doubted he knew I was there. There was a bitter smell in the air, which I assumed came from the fishing boats. It still irritated my nose, but not as badly as it had the day before. I guess I was becoming acclimatized. I walked aimlessly back and forth for a half hour, alternately staring at the sand and the water, trying to sweat off anger mixed with a hint of anxiety. The Jensons were the only ones who'd been overtly hostile, but I had a growing sense that the entire town was united against me. It occurred to me to wonder if Turner hadn't done some advance campaigning to prejudice his neighbors against me. I'd expected some reluctance to deal with an outsider, having grown up in the equally insular town of Managansett, but not open animosity.

I was ready to return to the car when I realized someone was watching me, spotted movement out of the corner of one eye. It was a young boy, probably ten or twelve years old, standing half concealed behind one of the supports of the town pier. He was wearing ragged cutoffs and a torn and badly stained T-shirt. His skin was burned dark by the sun and his arms and legs seemed unnaturally slender, as though he were suffering from malnutrition.

"Well, hello there!" I called out in as friendly a voice as I could manage, but carefully made no move in his direction.

Discovered, he stepped out into the open, but remained silent. He needed a haircut as well as a bath, I noticed. His eyes were dark and seemed planted unnaturally deep in his face. The mouth and chin were firm and unfrightened, surprisingly mature.

"My name's Steven," I offered. "I'm visiting for a few days." Suddenly I remembered the small footprints around my trailer and realized this was the first child I'd seen since arriving in Crayport. "Do you live around here?"

Stupid question, actually. Everyone in Crayport lived "around here."

"You're the one up on Sawblade Point, aren't you?"

"Yes. Was that you that came up to check me out yesterday?"

He didn't answer, just glanced back shoreward. "You planning to stay?"

"For a while. I'm looking for some land to buy. Know anybody who wants to sell?" I meant it as a joke, but the boy took me seriously.

"You don't want to live around here, mister. They won't let you." He turned and started to trudge back through the sand toward the road.

"Hey!" I called after him. "What's your name?"

He paused without looking back, as if considering whether or not my request was reasonable. "Sean," he answered at last, then resumed his trek without another word. I waited, bemused, until he vanished from sight, then returned to my work.

There was nobody home at the Caspar house, or at least no one answered my knock. If anything, their property was in worse condition than the rest. There was a pickup truck parked around the side, but all of the tires were flat and a crack in the windshield had spiderwebbed from top to bottom. The house had several broken windows and there were stray branches and bunches of dead leaves on the porch, which sagged alarmingly in one spot. It looked as though no one had lived there for a long time.

That exhausted my list of major prospects except for Crawley Island. My visual survey of the remaining shoreline hadn't suggested any new possibilities, and my initial attempt to approach the owners had left me depressed and uneasy. I planned to use the canoe to make an on-site inspection of the island, and only if that location looked promising would I approach the Crawleys about making an actual landing. I had been predisposed against even considering the island because of its logistical problems, but given the reaction to my initial efforts, it was starting to look as though I should reconsider. Based on my experience to date, the small staff might well prefer to be isolated from the local people by a band of water. One other remaining possibility was Sawblade Point itself, but there were other, perhaps insurmountable problems there because it was officially restricted from development by the Massachusetts Department of Environmental Management, and even if we could secure a variance, it would be expensive and time consuming.

The road surface improved dramatically once I was past the Caspar property. The pavement was narrow but had been resurfaced within the year. It became very steep very quickly and I had to downshift twice before I reached the first crest. The next half mile was a series of quick drops and rises through a rocky, heavily wooded area so overgrown with vines that I doubted it would be possible to hike through the area.

The Crawley place was larger and in better repair than anything else I'd seen in Crayport. The main house was sheltered in a ravine, and had been constructed straddling the bed of a narrow stream fed by runoff from the hills on either side. Smaller buildings were nestled against both ravine walls, and a wide ledge that was clearly artificial had been carved from one side, atop which stood a well-maintained utility building of considerable size with corrugated iron walls and no windows. This was all on the shoreward side of the road. There was a second, smaller house on the seaward side that crowded right up against the edge of the pavement. Adjacent to it was a stone-surfaced, wood-railed stairway that led down to a private pier that jutted out into the harbor. There was also a complicated structure of braces and cables that ran alongside the stairway, which resembled a ski jump cable car system. A large hook depended from a heavy chain near the upper end. It appeared that the Crawleys were either hauling something heavy up from the harbor, or perhaps sending something the other way. I enjoyed a brief moment of speculation about smugglers and drug dealers before deciding it was more likely used to haul small boats up out of the water in the event of storms.

The road deteriorated just past the house, and since I knew it came to an end a quarter mile farther on, I backed up and turned around in their driveway, which was not only paved but wide enough to accommodate three or even four cars abreast. No one came out to object, although I did notice someone moving up near the metal building. There was a large panel truck parked beside it, leased from a hauling company in Providence, although I didn't notice that at the time.

On the way back I impulsively stopped at the small cemetery at the north end of town. It was a large rectangle with the oldest graves near the front, the newest farthest from the road. As I wandered about, I noticed the same names over and over. Turners and Caspars, Thornes and Jensons, Abernathys and Blackleys, Wellesleys and Clarks, Harfords and Hewitts and Ryders and Hannigans. On impulse I searched for the most recent graves and there I found John and Martha Caspar, both of whom had died the previous year, along with their son, Sean, age eleven. No cause of death was listed, but obviously they must have met with some accident. The boy might have been a classmate of the Sean I'd met; they were about the same age. And then I remembered the tiny school building across the street from Turner House and realized that the local population was so small, the kids must have been grouped into at most two or three classes. Inevitably they would have known each other.

*   *   *

Diner was still closed, so I drove back to the trailer and made my own lunch, after first walking around to see if I'd had any more visitors. If so, they'd managed not to leave tracks this time. Even the gulls seemed to have abandoned me as a lost cause. I burned a couple of hamburgers and fixed myself a salad, ate it along with some of Pete's Wicked Ale from the cooler. I hadn't seen a package store in town, but I figured there must be one somewhere. I knew that if I had to live here all the time, I'd certainly need a steady source of alcohol.

After lunch I dragged the canoe down to the water, fetched my sample bag, and prepared to start the other part of my job here. Because of the peculiarities of the water quality, I was supposed to take small samples at different distances from shore at different times of the day. Although I lacked the equipment, as well as the expertise, to analyze these samples, I had instructions to ship them back to Providence every few days, where our lab would do the brain work. "It's not a big priority," Jane told me before I left, "but if you could find the time, we'd appreciate getting a jump on things." Which in Janetalk meant skip taking the samples only if you're in danger of your life, or you will be.

I spent a couple of hours taking the first set of samples. The harbor area was so sheltered that I could manage the canoe with no great difficulty. When I had checked off each and every item on my list, I packed everything securely and then began to paddle north toward Crawley Island. The town wharf was off to my left, and I counted the fishing boats, eight of them in the ten slips. Didn't they ever go out? No wonder the town was cash poor.

My muscles tightened up at first, but once I got the rhythm down, the exertion felt good. I was sweating heavily, but the heat wasn't enough to discourage me. The physical exertion helped soothe my frazzled nerves and I even admitted that, from a distance, Crayport was not without its charm. Even the acrid scent in the air bothered me less than it had.

The island loomed up suddenly because there was a low but thick mist that seemed to cling to it, reminding me of more than one cheap horror film. A few minutes later the effect was gone, and I suspected it was more of an optical illusion generated because the island lay so low in the water with its near shore covered by bright white sand that shimmered in the brilliant sunlight. The beach ended abruptly with a sharply eroded overhang fringed with tall, thick-stemmed grass of a particularly unattractive yellowish green. Beyond, stunted trees dotted the island, which swelled up to a cone in the center. I'd seen aerial photographs back in Boston and knew that it was a natural amphitheater with a hollow depression in the center, a product of wind and the occasional blustering storm, which often sent waves rolling from one end to the other.

It took another hour to circumnavigate the island, which presented much the same appearance from every angle. I noticed some activity near the Crawley pier; a small powerboat with at least two passengers was headed out to sea, but there were no other boats on the water. Someone was walking along the town beach, but it was too far for me to see if it might be Sean. My arms and shoulders were starting to hurt again at this point, so I pointed the nose of the canoe south and started back to Sawblade Point. By the time I arrived, after stopping several times for breathers, I was cursing myself for getting so ambitious on my first trip out. My arms and shoulders would be complaining all night.

I beached the canoe and dragged it right up to the trailer, then drove into town where, at last, I found Diner open. The menu was identical to the last time. So was the waitress. There also seemed to be two identical men sitting in the very same booth, although the beards made them so anonymous I couldn't tell for sure. This chili was no better than before, but I was ravenous this time and wolfed down two orders, although I passed on the soup. The waitress didn't seem surprised when I tipped her this time, but she didn't thank me either.

It was dark when I drove back to the trailer and, on an impulse, continued up the road. There were lights on at the Blackley house and I considered stopping, but I was tired, sore, and not exactly encouraged by my earlier experiences, so I turned around instead and returned to the trailer, where I found it easier to sleep than I had expected.

I am happy to say that if there were any strange sounds in the vicinity during the night that followed, I was far too deeply asleep to be aware of them.

Chapter Three

My third day in Crayport dawned overcast and blustery. I hadn't turned on the radio since arriving, so I'd missed the weather reports. I tried it now and eventually heard the bad news, intermittent rain and fog for the next forty-eight to seventy-two hours. Dandy. I had a quick breakfast and then wrote letters to the families I'd attempted to visit the previous day, requesting an appointment to discuss the purchase or lease of part or all of their property. I indicated my return address as general delivery, "or I can be reached at my trailer on Sawblade Point." I wrote to the Crawleys, explaining my purpose and asking for permission to make a quick physical survey of their island to appraise its suitability. I also wrote to the Blackleys but left that letter aside; I still

37

planned to make an unannounced visit first.

It was drizzling when I drove into town. Diner was closed, but the post office was open, and I paid the taciturn clerk for the stamps. I also inquired about a UPS pickup later in the week, when I would have the first package of samples ready, and the man reluctantly admitted that he could take care of that for me, "although they don't like coming way out here just to pick up one package." There was a pay phone just outside, the only one I'd seen in Crayport, so I decided to call my boss now. The hinges were stiff with rust and lack of use, there was no phone book, no printed instruction sheet, and the phone itself was practically an antique, but I managed to reach the operator and put through a collect call.

"I wondered when I'd be hearing from you."

"Good morning, Jane, and yes I'm fine, thanks. How are you?"

"Overworked, underpaid, and unappreciated. So what's the news?"

"Well, for one thing, the rumor that Crayport doesn't like outsiders was grossly understated. I haven't been tarred and feathered yet, but I've seen naked chickens in the neighborhood."

"Just turn on your boyish charm, Steven. By the end of the month I expect you to be elected mayor by acclaim. So have you talked to any of the landowners yet?"

I gave her a succinct and colorful report of the previous day's adventures, leaving out the frog fingers, strange sounds in the night, and other irrelevancies. "This is going to be a harder sell than we expected, Jane. This place reeks of inbreeding. They all look like cousins, and most of them probably are. And they don't like outsiders. Anyone stationed here should be eligible for hardship pay."

She ignored my whining. "You haven't talked to the Crawleys yet."

"No, but the island presents its own problems. You might check to see who's in charge of the Caspar estate. There's no one living there and it's possible the property has reverted to some distant relative who'd be more than happy to sell. Turner's notes claim the present ownership is unknown."

"I'll call the legal department. How about samples?"

"The first set is done, but it's gearing up to blow here for the next couple of days. If it clears, I'll go out."

"Don't bother. A storm will just stir things up and give us atypical results. Do the shore sampling if the weather's decent and put off the others until next week."

"All right. Anything else you'd like to tell me? Have I been reassigned out of this Third World enclave?"

"No, I'm afraid you're stuck there. Sorry. But take heart, I've just sent you a very nice present."

"I hope it's a bodyguard. I don't think these people like me."

"Well, sort of. You'll like it, though. I promise."

"All right. I'll call you back . . . when?"

"Today's what? Wednesday. Call me Monday morning unless something comes up before that. I'll try to have information on the Caspars by then."

"Will do." And I severed my only contact with the outside world by hanging up.

I checked out the local grocery store, imaginatively named Groceries, and picked through the produce section with something less than enthusiasm. I was able to find some acceptable cucumbers, radishes, carrots, and potatoes, although only the last would have passed muster at home. The lettuce was a complete write-off. All they had was iceberg, and it had not aged like fine wine. Only the mushrooms were notably good. They had a fair assortment of fish, but there was an unpleasant odor in that corner of the store that dissuaded me from trying any. None of the fruit looked remotely edible. I added a few canned goods, some relatively fresh bread, paid the preoccupied cashier, and drove back to the trailer, already plotting a provision run to Plymouth.

I stowed the groceries, waited out a half hour of heavy rain, then left again, this time determined to visit the Blackley family. The cloud cover was dark and heavy, and I was happy to see light pouring out of several windows when I rounded the curve and reached their property. The house wasn't far from the road and the driveway looked rough, so I pulled over to one side and parked. The rain had declined to a light misting, but there were standing pools of water that I had to navigate around in order to reach the house. There were the usual signs of decrepitude, but the yard was neat, the grass had been recently cut, and the car parked alongside the building was an older model but in good repair.

When I knocked, I felt a momentary urge to run back to the car, which I suppressed. There was a brief pause and the door opened, though only the few inches allowed by a security chain.

"Yes?" It was a woman's voice, low and tentative, her face almost completely obscured.

"My name's Steven Canfort. Would you be Mrs. Blackley?"

"Yes, I'm Edna Blackley. What can I do for you, Mr. Canfort?" She showed no inclination to unhook the chain. On the other hand, she hadn't ordered me off the property or threatened me, so I felt considerably heartened. In local terms, she was positively effusive.

"I've been sent to Crayport by the Sheffield Maritime Institute to negotiate the purchase of a parcel of land. I wondered if I might speak to you about your shorefront property."

There was a moment's pause during which I feared I'd lost her, but then she spoke in a firmer voice. "If you'll wait here a moment, I'll talk to my husband and see if he'd be willing to see you."

She left me standing on the porch, but compared to her neighbors, that was a model of good manners. Several minutes passed and I shifted my weight impatiently from foot to foot. The rain was picking up again, but the porch roof was sound and I didn't have anyplace else to be, so I waited. I could hear voices from somewhere inside, too indistinct to hear words, although it sounded quite animated. Then came a clattering from within and the door opened wide.

"Please come in, Mr. Canfort."

The interior was dim because the Blackleys had only two lamps lit, but even a cursory look told me these people took a lot more interest in their surroundings than did their neighbors. The room was neat and orderly, the furniture in good condition, the walls lined with neatly arranged photographs and paintings, most of them quite old.

Edna Blackley was a tall, slender woman of about forty who kept her hair pinned tightly to her skull. She wore an ankle-length dress with long sleeves that reminded me of the Puritan colonists. Her smile came and went, as though if felt uncomfortable on her face, and her eyes kept dancing around the room with what I felt sure was anxiety. Her husband, who introduced himself as William not Bill, was close to six feet tall, muscular, clean shaven and crewcutted. His Jimmy Stewart face was solemn but not unfriendly, and he had a nervous tic in his left eye. Their daughter also shook my hand briefly before moving to a chair from which she watched me intently for the rest of the time I was there, although she never spoke another word. Her name was Jennifer, she looked to be in her very late teens, and she was drop-dead gorgeous.

"Please sit down, Mr. Canfort. Can I make you some tea or coffee?"

I took the offered chair, admitted to a desire for coffee, and waited while William Blackley made himself comfortable at one end of an old-fashioned but well maintained couch. I was happy to notice that he, like his wife, had perfectly normal fingers, which I interpreted as another sign that this interview would go much differently than had the previous ones.

"Edna said you were interested in buying our property."

I summarized the plans of the Sheffield Institute and explained that I was their agent. "I'm not in a position to make you an actual offer yet, because we're looking at several different pieces of property. But I'm doing the preliminary negotiations and my recommendations will carry some weight."

Edna Blackley returned with my coffee, which was quite good. Neither of them joined me, though, which made me feel slightly awkward, though it passed quickly.

"Crayport has its eccentricities, Mr. Canfort." As if I hadn't noticed. "There's a great deal of resistance to the idea of selling to outsiders. The same families have lived here since colonial times. We've stayed largely isolated from the rest of the world, and most of my neighbors prefer that sense of insulation."

"I realize that there's concern about changing the town's character, but I assure you that there are no plans to build a major installation here. We're talking about a staff of three or four people, and they'll be rotating regularly. The structure will be low profile and, as much as possible, conform to the surrounding architectural style. You'll hardly know that we're around. Change is inevitable, Mr. Blackley. If we can't purchase an appropriate parcel of land, the institute will apply to the state to use Sawblade Point or the border of the wildlife refuge." This was a bluff, but I felt no remorse. "That would just delay things a few months, and then no one locally would profit from the situation."

The Blackleys exchanged looks, and I thought I glimpsed the passage of a great deal of secret, silent communication. Edna's face convulsed once with quickly suppressed enthusiasm, and her husband—after a momentary hesitation— seemed overcome by a sudden desire to be agreeable.

"And you'd be willing to buy outright, not just lease the place?"

"That's correct. But we do have budget limitations. What would you think would be a fair price?"

He named a figure that was slightly higher than the target we'd developed back in Providence, but not impossibly so.

"As I said before, I don't have the authority to actually offer you any money, but I will pass on that information. Unofficially, though, that's a bit high for three acres."

Blackley shook his head. "Six acres, Mr. Canfort. The property is six full acres, not counting the easement."

I realized then what he was talking about. "We're only interested in the undeveloped plot of land adjacent to Sawblade Point. As I mentioned, there'd be no problem with your continuing to live here. The station would be nearly invisible, and we'd be willing to plant trees to form a natural barrier, or take whatever reasonable steps would satisfy you."

Once again, his head moved back and forth. "All or nothing, Mr. Canfort. We'll sell, but only if you take the entire property." He licked his lips and glanced at his wife, who was sitting beside him with her hands in her lap, the fingers so tightly intertwined that I felt sympathetic pain. "And I might be willing to come down some on the price if we could resolve things fairly quickly. We'd . . . we'd like to relocate before the fall." His voice shook toward the last.

I nodded as if I understood, which I didn't think was true. "I'll speak to my boss within the next few days and possibly have an offer by early next week."

Edna Blackley looked briefly disheartened, but she recovered quickly. Her husband's expression never changed. I tried to sneak a look at Jennifer, but she was staring down into her lap and I couldn't read her expression.

"If that's the earliest, then we'll just have to wait and talk to you then."

I set my empty cup on the coffee table and started to rise. "It's been a pleasure speaking with you," I said with genuine warmth. "I hope to have some positive information soon." I had already decided to call Jane first thing in the morning. For whatever reason, the Blackleys were anxious to sell out, and to do so quickly. I was reasonably certain they'd accept the institute's first offer, and their property was one of the best on our list. It was a bit more isolated than the others, but based on my experience of the town of Crayport, we should move that from the minus to the plus side. The house could be used as living quarters for the staff, which would reduce construction costs for the station. There was a chance I could finish up this assignment within days and get back to Alyson, and civilization.

Mrs. Blackley saw me out, and I heard the chain engage before I was off the porch.

I was encouraged for the first time since arriving and even the thick, hot rain didn't completely dampen my mood. To be fair, I probably should have waited for a response to my letters before deciding the deal was done, but I felt no great inclination to go out of my way for the Harfords, the Thornes, the Jensons, or even the Crawleys, for that matter. The rain built steadily as I traced my way back to the trailer, and I sheltered inside, reading the latest P. D. James murder mystery until the weather and the third victim died off almost simultaneously early in the afternoon. WBZ reported no interesting news, but I was going stir crazy in that cramped space, so I drove into town and puttered around in the local drugstore, which unconventionally actually had a name—Liggett's, although the sign was so faded I didn't know if it applied any longer. Then two cups of rather bitter coffee at Diner, served by the same waitress, during which the rain increased once again to torrential proportions.

It grew even stronger as I made my way down Shoreline Road, waves of heavy rain coming in across the water in sheets that splattered against the first obstruction they hit on land, all too frequently my car. I slowed to a virtual crawl, my headlights and wipers useless, and actually stopped three times when I could no longer see the road ahead. The ten-minute drive I was used to took nearly an hour, and I was as exhausted as if I'd been driving all day, the muscles in the back of my neck so tense they felt like taut ropes. There was standing water where I usually parked, so I angled around to the other side of the trailer, which is the only reason I saw that there was another vehicle parked a few meters away, between two small dunes. It would have been invisible from the other side of the trailer.

It was too dark and rainy to see the car clearly, and I wondered if someone else was camped out nearby. Crayport was hardly what I would call a tourist spot, but Sawblade Point was listed as a free camping area, so it wasn't entirely unreasonable that someone on an economy vacation might go out of his or her way to avoid paying for a commercial site. It was a bit of a coincidence, but a happy one if the newcomers turned out to be more pleasant company than the locals. A nice, friendly ax murderer would be a positively pleasant diversion.

I was curious, but not sufficiently so to brave the storm. As it was, I was thoroughly drenched crossing the fifteen feet or so between my car and the trailer door. I hadn't bothered to lock it, so I was inside in a split second, dripping wet and out of breath.

I was stripping off my sodden clothes when some subliminal sense warned me that I wasn't alone and I turned to see a figure standing in the shadows at the far end of the trailer, apparently watching as I disrobed.

I paused with my pants halfway over my hips, groping for an appropriate course of action. Should I turn and run for help? Were my car keys in my pocket, or had I tossed them on the counter as I usually did? Before I could act, my mysterious visitor stole the initiative by reaching out and flicking on the interior lights.

"Wow! What I wouldn't give for a camera right about now."

"Alyson!" I stumbled forward, my pants

dropped down below my knees, and I nearly toppled to the floor. "What the hell are you doing
here?"

"And I'm glad to see you too."

Alyson Branford wasn't the reason I had taken
the job with the Sheffield Institute, although she
certainly provided a strong incentive for remaining there. She was a highly skilled lab technician
who had quickly become unofficial second in
command to Dr. Anthony, head of the organics
laboratory. We'd met in the course of our work
several times before we actually dealt with one
another as people, and my impression for a long
time was that she was just another in the ongoing
stream of short-term employees, of average looks
and intelligence. On the few occasions when
we'd actually spoken, the conversation had been
brief, professional, and toneless. I don't think we
made eye contact once during the first six
months she worked for the institute. If asked my
impression at the time, I'd probably have found
a polite way to call her an introvert with few in-
terests outside her work, destined to remain single unless she met an equally colorless co-worker
whose blandness complemented her own.

I had discovered my error the previous summer at the annual outing. The institute owned
most of Hawk Island out in Narragansett Bay, a
gift of the Sheffield family some years earlier,
which they had maintained largely undeveloped.
There was a small beach not far from the main
house, with a serviceable pier, but the rest of the

land was heavily wooded. The old stone walls that originally divided the island into three main and numerous subplots were in poor repair and provided no real barrier, and the one parcel still owned by another party was an infrequently used cabin on the opposite side of the island.

There were about fifty of us attending, staff and family, a lower than usual turnout because of the heavy cloud cover that loomed overhead. Of that group, families made up all but four of us, and Nelson Rodriguez and Kerry Bridges had recently become romantically entangled and had difficulty focusing on anyone but each other. I'd become bored quite quickly, wondering why I'd come at all, but it was rather difficult to leave early when returning to the mainland required the use of a boat, so I was forced to remain. I'd ridden in with the Kenners, and they were having such a good time playing board games in the main house, I couldn't very well ask them to make a special trip for me.

I ate a couple of hot dogs, some baked beans, and drank some beer, then decided to take a hike around the island to kill some time. One of the "wings" of the island ended in a high, rocky promontory that provided a panoramic, though at that time extremely hazy, view of the Providence skyline. Theoretically there were paths around the island, but there wasn't much wildlife and most Institute visitors confined their attention to the shoreline, so these were mostly overgrown. I took my time and consumed almost an hour before reaching the summit, a fairly extensive plateau, and looked around for a place to sit. That's when I discovered that I wasn't alone.

"Hi." Alyson was sitting with crossed legs on a shelf of rock, a backpack beside her. She always wore her long, reddish brown hair bound tightly to her head at work, where it was conveniently out of the way. Now it was down, sweeping almost to her waist, and my earlier impression that her face was too full vanished instantly. She'd tied the tails of her shirt in a knot just below her rib cage, leaving bare a well-tanned band of flesh above the belt line of her jeans. "Are you a fellow fugitive from the Monopoly tournament?"

"Guilty as charged." I walked over to stand just beneath her perch. The sky had grown steadily darker during the past half hour and the wind suddenly picked up, cool and damp. Alyson's hair began to stir and she blinked, turning away from the breeze.

"Maybe this wasn't such a great idea." She uncrossed her legs and stood up a bit unsteadily. "I think it's going to rain."

"Not according to the institute's weather report."

She gave me a sarcastic smile. "Dr. Sotheby's crystal ball has been known to err."

Paul was a friend of mine, so I offered a tentative defense. "He's consistently more accurate than the state weather bureau."

"Oh, well there's a challenging benchmark for you," Alyson replied archly. "I always wonder if weather forecasters ever consider looking out the window." She reached down for the backpack, and at that very moment the sky opened up.

We were drenched so completely and so quickly that seeking shelter would have been irrelevant if the wind had been less gentle. But it turned gusty almost immediately, and the water hit with stunning force.

"This way!" Alyson jumped to the ground and started running away from the trail up which I'd just climbed. Having no better plan, I did what I was told and followed her. We slipped and slid our way down a steep decline that already resembled a miniature waterfall, then scrambled across more level ground covered with waist-high bushes that tugged at our sodden clothing. Something dark huddled in the near distance, but because of the heavy rain I couldn't identify what it was until we were directly adjacent.

It was a small wooden shack with cracked windows and a sagging door, but mercifully a roof that only leaked in a few spots. We collapsed inside on a relatively dry floor, laughing spasmodically when we could spare the breath. Then we began to shiver as our adrenaline subsided. The walls kept out most of the rain but little of the wind, which was brisk, constant, and surprisingly chill.

Alyson had removed her blouse and was working on her slacks before I realized what she was doing, wringing them out and then spreading them to dry over some wooden crates at the rear of the small room. "You'd better get out of those clothes or you'll be using up your sick time," she told me, turning her head to one side so that she could squeeze the water out of her hair. She didn't seem the slightest bit uncomfortable about standing there in her underwear, which is more than I could say for myself. I doffed my shirt, and more slowly my pants, shoes, and socks. Feeling like an advertisement for Fruit of the Loom, I moved to a spot as far from Alyson as possible without being obvious about it. But at the same time I made sure I was in a position where I could sneak looks at my companion. Lab smocks aren't very revealing, and I was suddenly aware of the fact that she was a very attractive woman.

We spent two hours in that shack, waiting for the rain to stop and our clothing to shed the worst of the water, but the time went surprisingly quickly. I learned about the tragic death of her parents in a boating accident, how she had raised her sister Beverly, just turned eighteen, while finishing her own college degree. She'd been working for the institute since graduation, dated infrequently, was fond of folk dancing, computer games, spicy Chinese food, historical novels and spy thrillers, and Monty Python, the last of which had us swapping quotes for fifteen minutes. I regaled her with my own history, my inability to decide just what I wanted to be when I grew up, my fondness for classic murder mysteries, folk music, northern New Hampshire, and maple walnut ice cream. To my surprise, I found myself summarizing the series of intense but uniformly short relationships I'd had with women during the past two years, while she provided considerably less intimate descriptions of the two loves of her life, both of whom had eventually proven disloyal. "Bob was so immature he just couldn't say no when he had a chance to cheat on me, but I think Evan arranged for me to find out because he didn't want anyone to get too close to him."

By the time we had squelched our way back to the main house, our relationship had changed dramatically. Our first date was the following weekend. By the end of the summer we were sleeping together occasionally, but in such a relaxed and low-pressure manner that it was more like two friends sharing a common interest than an act of passion. I wasn't sure how to feel about what I perceived as an underlying shallowness, but Alyson seemed unconcerned.

"You're always looking for cloud in your silver linings, Steve," she'd told me on more than one occasion. "Relax and enjoy life. If I think it's time to change how we relate to each other, I'll tell you, and I expect you to do the same. But we don't have to obsess about it."

"What are you doing here?" I stood with my pants down around my ankles, trying to fit Alyson into the context of my temporary environment. "What about the Davidson project, and the Tin Island cultures?"

"Davidson's down with the flu and the cultures arrived contaminated and have to be redone from scratch. Jane dropped by and said something about how bored you were going to be down here by yourself. So I asked Dr. Anthony if I could take my vacation early, and since he was having trouble finding things for us to do, he jumped at the chance to get me out of his hair for a few days." She paused when the trailer literally shook as a blast of wind-driven rain slammed into it. "There must be something about us that attracts bad weather."

I finished removing my sodden clothing and began floundering through the closet to find a clean pair of pants. "Welcome to the Twilight Zone. You might regret coming down here. It's like stepping into a Monty Python skit without the jokes."

She came closer, leaned against the side of the closet where I was rummaging for a pair of clean pants. "I noticed on the way in. Looks like time stopped around nineteen-twenty. I asked three people for directions to your trailer. One ran off without saying a word, one insisted they didn't allow trailers in Crayport. Luckily number three was a young kid who might almost have seemed friendly if he could've managed a smile, and he did know where you were camped."

"Probably Sean," I replied.

"A friend of yours?"

"They don't allow friends in Crayport," I said in a mock serious voice. "Ah, here they are." I pulled out a pair of jeans and prepared to put them on.

"Don't go to all that trouble for me," she said quietly. So I didn't.

It *is* possible to make love in the lower half of a trailer bunk bed, but I don't recommend it even as a change of pace. Alyson lost some of her enthusiasm after banging her elbow against the wall, twice. But we managed, and I was feeling a lot better when we took advantage of a pause in the storm to run down to the beach for a quick dip in the darkness. We made love on the sand a little later, which was much more comfortable than the bunk bed, and then retreated hastily from a fresh burst of rain to open a bottle of wine.

I fell asleep in the upper bunk, by myself, but no longer feeling alone.

Chapter Four

I was first wakened by the sound of automobiles passing on Shoreline Road. There were at least four of them, one of which had a bad muffler. I glanced out the trailer window but didn't see their lights, which struck me as odd since they should have been visible unless the vehicles were driving with their lights off. Odd, but not odd enough to keep me awake.

My second wakening was because of a gunshot. It was distant and might almost have been mistaken for a backfire, but I was raised with shotguns and I know one when I hear one. My eyes drooped and I started to drift back to sleep, and there was a second concussion, just like the first. Alyson stirred uneasily below me but remained unconscious until the third shot, which was louder, closer than the first two.

"What's going on?" she asked sleepily, but before I could answer, someone shouted unintelligibly in the distance. There were answering cries from several spots southwest of us, in the general direction of the Blackley house. I climbed down and pressed my face against the window screen. The rain had stopped, although it was still pretty windy and the moon and stars remained cloaked by heavy cloud. There were a few more shouts, gradually fading away to the south.

"Something's up," I said calmly, glancing at my alarm clock. It was two-thirty in the morning, an ungodly hour to be up and about.

Alyson, who invariably slept naked, slipped out of bed and joined me at the window, which lessened my interest in whatever was happening outside. "It seems to have stopped now."

"It's probably nothing." Crayport was so filled with strangeness that a little more didn't faze me at all. I slid my arm around her waist, but she eluded me so effortlessly that I might almost have fooled myself that she didn't mean to.

"See you in the morning." And she was back in bed within seconds. After another minute or two I followed, but I didn't fall asleep right away. My stomach rumbled, and eventually I gave in and dropped quietly to the floor. Alyson's even breathing indicated she'd already fallen back to sleep and I didn't want to disturb her. I ate a slice of bread, liberally buttered, and washed it down with some apple juice. The rumbling subsided and I headed back to bed, pausing briefly to glance out the window. Five vehicles drove past, headed north on Shoreline Road. None of them had their headlights on.

Alyson is not an early riser, nor a happy one. I brought her a cup of coffee, which she sipped without getting out of the bunk, while I made myself toast and a small omelet. I'd long since given up trying to get her to eat solid food in the morning. "I'm going to drive into town and pick up a newspaper. Want to come along?"

"I'm on vacation. I'm not getting up until eight o'clock."

"It's almost nine," I pointed out.

"Whatever."

So I went by myself. But when I pulled out onto the pavement, I impulsively turned left instead of right and drove around the curve and up to the Blackley property. There was no sign of life, but there was something out of the ordinary. The driveway and part of the yard were churned to mud in several places. As though a number of vehicles had parked there during last night's rainstorm. Thoughtfully, I turned around and headed back toward town.

They carried the Boston papers at the drugstore, but they were two days old. I picked up three paperback novels, all mysteries, and paid the taciturn middle-aged man who stood behind the cash register. I was about to turn and leave when Jared Turner walked into the store, turned his head slowly until he saw me, then crossed to where I was standing.

" 'Morning, Mr. Canfort. How's your business proceeding?"

I doubted very much that anything happened in Crayport that Turner didn't consider his business, and I was even more certain that he already knew the results of my visits to his neighbors, although just possibly he didn't know about the Blackleys. I didn't think his expression would have been quite so smug if he'd known that despite his dire predictions I had found someone willing to sell. And while I was tempted to prick his arrogant balloon, something warned me to keep silent.

"About as you predicted, Mr. Turner. But I haven't spoken to everyone yet, and I'm still optimistic."

"I don't think you'll have any better luck than you've had already. This is a closely knit town, set in its ways and suspicious of the outside world. Maybe we lose something being that way, but we have a sense of community that seems to have vanished from the rest of the country. We all belong here, and we know when someone else doesn't. It's nothing personal, you understand."

"You can't freeze time forever, Mr. Turner. The world moves on whether we want it to or not. We can drag our feet a little, but keep them pressed to the ground too long and your soles will start to burn."

"We're quite confident about the status of our souls, Mr. Canfort," he replied somewhat huffily, and I realized he'd misunderstood the words I had used.

"I'll keep you posted on my progress," I said insincerely, and turned to go, but Turner hastily stepped to one side to partially block my escape.

"Terrible tragedy here last night. I don't suppose you've heard."

"No," I said, and something subliminal warned me that this was the reason why Turner was talking to me, that this entire meeting had not been simple chance.

"It happened right down past where you're camping, at the Blackley place. I thought you might have heard something during the night."

He waited until I answered, and I had an instinctive urge not to reveal anything I'd heard or seen. "Not that I remember. What happened?"

"William Blackley, a fine, decent man, apparently had some kind of a breakdown. Took down his shotgun and killed his wife, then himself. The daughter's missing. Either he killed her as well and hid the body or she ran off in shock. Wouldn't be surprised if she was scared right out of her wits, hallucinating or worse. If you see anything funny out that way, I'd appreciate it if you'd pass word on to myself or the local police. Funeral's tomorrow. Closed casket, of course."

I was shocked but tried, probably without success, to keep my feelings off of my face. I had talked to those people yesterday and now they were dead, and I had the sudden, uneasy, unjustifiable feeling that perhaps they were dead exactly because I had talked to them. I dismissed it right away, of course. That kind of melodrama only happens in Hollywood, not in the real world, but the coincidence was still enough to make me uneasy.

"I'm sorry to hear that. As you know, the Blackleys owned one of the pieces of property we're interested in." If alive, the daughter was presumably the owner now, but the land's disposition would be controlled by whoever ended up as her legal guardian if she was under age. At best, it would be months before we could even talk about purchasing the property, although I'd certainly have Jane run this by the legal department. More likely custody would pass on to another of the Neanderthal personalities I'd already encountered. And if she was dead, the result might be the same or worse.

"William's brother James inherits if the girl's dead," remarked Turner, as though he'd been reading my thoughts.

"Then perhaps I should talk to him at some point. I assume he lives here in Crayport."

Turner nodded. "You can talk to him any time you want. That's him right over there." And he gestured toward the solemn cashier who stood watching us. I could see the resemblance now that it had been pointed out, although the strong features I'd seen in his brother's face were softened, and James's skin was riddled with acne scars. But there was one other physical difference that set the two brothers apart. James had frog fingers.

Alyson was up and dressed when I got back to the trailer. She read the expression in my face, but in order to explain adequately I first had to summarize everything that had already happened during my visit. That took a while, but she didn't interrupt until I was done, and then asked questions about details I'd forgotten to include.

"Sounds positively gothic," she said at last. "You don't really think the Blackleys were murdered to keep them from selling to the institute, do you?"

I was tempted to say yes, but truthfully, I didn't believe it. "No, I suppose not. They were under a lot of strain. That was obvious when I was talking to them. Maybe I'm responsible somehow. These people are all tied to the land, and maybe the thought of actually selling out pushed Blackley over the edge."

"Then why not just refuse to sell, like all the others?"

"I don't know. Maybe they were in a real financial pinch and saw this as the only way out. Maybe it's because this is the last year of the millennium and strange behavior doesn't need a justification. And maybe it's just a totally unrelated act that coincidentally sinks the best prospect I had afloat. Whatever the reason, the end result is that the only tentative seller in town is dead and I have no other leads."

"But you haven't talked to everyone yet."

"No, I haven't. But it's almost as if everyone in town got together in advance to make sure I failed."

"Everyone except the Blackleys."

"Yes, well, maybe they held out for some reason, and the town punished them." I meant it as a dark joke, but it didn't seem funny even at the time.

The morning remained cloudy as it edged toward noon, spitting rain in short, feeble bursts that lasted only a few minutes each. Alyson helped me take a few soil samples along the beach, and I noticed that the depression I'd discovered the first day was now almost entirely obliterated. We had an early lunch, since Alyson had had no breakfast, and then I took her on a drive around town, pointing out the properties that mattered to the institute. We tried the Harfords again, but as before, there was no answer to my knock, and this time we didn't see any furtive movement from inside the house. A flock of gulls raucously quarreled over something they'd found out in the yard, a small dead animal no longer identifiable.

I really should have driven out to the Crawleys then, but the sun broke through just after noon, Alyson was in a good mood, and I just didn't want to deal with more unpleasantness, particularly after we passed the cemetery and I noticed that they were digging fresh graves. Three of them. I assumed they must have found young Jennifer's body.

"What do you feel like doing today?"

"Well, sir, what are my choices?"

I thought about it. "We could drive into Boston for dinner in a nice restaurant and maybe a movie. We could sit on the beach with a couple of good books." I glanced up at the sky, which was rapidly clearing. The wind had already died down to a gentle breeze. "We have a canoe and a radio, no television. I have my laptop, but the only game on it is solitaire."

"Ummm, boy. With all those attractive choices, how can I decide? How about packing a picnic lunch and hiking up into the hills south of us?"

That sounded good, actually, and in fact it turned out to be a very nice afternoon. Alyson had the very same backpack she'd worn on Hawk Island in the trunk of her car, and we alternated wearing it as we explored the steep, overgrown hills beyond Sawblade Point. I hadn't realized how stunted and colorless the foliage was in Crayport. When I thought about it, I couldn't remember seeing a single flower garden, not even a flowering plant anywhere within the town limits. Up in the hills, there was a riot of color, including wild roses, wisteria, trumpet vines, and other flowering shrubs, and there were violets and buttercups underfoot almost everywhere.

The ground was muddy in spots because of the intense rain, but we were careful about our footing and avoided most of it, and the sun grew warm and friendly as we climbed, gradually drying the air. We ate our sandwiches and drank cool beer on a stretch of bare rock that looked back down on Crayport, which from this distance appeared quaint, though it was far from a postcard town. In fact, the downtown area seemed to hunker together protectively, like wagons circled against the Indians, and even the waterfront was drab and uninviting.

We started back shortly after that, following a route roughly parallel to the one we'd taken on the way out, and by the time we were back at Shoreline Road I was pretty tired, although it was the pleasant kind of fatigue that comes from steady physical exertion. Alyson seemed as rested as when we'd started out, but I noticed that she walked to the beach when we got back to the trailer rather than ran, and she was lying on the sand with one arm covering her eyes before I stopped swimming and joined her.

"Are you glad I came out here?"

I laughed. "Are you kidding? This is the end of the universe, the armpit of creation, the innermost circle of Hell for the mediocre. But you make it all seem bearable. Just."

"That was the right answer. So what's the plan for tomorrow?"

"Well, unless something better suggests itself— and feel free to jump in at any time if something occurs to you—I suppose a visit to the Crawleys is next on the agenda. By now I'm sure everyone in town knows why I'm here, but they may not realize we're interested in the island. I'd like to get permission to look it over on foot, then feel them out about selling it, or a portion thereof."

"And after that?" She rolled over and brushed her knee against my thigh.

"I'm open to suggestions." She had one, and I approved of it. But our plans got changed for us.

We dozed on the beach for an hour or so and woke up in the dusk. Feeling a bit silly, we walked hand in hand back to the trailer. I was reaching for the door handle when Alyson grabbed me by the arm. "Someone's watching us," she whispered.

I paused, glanced around. "Where?"

"I just caught a glimpse as they ducked behind the trailer."

"All right. You stay here and I'll investigate."

"No way. Remember your horror movies. They always get you when you split up." It was meant to be funny, but somehow it wasn't. Graveyard humor never seemed to work in Crayport.

We advanced cautiously, giving the trailer a wide berth as we moved around the far end. Sure enough, there was clear evidence in the sand that someone had been standing there, although the sea breeze had already partially obliterated the footprints. Whoever it was had retreated toward the dunes where Alyson had parked her car.

Since no one had jumped out at us, I was feeling a bit bolder, so I picked up the pace. We found her car, apparently untouched and still locked. Sand had drifted up in mini dunes around the tires. The tracks disappeared where a skirt of grass started. I climbed a dune and scanned the area. From my vantage point, I could see all around us. The shadows could have concealed someone, but it didn't seem likely. Maybe the prints were older than we thought and Alyson had just seen a dog or a cat, although I hadn't noticed either since arriving in Crayport, another oddity to add to the list.

"Well, whoever it was appears to be gone." I half walked, half slid back down to the car. "Let's remember to draw the blinds tonight, just in case. And lock the door."

"Yeah." Alyson looked thoughtful and, for the first time ever in my experience, a little nervous.

We turned back to the trailer and found someone standing in our way.

"Sean? Is that you?" He was standing in the shadow of the dune, but I recognized him immediately. He was still wearing the same clothing.

He stepped forward, face solemn, and glanced at Alyson. A few seconds passed silently before he was satisfied. "We need help."

"What kind of help?" That was Alyson, as I asked, "Who's we?" Different priorities.

"Jennifer and I. They've forgotten about me, mostly, but they'll kill her if they can. She needs to get away from here. Far away. You could drive her out to someplace where she'll be safe."

"Who's Jennifer?" I asked, but even as I spoke I realized it had to be Jennifer Blackley.

Sean confirmed it. "They killed her mom and dad, but she climbed out the window and got away. They always forget about the kids until later, and sometimes not even then."

"Who are we talking about, Sean? Who killed the Blackleys?" I don't think I believed him, not then anyway. Turner was authority, and I'd been brought up to defer to authority in matters like this.

"Those Who Serve," he answered. "Those Who Serve the Servants." I could practically hear the capital letters in his voice.

I started to ask another question, but Sean shook his head. "We can't talk here. They're probably watching you."

"Where should we go then, Sean?" Alyson sounded cool and calm again. "Down by the water?"

He shrugged. "That should be okay. Sometimes the sounds the waves make confuses them. They remember the Gatherings, and that pushes other stuff right out of their minds."

I ignored the last of this, having reached weirdness overload. We walked down to the shore in the deepening darkness while Sean told us his version of what had happened at the Blackley house the previous night.

"They figured out Mr. and Mrs. Blackley were

talking to you about selling, so they came for them after dark. Jennifer's mom stopped coming to the Gatherings a few months back and told one of her neighbors that they were thinking about leaving Crayport. Jennifer says no one would speak to them after that and people were coming by the house all the time, but never stopping or saying anything. Anyway, last night Jennifer woke up and heard her father shouting at someone. He'd made her practice climbing out the window and crossing the roof so many times that she got away before they found her. Some of them searched for her later, those that hadn't already forgotten, but she and her father had dug this hidey hole in the woods. They walked right over her a couple of times, but she stayed quiet and they left."

I wasn't sure how much if any of this to believe, but Sean's quiet, confident delivery was difficult to completely discount. "So Jennifer thinks that some of the people from town shot her parents?"

Sean shook his head. "They fired the shotguns outside the house after her mom and dad were already dead. Jennifer thought maybe they were shooting into the woods, hoping to scare her out of her hiding place."

Or, I thought, maybe they were fabricating a cover story, in case the unwelcome visitor camped nearby heard something in the night.

"But if they didn't shoot the Blackleys . . ." I let the unspoken question hover in the air.

He hesitated and looked out to sea. "Those

Who Serve didn't use guns to kill my mom and dad either. I don't know how they did it exactly, but they did it."

"Where is Jennifer now?" asked Alyson.

Apparently Sean still didn't entirely trust us, because his only answer was "Someplace safe."

"So what do you want us to do, Sean?" I wasn't happy with the situation. I still couldn't believe that the Blackleys had been murdered, but clearly something unusual surrounded their deaths. More likely Jennifer had misconstrued whatever she had seen or heard, entirely possible given the traumatic nature of her experience.

"You've got a car. You could drive her out of town to someplace safe," he repeated.

I mulled over that one. I wondered if Jennifer was eighteen yet. If she was still a minor, I could see myself being hauled into court for transporting an attractive young girl without the permission of whoever was responsible for her now. And after being told by the town manager that she had been traumatized and was potentially unstable. A little devil not very deep down inside was insisting that this wasn't any of my business, and to my shame, I was listening.

"Why doesn't she just go to the police?" There was a police force in Crayport. I'd passed the station several times, although come to think of it, I'd never actually seen any uniforms or marked cars anywhere in town.

I could sense Sean's exasperation, perhaps even alarm. "They wouldn't help," he said at last.

Don D'Ammassa

"Can you take us to her? I need to talk to her first." I wanted to hear what Jennifer had to say before I made any decisions. Sean seemed to be in earnest, but he was clearly a strange kid, and I wasn't sure how much I could rely on what he was saying. I doubted that he was consciously lying, but for kids sometimes the truth is more malleable than for the rest of us.

"I promised her I wouldn't tell anyone where she is."

"You'll have to tell us if we're going to help," interposed Alyson quietly.

"*Are* you going to help?

I hesitated, which probably hurt my credibility, then pushed on in an attempt to recover. "We'll do what we can, but you have to see that we can't just take your word for all of this. If you don't want to talk to the police, then you have to at least let us talk to Jennifer. Then we'll decide what to do. But I promise that we won't do anything without telling you first." I hoped that was a promise I'd be able to keep.

"All right, but I won't tell you where she is. We'll be at the cemetery tomorrow night, nine o'clock, back where they're burying her parents. Don't park on the road. Someone will see your car. You can park downtown and cut across the fields. No one farms there any more, so no one will be around."

"All right, we'll meet you there. Can I give you a ride home?"

Sean shook his head. "No. I'll be okay. Remember your promise." And with that he was gone, so quickly that it was almost as if he'd turned into a vampire and vanished in a cloud of mist.

"Well," I said, "the fun and excitement never cease in Crayport, Massachusetts."

"I don't think there's anything funny about this." Alyson sounded distinctly annoyed and I regretted my tone.

"Sorry. When I get nervous I tend to make inappropriate jokes to relieve the tension. You realize the awkward position we're in, don't you? Sean is underage and Jennifer might be."

"And both of them are in trouble."

"And maybe so are we."

The comparatively good mood of the afternoon had been fatally wounded by Sean's visit, and we retreated to our separate bunks without any amorous byplay. Alyson seemed unusually thoughtful and I was feeling rather tense myself. This wasn't my kind of situation. I'm not a physical coward, but neither am I the heroic type. I'd always outsmarted or outrun bullies rather than stood up to them, and I was more likely to write an angry letter to the editor than take a position at a public meeting or join a protest group.

But I liked kids. I'd been an assistant troop leader in the Boy Scouts until I broke with them over their refusal to admit atheists, and I led a reading group at one of the branch libraries in Providence and helped out at the Boys' Club. Sean struck me as a troubled kid, possibly an abused one, although I had no evidence other

than the poor condition of his clothing. And I'd
seen more than one adult in Crayport whose garments were even less reputable. If he was telling
the truth, he was an orphan as well, and must
have been fostered with someone else in town. I
couldn't imagine him living with the Harfords or
the Jensons or the Thornes or anyone else I'd met
since arriving. I wanted to help, but I wasn't sure
what that help should consist of, and I didn't
want to get myself in trouble in the process.

My mind was still going over the same small
collection of options when I finally fell into a
troubled sleep.

I'm not sure what disturbed my rest that night.
Alyson never stirred, and the night was almost
completely silent. I felt a vague but palpable
sense of unease that refused to go away; my heart
beat wildly and my mouth was dry, the kind of
anxiety attack I hadn't experienced in years. Quietly I climbed down, walked barefoot across the
carpeted floor into the tiny kitchen. There was
still some apple juice left and I drank a small glass
of it, swishing the liquid around the inside of my
mouth before swallowing. Then I crossed to the
seaside window and pushed the curtain to the
side. We'd been keeping the windows open to let
in the night air, and only a fine mesh screen separated me from the outdoors.

The sky had cleared, the moon was half full,
and the stars were unusually bright. The sea smell
was strong, and I had to concentrate to pick out

the bitter scent, although Alyson had remarked on it twice during the day. Either it had weakened since my arrival or I was becoming inured to it. I was about to turn back to bed when I noticed a light moving out on the water.

It was a pale yellow glow, barely visible, and from my perspective it moved from left to right. After a minute, I noticed a second, and then a third. They moved in unison, and eventually I realized that they must be mounted on a boat leaving the town wharf. Judging by the spacing, it was a largish vessel, almost certainly one of the fishing boats. Perhaps, I thought, this explains why I never saw an empty slip. Crayport's fishermen only went out at night. The clock read just after midnight. Was that time to gather their nets, empty and re-lay them? I had no idea. My father was a lawyer who'd never been fishing in his life, as far as I knew. I'd canoed in Maine and New Hampshire ever since high school but hadn't been out on saltwater until I started working at the institute. We passed fishing vessels on almost every trip out to sea, but I'd never been interested in the mechanics of the process, which looked to me to consist of difficult, dirty work at awkward hours for insufficient pay.

I stood there for about twenty minutes, at which point the lights were no longer visible, waiting to see if the other ships followed. But perhaps they had preceded it, because that was the last activity I detected that night, and finally fatigue caught up to me and I climbed back up into bed.

Alyson never stirred and it never occurred to me to mention it to her the following day, although even if I had, there was no reason why she might have found it significant.

Chapter Five

The problems presented by Sean's revelation col-
ored our mood the following morning. Alyson
was up and about uncharacteristically early, and
even more surprisingly she ate some toast with
me. By unspoken agreement we didn't discuss
the previous day's events, and spent the morning
taking a second set of soil samples on the beach
and catching up on some overdue housekeeping
in the trailer.

Alyson volunteered to drive into town for milk
and a few other things I'd overlooked, and to try
to call her sister Beverly. The two of them had
been close even before the death of their parents
and had rarely spent a night under different roofs.
Personally, I found Beverly a little bit unsettling.
She had sharper edges than her sister, was more

outspoken, more certain of her positions, less patient with the shortcomings of other people. When we'd first met, it was quite obvious that I was being examined critically to make certain I was a worthy companion for Alyson. I still didn't know if I had passed or was merely on probation. Most startling of all was my discovery that Beverly made most of the important decisions for them both.

"She knows where she's going and how she wants to get there," Alyson told me once. "Most of the time I tag along for the ride."

While Alyson was gone, I caught up on the report I was supposed to be writing. She was back sooner than I expected, complaining because the freshest milk she'd found had an expiration date only two days off.

"Did you reach your sister?"

She shook her head. "No one home. I left a message on the answering machine. I also took a quick look around while I was there," she informed me conspiratorially. "We shouldn't have any trouble finding the back way into the cemetery in the dark. It's pretty much overgrown, but there's a little brook that runs down behind the last of the buildings and right around the nearest row of gravestones."

"This thing could blow up in our faces, you know. Technically, it's none of our business. The girl is a runaway, possibly suffering from shock."

"I know. But something funny is going on here. Doesn't it strike you as a huge coincidence that

Mr. Blackley blows his stack right after you talk to him, particularly considering he was the only one in town who would even consider selling his land?"

"Of course it does, at least in bad movies and mediocre novels. But coincidences do happen, and even if there's something more sinister involved, we don't have the authority, or the resources, to deal with it."

Once the subject had been opened, the informal taboo no longer held, and we argued about if off and on for the balance of the morning, resolving nothing, finally agreeing that any decision would have to wait until after we met Jennifer and judged her state of mind.

I made tuna fish salad for lunch, dicing the almost fresh radishes to give it some texture. We used up the last of the almost stale bread making sandwiches, washed it down with almost cold beer.

"So what's on the agenda for this afternoon?"

"I think it's time to visit the Crawleys. I'm not scheduled to call Jane until Monday but I might try later today just to let her know what's been happening so she can sic her legal department on the Blackley estate, and she'll want to know if I've spoken to them. You're welcome to come along. You're an institute employee, so I think I can justify recruiting you as assistant negotiator. Besides, they might have more trouble being rude to an attractive woman."

"Sexist."

"Guilty as charged. I'll take advantage of any asset I can find right now."

We stopped at the post office on our way in, but as I had expected, there were no responses to my letters. For all I knew, none of the recipients were even literate. Nothing would surprise me now. We were on our way out to the Crawleys, uninvited, when Alyson touched my arm. "Pull over for a minute."

I did so, not knowing why, and came to a stop directly across from the cemetery. "What's up?"

"Let's take a walk. Scout out the territory."

With a little care, it could have been an attractive, even picturesque cemetery. The central section was level, with rows of variegated headstones laid out in fairly conventional fashion. This was flanked on both sides by gently rolling hills capped with trees, mostly Japanese maple and oak, although sumac and ash were both battling to supplant them. There were even clumps of forsythia gone wild, though none sported flowers. Sprinkled throughout the small summits were burial vaults, some of them quite large, all in a state of very obvious disrepair. Oxidation discolored many, and windblown debris filled every nook and cranny. There were dead branches in most of the trees, which badly needed pruning.

Deeper still, the level ground also gave way to hills, and here invading foliage had displaced most of the original plantings, so that we didn't realize how far the cemetery extended until we spotted gravestones sprinkled through the brush. There was one comparatively clear area that showed evidence of recent activity, and as I expected the markers were for William and Edna Blackley. Mrs. Blackley had been thirty-six, her husband forty. A third plot, almost concealed from where we stood, was unmarked and unfinished, presumably intended for Jennifer in the belief that her father had hidden her body somewhere.

"They bury them fast around here," Alyson observed with obvious displeasure, then drew in her breath sharply. She'd just spotted the third grave.

"It looks like someone's anticipating a third body," I said quietly, but my voice wasn't entirely steady.

"Sean's story sounds a little more credible now."

"Don't jump to any conclusions. Turner told me that they believed Blackley killed his daughter and concealed the body. It might be in poor taste, but it could still have an innocent explanation." I don't think I believed it even then, because in the back of my mind. I was trying to decide if I was justified in bundling the two kids into the car tonight and driving all four of us out of this crazy town, never to return. Or at least not without the police, the Marines, the French Foreign Legion, or something along those lines.

"It's more like being dragged to a conclusion

against my will. I didn't notice any evidence of a search party, did you?"

I hadn't, and we could hardly have missed the activity if anything organized was under way. That realization was, I think, the point where I started to believe that something in Crayport was more than just wrong. It was dangerous as well.

We returned to the car in silence. As I was pulling away, I noticed someone standing on the beach, watching us with obvious interest. I was pretty sure it was the younger Jenson, the one who had threatened me, and I felt his eyes burning into the back of my neck until he and the cemetery had disappeared from my rearview mirror.

We wound our way up into the hills, pulling over once when a large panel truck approached from ahead. I recognized the stylized polar bear emblem on the side; Polar Trucking operated out of Providence and specialized in refrigerated trucks. I wondered if the Crawleys imported their own groceries and produce. I wouldn't have blamed them after my own local shopping, and clearly they were more closely attuned to the twentieth century than their neighbors, judging by the condition of their property and the modern motor launch at their private wharf. I felt as though I were approaching the local lord's keep after unsuccessfully negotiating with his serfs.

There wasn't much activity at the Crawley place when we arrived, at least not visible activity. There were two more trucks parked just below the corrugated metal building I'd noticed earlier, and there were sections of unpowered roller skate conveyor strung together from the overhead doorway above to the first of the trucks, but there was no sign that anything was being actively unloaded. We had our choice between the larger house on our left and the smaller to the right, but since the driveway was adjacent to the former, that's where we started.

As usual, there was no doorbell, but someone answered the door almost immediately, and he greeted us with what might actually have been a smile. "Yes? Can I help you?"

I introduced us both. "I sent a letter the other day. I was wondering if I could talk to someone who would have authority to let us visit your island."

"Oh, yes, the prospective buyer. Come in, please. I'm Edward Crawley. My father owns the property."

We were ushered into a quite pleasant front room. Through an archway to our left I noticed what appeared to be a library or den; the walls were all fitted with floor-to-ceiling bookcases, and there weren't many gaps. Crawley led us off to the right, into a largish room fitted with three oversized sofas and some comfortable chairs. "Please make yourselves at home. Can I get you something to drink? Lemonade, iced tea, a soft drink?"

"Iced tea would be wonderful," admitted Alyson, and I nodded as well.

We both examined the room with undisguised curiosity while he was gone. The furnishings were a bit old fashioned but in impeccable condition. The drapes were drawn over the windows, probably to keep out the heat of the day, although the house was so sheltered by the surrounding trees that it was almost entirely shaded. The one incongruity was the large painting mounted over the fireplace, a striking piece of nonrepresentational art, filled with swirls and vortices and odd twists and turns that fooled the eye. The paint had been laid on heavily—I could see the ridges from several feet away—and the colors tended toward the dark. It had a hypnotic quality to it and I found it difficult to look away. On the whole, I thought it rather unpleasant, certainly not something I'd want to have hovering over me while I was trying to relax with the newspaper.

A thin, colorless woman who was quite obviously a servant brought our iced tea, each with its small individual tray. She didn't respond to our thanks, just turned and vanished back into the recesses of the house, moving so silently I couldn't hear her feet touch the carpet. The tea was cold and refreshing, though a trifle bitter for my taste, and we had time to consume most of it before our host returned with his father.

Edward Crawley was an attractive man, the kind who impresses you with his self-confidence and convinces you that he's competent even before you have any proof. He had a full head of dark black hair that was stylishly cut, and although he wore casual clothes they were clearly of good quality. I estimated his height as just under six feet, and he was built solidly, without any obvious tendency to fat. The executive type, I suspected, though I couldn't imagine any commercial activity in Crayport that would be sufficiently challenging to hold his interest. His demeanor was so different from that of his neighbors that I felt mildly disoriented, my expectations having been skewed by the events of the past two days.

But if Edward Crawley was imposing, his father Joseph was dominating. At least three inches above six feet, the elder Crawley sported a shock (and that's the right word) of snow white hair that spilled down below his ears. He wore a dark business suit that seemed to have difficulty restraining the powerful frame beneath it, for the man was even more solid than his son. If Edward was in his late thirties, then Joseph must be close to sixty, but he looked at least ten years younger. His most striking feature, however, was his eyes, which seemed a trifle too large for his face, even though they were dark and deeply set.

"Mr. Canfort, Miss Branford." He greeted us both, shaking our hands until our teeth rattled. "Welcome to my home. I received your letter, of course, but haven't had the opportunity to respond."

"I hope we haven't come at an inconvenient time, Mr. Crawley."

"Not at all. We have lots of time in Crayport;

that's one of our greatest assets. We live a much more relaxed, protected life than does the outside world."

"It certainly does appear to be a unique community," I replied diplomatically.

He chuckled and took a seat opposite us, while his son stood quietly to one side. "Which means we seem very insular, if not openly hostile to outsiders."

I refused to be embarrassed. "I haven't exactly felt welcome here."

He allowed himself a small sigh. "You have to understand how rare it is for us to have to deal with strangers. Some of the local people haven't spoken to anyone outside the town in their entire lives. The only television set in Crayport is in this house, and it's rarely used. My neighbors feel awkward at best, occasionally defensive, and I suppose some even suffer a mild xenophobia. You shouldn't take it personally."

"I didn't come here to make friends, Mr. Crawley. If you've read my letter, you know that already. The institute has no desire to change the character of your town in any way; in fact, our intentions are entirely the opposite. We want to study the unique conditions in the waters of your harbor and just beyond. The installation is designed to be unobtrusive and to avoid any activity which might affect the subject of our investigation."

"I don't doubt your intentions at all, Mr. Canfort. I wish you the best of luck. But to be frank,

I doubt that you'll find anyone in town willing to part with their property. There hasn't been a change of ownership in generations other than through inheritance."

"What about the Caspar home?" I asked impulsively. "I gather that family line is extinct."

"Ah, the Caspars. A terrible tragedy. Yes, you're correct. They were the last of their line. Under the terms of their will, the property went to Ted's cousin, Jared Turner. But I don't think you're likely to have any luck there. Jared's son is almost of an age to strike out on his own, and I believe Jared is holding the house for him."

I mentally scratched another possibility off my list, then reinstated it. Turner was a lost case, but perhaps his son might be tempted by the money. It was a long shot though, and Crawley had implied the boy would still be a minor for some time yet.

"And how can I be of assistance to you?"

"Your family holds title to Crawley Island."

"Yes, the island has been part of the family holding since the town was founded back in the seventeenth century. It's a pretty desolate place, essentially a sandbar laid across a bed of rock."

"I wondered if you would have any objection to our landing on the island to look it over. There's a possibility that it might be suitable for the installation, although obviously the mainland would be more convenient."

Neither Crawley reacted in any tangible way, but somehow I felt the atmosphere in the room change, as though someone had turned up the air conditioning. Several seconds passed before Joseph resumed the conversation. "Of course I have no objection to your visiting our island, although I can't imagine why you would bother. It's terribly exposed; the outlines have changed several times in my lifetime. My grandfather built a hut there one year and it blew down within a month. There's absolutely no protection from storms, and unless you were willing to excavate down to the bedrock, you'd be floating on a sea of sand and loose soil. You'd have to bring in the construction equipment by ship and off-load it at an uncertain anchorage. Plus, as I imagine you've already realized, it would be a logistical nightmare for your staff to be isolated from the amenities ashore."

I considered the latter a plus rather than a minus, but refrained from saying so. "I admit that it's not the most attractive possibility, but given our lack of success elsewhere, I'd be willing to explore the option. The property is clearly of no value to you, Mr. Crawley, and my employers would be willing to pay quite well for either a lease or an outright purchase."

Edward remained motionless, but Joseph put his hands on his knees and slowly rose to his feet. Without looking at us, he walked across the room until he was facing the unusual painting I'd noticed earlier. He stared into it for several seconds before turning around. "Crawley Island has been part of this family for many generations. I'm sure this will make you think us as provincial as everyone else in town, but I have to tell you that you're wasting your time. Under no circumstances could I be persuaded to part with it."

"Then perhaps a lease . . ."

But Crawley was shaking his head. "No, I think not. Legally it would still belong to us, but you would alter its character. I'm sorry to disappoint you, Mr. Canfort"—he turned to Alyson—"and Miss Branford, but it's entirely out of the question. I don't need the money and I don't like changes that are outside my control. It is perhaps an old man's conservatism, but I fear that nothing you could say would persuade me otherwise."

Briefly I entertained the possibility that his reluctance was a ploy to force us to increase the size of our offer, but I caught his eyes briefly and there was something in them—a cold, calculating determination—that warned me off. I rose to my feet, and Alyson followed suit.

"Well, then, I'm sorry to have wasted your time."

"Not at all." He was suddenly affable again, at least everything but his eyes. "We get visitors so rarely out here, it always makes an interesting diversion. Perhaps I'll see you again before you leave." There wasn't a trace of sincerity in his last statement, and he knew I recognized that fact. He shook our hands and walked out of the room, leaving Edward to escort us to the door and beyond.

Although it was still hot, the air had been con-

siderably drier since the storm, and it was actually rather nice outside the house. Crawley the
younger was trying to shepherd us directly to the
car, but Alyson eluded him, attracted by activity
across the road. The elaborate rigging system that
I'd noticed on my previous trip was in operation,
and we could hear a powerful electric motor running down near the water.

The winch had almost drawn its burden to the
top of the hill and I paused, ignoring Edward's
small talk to glance in that direction, while Alyson actually crossed to the opposite side, staring
down at a bulky object that was rapidly reaching
the summit. "That's quite a mechanism you have
there."

He stopped in midsentence, followed the line
of my eyes. "It's a bit primitive, of course, but it
gets the job done."

The entire system was straining with the weight
of the large crate that was being lifted from the
shoreline. I noticed that what I had mistaken for
ropes anchoring the device were actually metal
cables that had cut deeply into the wood of the
trees that served as braces. Metal stanchions had
been installed as well, and presumably these
took the worst of the strain. Three glum-looking
men in coveralls were standing near the top; but
not one of them glanced in our direction.

"We're moving some furniture up from the
lower house," Crawley explained without being
asked, and for the first time since we'd met I detected a note of uncertainty or nervousness in his

voice. I knew intuitively that he was lying. "We're taking it to Boston for sale."

"Looks pretty heavy for furniture," I said with feigned disinterest.

"Yes, I think we tried to cram too much into a single lift. But we wanted to be sure it would all fit into one load." He gestured toward the parked truck. "The family has acquired quite a few valuable antiques over the generations. Dad finally decided to take some of them out of storage and sell them. This way someone will put them to actual use. Even carefully stored, they deteriorate in the salt air here. My father deplores waste."

"But he doesn't mind wasting an entire island," I replied pointedly.

"We all have our inconsistencies, Mr. Canfort. That's what makes life so interesting. And I'm not sure that preserving this town from outside intervention, however minimal and well intended, is wasteful."

A moment later Alyson and I were in the car, driving slowly back toward the heart of Crayport. "Well, that was certainly . . . interesting." Alyson, who had said barely a word during our visit, was shifting back and forth in her seat, a mannerism that I knew meant she had something significant to say. "I don't think I've ever been lied to so earnestly before."

"You don't believe Edward Crawley either, I take it."

"Edward or Joseph. The meaningful pauses, the earnest looks. I felt like I'd walked into a stage play by accident. A glib, well-written play, but a sham nonetheless."

"The crate caught them by surprise though. Edward had to think fast to come up with a story for that. You saw the flaw, I take it?"

"You mean, why are they paying for refrigerated trucks to move furniture?"

"That's the one. Come to think of it though, what are they transporting? Fresh fish? I can't think of anything else."

She shook her head. "Doubtful. No reason to conceal that, unless they're dealing with a protected species or something."

"Whatever their reasons, it's obvious that they have no intention of letting us lease the island. If they're up to something crooked, maybe they're using the island to store illicit goods. Do you suppose they're drug runners, adapting smuggling techniques from the last century?"

"Possibly. Put a patch over his eye and Crawley the elder would make a formidable pirate. But I don't remember ever hearing that drugs needed refrigerated trucks."

"Maybe it keeps them fresh." She shrugged and pressed the tips of her fingers to her lips. "Maybe it's just a clever way of disguising the shipments. I'd love to take a look at that island."

"Well, I don't see how we can justify doing it without his permission. I'm not in the mood to spend time in jail for trespassing, particularly in this town."

"Actually, he said he had no objection to our

visiting the island, but that we were wasting our time. I'd say we have his permission."

I thought about it and she was right. That was what he said. It might be embarrassing to be caught there, but we could always say we were out in the canoe for the fun of it, and just decided to stop and look the place over while we were nearby.

"Are you sure you want to do this? If they're the bad guys, we might get into trouble." I had contradictory feelings about the whole thing. On the one hand, I disliked any kind of personal confrontation, however slight, and I'd been through more than my quota since arriving in Crayport. On the other hand, I was sufficiently annoyed by the way I'd been treated that an opportunity to tweak someone's metaphorical nose had its appeal.

"We go right now, in broad daylight. We don't sneak around, and if we see anybody out there, we don't put ashore. And we can call Jane before we go."

So that's what we did. I briefed the boss on the situation, but left out most of our suspicions and everything about Sean and Jennifer. She confirmed what I already knew about the Caspar property. "Quite a coincidence this Blackley fellow going off his nut just when it looked like he might sell." Jane was sharp; she didn't need my suggestion to smell a rat.

"I thought so too, but he did appear to be under considerable stress when I spoke to him." I wanted to level with her, but the part of the story I hadn't told her wasn't likely to boost her confidence in me unless I had some concrete evidence. Jane was sharp enough to interpolate at least some of my misgivings, however.

"Maybe, but watch yourself out there, Steven. We'd be hard put to find someone else who works as cheaply as you."

"I'll remember that when my annual review comes up."

"I gather you don't think there's much chance of getting Crawley to change his mind about the island."

"Not a whisper. This whole town needs an enema, Jane. It's like something out of a bad horror film."

We drove back to the trailer, changed clothes, and then launched the canoe. The rain clouds had blown away, though it was still overcast. There was an occasional breeze that was more of a tease than a refreshment, and we were both sweating profusely a short time later. We swung wide of the town wharf, the usual number of fishing boats in their usual spots, then headed directly toward the island. It was cloaked with mist again, though not as thickly as it had been on my previous visit. We gave it a wide berth initially, surreptitiously checking out more than half of its beach before approaching from the seaward side.

There was a deep but narrow groove there,

and we dragged the canoe well up into the dunes. I had no intention of being marooned. A handful of gulls circled us curiously but lost interest quickly and flew back toward shore. We started inland up a slope that was gentle at first but grew increasingly steep. The fine sand didn't provide much purchase for our feet and we both felt the strain in our legs well before we reached the summit of the grassy ridge that concealed the center of the island. The handful of stunted trees we'd seen earlier were completely missing from this side, although we saw clumps of them in the distance.

We reached the crest and found ourselves looking out across an enormous concavity, a kind of natural amphitheater whose circumference was broken at only two places, one facing north toward the Crawley property, the other southwest, approximately in the direction of the town wharf. The interior slopes were smooth and gradual and we had no trouble climbing down despite the fine sand. It was a remarkable enough sight in itself, made more so by the footprints that covered much of the interior. There were a lot of them; created by at least a few dozen people, maybe more than that. And they were fresh. The wind and rain from the recent storm would have wiped them out otherwise. I remembered the fishing boat I'd seen moving out into the harbor in the middle of the night and wondered just exactly what was going on in Crayport.

"Well, this ranks pretty high on the weirdness

scale." Alyson shaded her eyes with one hand, her long hair blowing in a sudden breeze, and slowly scanned the perimeter. "Looks like they came in from that end and spread all around the inside."

Now that she pointed it out, I saw that the tracking was much heavier at the southwest notch. The northern one was only slightly disturbed. "Maybe they came out for a party." I stood motionless while Alyson began walking across the interior, her head down, pausing occasionally to dig into the sand with her toes. "What're we looking for? Blood? Human sacrifices?" It didn't sound funny, even to me.

"They all stood around in a big circle, so what was in the center?"

I walked out and joined her, but insofar as I could tell, there were no distinguishing features at all, just an expanse of soft white sand.

"Owww!" Alyson began hopping around on one foot.

"What's wrong?" I glanced down but couldn't see anything that could have caused an injury.

"Stubbed my toe, that's what's wrong." She stopped hopping, put her foot down gingerly. I got down on my hands and knees, felt around the sand, and sure enough, there was a roughly circular plate of stone perhaps a meter in diameter concealed there. Or covered at least. It was featureless, unremarkable, and other than being surprisingly close to a perfect circle, entirely natural.

"It seems to me that the Crawleys aren't holding on to the island just because of tradition."

Alyson nodded agreement. "They're using it for something. But what?"

I had no answer to that, and both of us lapsed into an uneasy silence that wasn't broken for the remainder of our stay on the island. Not that we lingered. Convinced that there was nothing more to find, we launched the canoe and paddled back to shore, each of us wrapped up in our own thoughts and speculations.

Chapter Six

We found the chief of police waiting for us when we got back to the trailer. He was sitting in an unmarked car and climbed out slowly when he saw us walking up from the beach. He wasn't very tall but he was solid; broad shoulders, massive arms and legs, running perhaps a trifle to fat, although most of it appeared to be muscle. He wore a neat crew cut and no hat, but he wasn't sweating at all despite the hot sun and his dark uniform. I felt a momentary alarm when I spotted him, wondering if our expedition to the island had attracted attention after all, a queasiness that didn't completely go away even after he introduced himself and we realized this wasn't an official visit at all, at least not in the usual sense of the term.

" 'Afternoon, folks. I'm Ralph Weathers, chief of police here in Crayport." We shook his hand, which was large and hot but perfectly normal, and gave him our names, although I'm sure he already knew them both.

"Mr. Turner told me you were looking to buy some land in the area." His expression told us that we were crazy even to contemplate such a stupid course of action.

I nodded my head. "We work for an oceanographic institute that wants to build a small research station here. Our job is to sound out the local landowners and do a preliminary survey of the possible sites. Not that I'm having much luck finding anyone willing to sell."

Chief Weathers nodded with mock sympathy. "People hereabouts are pretty set in their ways, and they're land proud, most of them. They don't like things to change. It makes them uneasy, suspicious. They figure things have been fine for their families for generations, so there's no good reason to try anything new. I doubt you'll have any luck at all."

I was getting pretty tired of what appeared to be the local party line. "The only alternative to change is death. And I'd say Crayport is pretty close to being terminally ill. A little new blood in town might be just the thing you need."

"Well, there's change, and then there's change, if you see what I mean. Now, if we were to come down to your institute and tell you we thought maybe you were investigating the wrong things, you'd most likely get annoyed and stubborn and tell us to peddle our advice elsewheres. Same goes for us. You see, we got balance here. There's not a whole lot of money and we don't have what you'd call a lot of modern conveniences, but we don't miss them. We don't spend all our time trying to get ahead of the next guy or gal. Our goals might not be as ambitious as yours, but we reach them a lot more often than most people do. I've got two deputies working for me, and they spend most of their time playing cards. Crime's another thing that we don't have much use for in Crayport."

"Seems to me I heard you had a murder and a suicide just the other night."

For just a second I thought someone else was looking at me out of Chief Weathers's eyes, a darker version of himself, but it was gone almost immediately and his calm voice remained the same. "Sad thing, that. William never was quite right in the head. Spent too much time by himself, worrying over things that didn't matter. Started thinking his neighbors had something against him and had his wife half convinced the same. I'd call it more a tragic sickness than a crime, Mr. Canfort."

"Has their daughter been found yet?"

"Their daughter?" He looked momentarily puzzled. "Jennifer, you mean. No, she hasn't turned up. If William didn't shoot her and throw her into the ocean, then maybe she fell into a ravine up in the hills somewhere. Wouldn't be surprised if she was half crazy herself, after everything that's happened."

Alyson quickly changed the subject. "Is there something specific you wanted to talk to us about or is this just a social visit?"

"Courtesy call is all. I make it my business to keep track of what's happening here in town. An ounce of prevention, you know."

"We're not here to cause any trouble," I said quickly, suppressing a flash of nervousness.

"Didn't say you were." Weathers let his eyes wander around our campsite and down to the beached canoe. "Not the safest transportation you could have found. The waters around here are misleading. They look nice and gentle, but the currents run deep and unpredictable. I wouldn't venture out too far if I were you. Sudden storm might come up and you'd never be seen again."

"We're careful to stay near the shore." Wondering if that was a veiled threat, I felt a sudden need to soothe this man, anything to encourage him to leave. His very presence was suddenly making me acutely uncomfortable. There was nothing specific that I could put my mental finger on, but there just seemed to be something wrong about the situation. Dangerously wrong. It was irrational, but I didn't doubt my instincts for a second. Chief Weathers was formidable and, like the Crawleys, he didn't seem the kind of man who would vegetate his life away in a backwater like Crayport. "We appreciate your taking the time to stop by." I took a tentative step toward the trailer.

"I just wanted to caution you folks." He was still smiling, but his voice had changed tone. "People around here aren't used to outsiders. We've learned to respect each other's privacy, and most of us are pretty stubborn about keeping things to ourselves. If you push where you're not wanted, even with the best of intentions, you might get yourselves into trouble. None of us wants that to happen. If I were you, I'd fill in whatever report you're called on to make and recommend trying elsewhere, someplace that isn't quite so protective of itself."

"We'll be careful not to step on any toes," I replied quietly, not entirely suppressing a sudden desire to challenge the man's thinly veiled threat. "But we have a job to do. If no one wants to sell to us, that's their prerogative, of course, and we'll respect their wishes and build on public land. I don't intend to pressure anyone, and my employers would fire me if I did. So there's nothing for you to worry about."

"I'm happy to hear that." He didn't sound that way. "I'll be seeing you folks around, I'd imagine." And he left then, but his presence lingered palpably behind, an oppressive wraith that clung like fog.

"That man doesn't like us very much." Alyson handed me a cold, or at least cool, beer from the icebox, then opened one for herself before handing me a sandwich.

"Doesn't seem like anyone in Crayport likes us very much, or even a little." I took a long drink and stared out the window. The sun was low in the sky, but it was still quite light out. A glance at my wristwatch told me we had about two hours before our scheduled rendezvous. The drive would take ten minutes, the walk maybe fifteen if we took our time and were careful to avoid being seen. I had no intention of spending time in downtown Crayport. Not only was it depressing, but it would draw attention to ourselves that I thought unwise. I still couldn't credit Sean's story that the Blackleys had been murdered, but I suspected that we hadn't been told the entire truth about their deaths, and I was perversely heartened by the prospect of doing something that Turner and Weathers and the rest of Crayport would certainly find objectionable. The wait seemed too long to bear and I had to do something to bleed off some of my nervous energy.

"Feel like taking a walk along the beach?"

"Sure. Let me grab a bag for our trash."

We walked south, away from Crayport, eating our sandwiches and drinking beer. The night had cooled to an almost comfortable temperature and the sky was unusually colorful, lines of red deep as blood near the horizon, fading through a sequence of colors through the ascending sky. There were a few clouds, but they were long and thin, and drifted so slowly that they seemed motionless. We walked right at the water's edge, because the beach narrowed once we were past

Sawblade Point, the land rising abruptly on our right into low cliffs studded with eroding rock. We saw occasional blueberry bushes, a lot of laurel, patches of poison ivy so elderly that they were virtually small trees, and occasionally swaths of intrepid violets crowding into the comparatively sheltered areas.

We were approximately fifteen minutes away from the trailer when I noticed something unusual ahead of us.

"What happened here?" Alyson had spotted the same thing.

The moon was near full and the sky was clear, so we could see surprisingly well. There was, or rather had been, a small cabin nestled in a rocky notch just high enough to avoid high tide. It obviously had never enjoyed electrical power or plumbing or a telephone, but the wooden frame looked sturdy enough. At least what we could see of it. Something had smashed the building almost completely flat, as though a gigantic weight had fallen from the sky. The roof was almost intact, but the center was lower than the edges, which had flexed upward as the main structure hit the ground. The walls were shattered into splinters, and only a few boards had survived relatively undamaged. These must have exploded outward from the structure at the time of its demise, for they were scattered several meters away from the rest of the wreckage, one of them caught in the branches of a nearby tree.

We had no difficulty climbing up to the ruins,

but we had to be careful walking about because of the many jagged splinters and loose nails. Alyson spotted the leg of what was probably a small table peeking out from under one corner of the roof, and I found a few scraps of cloth that might have been curtains.

"Collapsed in a storm?" I suggested, not entirely believing it. The damage was not recent, but neither had it happened many years in the past.

Alyson looked doubtful. "None of the trees are damaged. It looks as if something fell on it."

"Maybe that's Crayport's hidden secret. They have a giant living in the hills."

"You don't suppose there's someone, you know, *in there*, do you?"

"Of course not!" But once she'd planted the idea, I was suddenly struck with the image of pale white bones hidden under the wreckage. I tried lifting one corner of the roof, but the weight was too much for me.

We poked around for a few more minutes without making any further discoveries, then made our way back to the trailer. Alyson disposed of the trash while I refilled the generator's tank. It was almost time to leave.

"Mind if we take your car this time? I'm almost out of gas." Crayport didn't have a station as such, but I'd been told I could buy gasoline at the mariners' supply shop adjacent to the town wharf. It had been dark and apparently closed each time I'd passed it, but I would have to do something about it tomorrow or learn to walk a lot faster.

"Sure, but I get to drive."

As the time approached to leave, I felt increasingly nervous. Almost certainly something strange, probably illegal, possibly deadly, was happening behind the scenes in Crayport. I still couldn't convince myself that the Blackleys had actually been killed by their neighbors, but neither was I comfortable with the concept of solemn William Blackley committing murder and suicide. Still, I'd had a college friend who quite calmly threw himself in front of a train one night, leaving behind a suicide note that said simply that he was bored and saw no point in continuing with his life. Jennifer Blackley might well be in a hysterical state, even if she supported Sean's implications about some mysterious conspiracy. There was a conspiracy, of course; the resistance to my efforts to purchase land in the area was at least tacitly organized, instigated almost certainly by Jared Turner and perhaps with the collaboration of the Crawleys. But I could understand if not sympathize with the kind of xenophobia and resistance to change that occurs in insular communities like this. I'd grown up in Managansett, Rhode Island, which in its quiet and unassuming way was every bit as peculiar as Crayport. It was annoying and frustrating to outsiders, but hardly alarming. I also suspected that the Crawleys were involved in something that was at least marginally illegal. They were smuggling something, I was certain, or perhaps disposing of treasure recovered from a sunken ship to avoid paying taxes. That would explain the size and weight of the crate we'd seen being hoisted from the beach. That might involve enough money to risk some rough stuff.

A bank of dark cloud rolled in just as we were getting ready to leave, obscuring the moon and stars and making the evening prematurely dark. Alyson drove slowly into town, then took the side road where I'd first met Jared Turner. She pulled into an unpaved cul-de-sac just past the abandoned building I'd noticed that first day, after we'd both looked around thoroughly to ensure we weren't being watched. In fact, we'd only passed three pedestrians on the way through town, and not one of them had so much as turned in our direction. Not for the first time, I had the feeling that we'd wandered into a movie set, a cross between rustic fishing village and Wild West ghost town.

Feeling melodramatically clandestine, we locked the car and took the path that Alyson had spotted earlier, moving as quickly as possible until we were concealed from view by trees, then slowing to something approximating a normal walk. Neither of us spoke more than was necessary, and I for one began to feel a depressing sense of wrongness. I'm not sure whether it was a burst of precognition about what was to come, or just a growing doubt about the actions we had chosen to take. Here we were, after all, skulking in the dark, on our way to a pair of freshly filled graves, and all because a ten-year-old boy had told us that someone was chasing a missing girl who might be suffering from hysterics, if she was here at all.

"I have a bad feeling about this," I whispered when we reached the edge of the cemetery.

"The Force will be with us," she answered solemnly.

It took longer than we expected to find the right gravesites, even though we'd scouted the area during the day. Full darkness was nearly upon us, and already the landscape was shrouded in inky shadows that seemed to move of their own volition. I was frankly spooked, and Alyson's occasional whispered monosyllable also seemed increasingly freighted with tension. Eventually we came to what I thought was the right spot, and Alyson confirmed it by briefly illuminating one of the headstones with a flashlight she'd thought (and I hadn't) to bring along.

There was no sign of Sean or Jennifer.

Alyson made herself reasonably comfortable leaning against a headstone, but I was too nervous to remain still and prowled back and forth for the next few minutes, which dragged out to more than a few. My watch read almost half past nine, and I was beginning to feel foolish as well as nervous.

"Do you suppose we've been stood up?"

Alyson was spared answering me by a rustle in the bushes that brought her quickly to her feet. I spun around, trying vainly to see who or what was moving there. "Sean?" I dared not raise my voice much above a whisper.

"I'm here."

I wasn't sure whether to be pleased or disappointed by that confirmation. A feeling of intense weariness was settling over me. "Where's Jennifer?"

"Close by. I wanted to make sure you came alone."

"I don't think anyone saw us," Alyson reassured him. "There was no one in sight."

"You can't always see Those Who Serve," he answered quietly. "But I think we'll be all right. Come this way."

Following a ten-year-old boy through the overgrown bushes that were slowly reclaiming Crayport's cemetery from civilization was not a walk in the park. We ducked and crawled and got scratched and stabbed by thorns. He led us through the brush and down a relatively gentle slope to an older part of the cemetery. Mausoleums were deeper shadows among the darkness, and I had to suppress the image of Bela Lugosi or Christopher Lee preparing to jump out from behind one of them with bared fangs and groping hands. It was to one of the largest of these monuments that Sean eventually led us. A wrought-iron fence surrounded it, but one section toward the rear was damaged, and I was just able to squeeze through without scraping off significant portions of my skin.

The door was shut when we reached it, but the

lock was broken. Sean pulled it partly open. "You can use your light once we're inside."

He closed the door behind us and Alyson clicked on her flashlight. We were in a fairly good-sized enclosure, the walls lined with shelves, most of which were occupied by coffins. There was a thick layer of dust covering almost every surface, but a small alcove at the rear was relatively clean. When Alyson swung the light in that direction, I saw a small collection of candles, a box of cookies, and a small pile of clothing set to one side. On the floor, a sleeping bag had been rolled out on the floor with a pillow arranged at one end. Apparently someone was living here.

"Where's Jennifer?" I asked quietly.

"Right here." She stepped out from a dark corner, startling us both. Sean quickly lit two candles, and the light grew bright enough for me to recognize her, although she was greatly changed from the last time I'd seen her. Her long hair was tangled and unkempt, her face was smeared with dark stains, and one sleeve of her blouse was badly torn. She was wearing jeans and sneakers and looked a great deal younger than I remembered her.

"This is Alyson, a friend of mine. We're here to help."

"No one can help." Her voice was flat, emotionless, and reinforced my suspicion that she was suffering from shock.

"They've got a car. They can take you out of

here." Sean crossed to her side and grabbed Jennifer by the arm.

"What good will that do? Jessie Ames went away, and they brought her back. My father tried to leave and they killed him."

Alyson spoke up then, her voice deliberately calm and reasonable. "Why don't you tell us what happened to your parents, Jennifer?"

The teenager sighed and looked away, and there was a catch in her voice when she spoke again. "We talked about it, and Dad thought that maybe if we moved fast enough and far enough, it wouldn't be worth their time to track us down. He planned to send a letter to the Crawleys, telling them that we wouldn't say anything about what was happening here."

"What *is* happening here?" I interrupted, but Alyson gave me a dirty look and I subsided. Jennifer, lost in her thoughts, didn't seem to have heard me.

"After you left we started making a list of what we were going to take with us. Most of our stuff would have to stay behind because there wouldn't be much room in the car, but Mom said we'd have enough money to replace everything except a few old family things she wanted us to keep. I was up in the attic, going through stuff, when I heard them come."

"Who came, Jennifer?" asked Alyson.

"Them. The Servants and some of Those Who Serve. There was Mr. Turner and Mr. Weathers and one of the Crawleys. They knocked on the

111

door, and I ran over to the air vent and listened to what they were saying. Mr. Turner told Dad he knew we'd had an offer and hoped we were loyal enough to the town not to have sold out. My dad doesn't lie real good and he knows it, so he just told them you'd made an offer and he was considering it, but that he hadn't agreed to anything yet. Then Mr. Crawley said something about how disappointed he was that we would consider letting outsiders move into Crayport, and Dad got mad all of a sudden and told him it was his property and he'd sell it if he wanted to."

Jennifer paused then, reliving that terrible moment. None of us said anything, and after a minute or two she continued, her voice once more level. "Dad told them to get out of our house, and then I heard Mom shout something, and there was a lot of running around and shouting. Then everything got real quiet. My legs were starting to cramp and I was trying to decide what to do when I heard this awful explosion and there was glass breaking. Then there was another one, and after that I heard talking downstairs, but it wasn't Mom or Dad. Someone went out into the front yard and fired the shotgun again, but I don't know why. I heard footsteps coming up the stairs toward my room, so I climbed out the attic window and went over the roof to the other side of the house. I think I heard Mr. Turner calling my name from inside, but I just hid behind the chimney and pretty soon they went back downstairs, and a little while after that they all drove away."

She ran her fingers through her hair and threw her head back. "I came down later, after I was sure they were all gone. My parents were gone too, but I know what happened to them. There was a lot of blood." Her voice broke and I knew she was crying. "So I took some stuff and ran off before they came back for me." Her voice trailed off.

"I found her down on the beach and brought her here. They never come inside the cemetery unless they have to, and I knew as long as she stayed out of sight for a while, they'd forget about her. They always forget about us kids."

Something way in the back of my mind connected to something else that I'd forgotten, and I had a momentary flash of insight. "You're Sean Caspar, aren't you?"

He nodded slowly. "They're stupid about some things. When I filled in the grave, after they killed Mom and Dad, they stopped looking for me. I guess they kind of think I'm buried out there." He shrugged. "Most of 'em aren't real bright, at least Those Who Serve aren't."

"Who are we talking about, Sean?" I asked. "Is everyone in town a part of . . . whatever this is?"

"I don't know exactly. There're only a few Servants; I don't know how many have become Those Who Serve. You know, the ones who act like zombies."

"Zombies?" Alyson and I reacted identically.

"They're not really zombies, I guess, but they act different after the change. I don't know ex-

113

actly what happens to them, but they stop doing much except sit around and wait to be told what to do. And their hands get all funny. Sometimes that happens to the Servants too, like Mr. Turner." I thought of the people with frog fingers and realized what he was talking about.

"Mom used to be really good friends with Mrs. Harford before she got changed," added Jennifer. "That's what made her afraid to stay. That, and when Old Davy got killed. They were the only friends she had left in town, and she figured that we were next."

"Who's Old Davy?"

"He was kind of a hermit," explained Sean. "Lived in a shack down the coast a little way. He used to take me with him hiking up in the hills sometimes, and we'd go fishing together once in a while. Old Davy was never really a part of the town after his family died, back before I was born, and he kept pretty much to himself until he started seeing things out on the water. He told some people that he was going to get a camera and take pictures, but I guess he never got around to it. A few days after that I went out to see him and he was gone, and his place was all smashed up. My dad told me it was probably hit by lightning or a waterspout or something, but I think he was just trying to make me forget about it."

Alyson and I exchanged looks. Undoubtedly the ruins we'd seen earlier in the day were what remained of Old Davy's cabin.

"So let me get this straight," I said, trying to sort things out in my own mind. "Turner and the Crawleys and some of the other people in town have this secret organization that murders people."

"They call themselves the Servants," Sean answered, nodding.

"Why do they call themselves that?" asked Alyson. "The Servants of who, or what?"

Sean shrugged. "I don't know. My mom and dad never wanted to talk about it when I was around."

I was still trying to arrange my thoughts. "And then there are the zombies, the people who have been changed. How do they fit in?"

This time it was Jennifer who answered. "Dad thinks . . . thought that they were the ones who wanted to be Servants but who failed some kind of test. They pretty much do what the Servants tell them to do. The Servants call them Those Who Serve. The change always happened after they were missing for a few days. They'd show up again, but they weren't the same. Never went back to their jobs, stopped working in their gardens or fixing up their yards. It was like they just weren't interested in anything anymore. Except the festivals."

"Festivals?"

But I didn't get an answer to my question, because Sean suddenly whispered for us to be quiet and blew out the candles. In the darkness I heard the creaking of the iron gate outside the mausoleum. Someone had just swung it open.

115

Chapter Seven

I froze, as though by not making any noise we would escape notice. Obviously the very fact that someone had opened the gate indicated that they knew we were here. I heard something scuttling away from me, but before I could react, the door was flung wide, and what appeared to be a very bright light flooded into the room. It was a gas lantern, and as I blinked and retreated toward the rear of the mausoleum, a second came into sight, accompanied by at least two flashlights.

"It appears that you were right, Jared," said a man's voice, a voice that sounded very familiar. Edward Crawley stepped into view, followed promptly by Jared Turner. "All of our fishes in one net. I must say that I'm impressed with your tenacity, Mr. Canfort, and yours, Miss Branford, although regretfully it's necessary to remove you from the game before you do any more damage than you have already."

"What's this all about, Crawley?" I tried to sound sure of myself, but there was a tremble in my voice. He acted as though I hadn't even spoken.

"Outside, all of you."

I thought about refusing, but then decided the odds were better for us out in the open. I counted at least six people opposite us, and there might be more beyond the vault's doors, but at least outside there'd be some place to run to if the opportunity arose.

Alyson and Jennifer preceded me, and I hesitated for a second, realizing that Sean was nowhere to be seen. I remembered what the boy had said about the adults forgetting the children existed and entertained the faint hope that they might not have realized he was with us. I followed the others quickly lest they be tempted to search the mausoleum.

The sky was still dark, but the lanterns and flashlights provided enough illumination for me to confirm that there were in fact only the six men confronting us: Turner, the younger Crawley, and four I didn't recognize, although I thought one of them might be Jenson, the man who'd threatened me.

"Take those two in your car, Jared," ordered Crawley. "Mr. Canfort will ride with me."

"We're not going anywhere with you, Crawley.

You have no right to interfere with us in any way."

He sighed theatrically. "Mr. Canfort, you will do exactly what we tell you to do or we will hurt you, is that clear?" To prove his point he removed a small revolver from his jacket pocket.

"What's this all about, anyway?"

He laughed unpleasantly. "Right, this is the point where I'm supposed to reveal the details of my sinister plot, confident that you cannot escape, so that you have crucial information when you prove me wrong, overwhelm your captors, take my gun, and turn the tables for the dramatic and heroic finish. Sorry, Canfort, but I've read that script and I didn't care for it. No imagination. I have no interest in trying to explain something to you that you probably haven't the intelligence or desire to understand. Now, do as you're told, or remember where we're standing. I assure you the ground is nice and soft this time of year, and it wouldn't take long at all to dig a grave for you."

That's when Jennifer bolted. She twisted away from the two men standing beside her and started to run for the woods. Only Jenson—by now I was certain of his identity—had a chance to grab her and he reached out. I felt a moment of exultation as I realized that his fingers would fall just short, but even as I allowed that hope to rise it was dashed. Jennifer cried out in obvious pain and jerked to a halt, then stumbled as Jenson yanked his arm back, dragging her close. I was startled and dismayed, startled because obviously some trick of the shadows had led me to believe she was beyond his reach when she actually wasn't. Abruptly she turned about and kicked her captor in the shin, the blow landing solidly enough to be audible, but Jenson reacted only by tightening his grip, apparently with painful force because Jennifer cried out again and collapsed, held erect only by Jenson's grip on her upper arm. One of the others closed the distance quickly and caught her from the opposite side, and she must have fainted because she went completely limp.

"Leave her alone!" demanded Alyson. "She's just a child!"

Crawley moved the revolver to point roughly in her direction. "She hasn't been seriously hurt, I assure you. Not yet. Now please follow Mr. Turner before we are forced to use even less pleasant tactics."

There was no viable alternative, so Alyson and I meekly allowed ourselves to be herded down to Shoreline Road, where two vehicles were parked bumper-to-bumper. Jennifer's now unconscious form was bundled into the back seat of the first vehicle, and Alyson climbed in beside her. One of the silent men joined them and another climbed into the front passenger seat opposite Turner, who started the engine without closing his door.

"Take them up to the house," ordered Crawley. "We'll be right behind you."

Turner drove off while Crawley opened the

rear door of the second car. "If you please, Mr. Canfort."

One of the remaining two men was already walking around to the opposite side of the car, but the last, Jenson, was right beside me. I suspected I could outrun him given a few steps head start, but there was no way I could outrun a bullet from Crawley's weapon. Reluctantly I started forward, preparing to clamber inside. Crawley was smiling broadly and had even started to replace the revolver in his pocket when something flew out of the night and struck him in the forehead. He staggered back against the side of the car with a cry of outraged pain.

If I'd stopped to think, I probably wouldn't have acted quickly enough. But when I saw his gun arm drop, I twisted away from Jenson and started to run back into the cemetery, weaving my way through the gravestones, bruising my shoulder when I cut too close to a tree. Someone shouted behind me and I heard a sharp crack like a snapped branch that was probably a gunshot, but as far as I could tell it came nowhere near me. Apparently Crawley could see in the dark no better than I.

I was certain that Sean had thrown the stone that had won my freedom, and I hoped he was making his escape as well, but I had no time to think about that now. Away from the lanterns, I could barely make out the shapes around me. I fell over a grave marker once, banging my elbow, and lost my balance on a sudden sharp slope, this time bruising my right hip so badly that I limped slightly when I regained my feet. Fear helped me ignore the pain, however, and I finally reached thicker brush, pushing through it even when sharp thorns tore at my clothing and skin. I'm not sure just how long my panicky initial flight lasted, but when I finally collapsed, out of breath, drenched with perspiration, I was near the crest of a sizable hill with no idea where I was in relation to anything else.

I made my way more slowly to a high spot, then climbed a jagged rock to an outcropping from which I had a fair view of my surroundings. I was north of the town but not very far from shore, around which curvature I had advanced far enough that I could see distant lights to my left that were probably from the Crawley property. Seeing those lights reminded me that Alyson and Jennifer were still prisoners. My first inclination was to go for help, but upon reflection I realized that wasn't as easy as it seemed. The Uncohasset River forked to the west, and its two branches ran down to the sea above and below Crayport. The only bridge I knew of was the one across which I'd come when I'd first arrived. Crawley would have to be very stupid not to realize the same thing, and I suspected that a guard was already posted there.

The local police? I hadn't been favorably impressed by Chief Weathers, who was probably one of Crawley's stooges. If he had this town tied up as neatly as I suspected, the chief of police was a crucial position for him to control. Even if I swam the river, and I wasn't sure I could have managed that, and even if I could find someone in authority and get them to come investigate, it would be a simple matter for Crawley to deny everything. What evidence did I have, after all, considering that he could probably get everyone in town to support whatever story he chose to put forward?

That was as far as my thoughts had progressed when I realized I had more immediate and more serious problems. Lights began to dance through the woods back the way I'd come. Lots of lights. I counted at least a dozen, and there were probably more. It didn't take a great leap of insight to realize what they were looking for. I rounded the crest of the hill, planning to outflank them and slip back into town, but I spotted more lights below, working their way around to cut me off. I turned northeast instead.

With a conscious effort to suppress a new wave of panic, I refrained from running this time, made my way carefully but as quickly as possible over a series of rises and dips, through brush and small trees, across two fast-moving brooks. It was difficult in the pitch darkness, but even if I'd had a light, I wouldn't have dared to use it. Behind me, my pursuers seemed to have gained considerably because their lights were brighter and even more numerous. If they were communicating with one another, it was silently, because I heard none of the shouting that normally accompanied searches of this kind. I had the distinct feeling that I was being herded, but I couldn't think of anything that I could do about it.

I considered heading for the Crawley property. Perhaps they would be surprised by a direct assault, so to speak. I never really had the opportunity. I did see the outline of the large metal building, silhouetted against reflected lights from below, but still another search party was climbing up from the coast, apparently attempting to close the trap. They had, however, underestimated my progress, and I was able to slip around their line, although this seemed only the briefest of respites. A few minutes later I realized that I had moved past the end of the developed shore. I was now caught in a triangle of freedom surrounded by the ocean, the river, and Crawley's minions.

I was also exhausted. The pursuit had lasted long enough that my adrenaline high had subsided. In addition to scores of scratches and aching muscles, I was also being eaten alive by mosquitoes. I had doubted my ability to swim the river early on; at this point I knew it was impossible. So I headed toward the ocean, hoping that when the two pincers of the search met, they'd assume I had doubled back.

As it turned out, either they dismissed that possibility or hedged their bets, because when I finally reached the end of the line, a row of steep cliffs overlooking a rock-strewn shoreline, I could tell that the lights were moving in my direction once again. Frantic, I ranged back and forth, looking for someplace where I could climb down. There was a slight ledge a meter or so below, but the darkness prevented me from finding any negotiable route by which to descend any farther. I climbed back to the summit and promptly stepped on a rock that turned under my foot. My knee hit a tree stump when I fell, hard enough that I knew I wouldn't be doing any running for a while, although I could still manage an unsteady walk.

Out of breath, out of running room, out of time, I felt a sudden wave of hopelessness and sat down on the very same tree stump that had injured my knee. It rolled away, leaving me sitting on the ground. I started to laugh and suppressed it, afraid that I was getting hysterical. Somewhere in the distance I heard a brief shouting. They were getting close now. Very close. But as I staggered to my feet, I realized I was too exhausted, emotionally and physically, to prolong this much longer. Unless some marvelous escape plan suggested itself to me, they were going to catch up very shortly and I'd be a prisoner again, assuming they didn't just throw me into the ocean and have done with it.

And then I had a thought.

It required patience, good timing, and more good luck than I deserved, but I couldn't think of anything else to do. It was tedious rolling the rotting stump to the right place, but I needed a spot from which it would drop straight into the breaking waves. I positioned it by touch as much as by sight, knowing that I'd have only one chance. When the searchers were close enough, I would have to tip it over the brink, then conceal myself by dropping to the ledge and squeezing under the narrow overhang, far enough back that they wouldn't be able to spot me with their flashlights. If they climbed down and checked, then it was all over. Not the greatest plan imaginable, but it was the only thing I could think of.

And to my immense surprise, it worked.

I heard them rustling in the brush only a few meters away, and the beams of their lights were already probing in my direction. I dared not delay any longer; if they spotted me at the wrong moment, the game would be up. I pressed my shoulder against the stump, braced my legs, and thrust the stump seaward with such force that I almost followed it over the edge. Then I let out the most bloodcurdling scream I could manage as I dropped down to the ledge, letting it taper off theatrically and end with the splash of the stump hitting the surf. It wouldn't have fooled most people, I suspect, but Crawley's followers had so far failed to impress me with their intelligence, and I thought I had a decent chance of fooling them.

I had a bad moment when footsteps approached the cliff above me and beams of light dropped down to sweep the roiling waters below. Cringing against the earthen wall, I kept my breathing low and my body motionless. They seemed to stand there an inordinately long time, and I heard more rustling from both sides as additional searchers joined them. Eventually the lights became less numerous, and I realized that the party was starting to move off, exploring the cliff face to either side, probably looking for a way down. If so, they had no more luck than I, because ultimately they all trudged back toward the Crawley property.

I decided to wait for an hour to be sure they were really gone, checking my watch to mark the time. To my amazement, it was almost two in the morning; the pursuit had lasted close to five hours. Then I must have dozed off, because when I opened my eyes and stretched my cramped limbs, the sun was beginning to rise, a fiery red eye that dripped blood over the ocean as it broke through the thinning curtain of ashen clouds.

Both my knee and my hip loosened up once I had walked around a bit. I remained cautious, and frankly terrified. My pursuers wouldn't be carrying lights now if they still searched for me, so I wouldn't have that warning. With frequent stops to listen for indications of undesired company, I reversed my course, angling back toward the road. I breakfasted on some wild blueberries and drank from a brackish but cool brook, splashing water onto my face. Despite everything, I began to feel a little more optimistic. I had, after all, outsmarted them. There was a good chance they thought I was dead. Even if they entertained the possibility that I was alive, I doubted they'd expect a frontal assault. But they still had Alyson, and I wasn't leaving without her.

Was I in love with Alyson? That's a tough question. Certainly I liked her and admired her immensely. I'd hardly call our relationship casual, but it was free of the kind of sexual tensions I often detected in other couples. But she was certainly at least a very close friend, and I didn't want anything to happen to her. What's more, I felt responsible. She'd only come to Crayport to be with me.

On the other hand, saying that I was going to rescue her and coming up with a plan for actually doing so were two entirely different matters.

I avoided the large, modern building and descended toward the main house from the rear. One of the two refrigerated trucks was still there, this one with its rear doors open, revealing an empty interior. Two men were washing it out, and I carefully stayed behind thick cover while I passed their position. There were two cars parked out front when I first arrived, but while I lay in the bushes watching, Jared Turner and three other men came out of the house and got into one of them. It did an abrupt U-turn and vanished back toward the town center. A few minutes after that two more men came out of the house, crossed the road, and descended out of my line of sight, probably using the stairway that led to the shore.

I waited for half an hour without moving. The

men washing the truck finished their work, closed the back, and started the engine. They backed it so that it straddled the road, then both followed the others down to the water. There was a small porch at the rear of the house, with a pile of kindling wood arranged at one end. I selected a stout length from among these as a makeshift cudgel, and hoped fervently that I'd have an opportunity to try it out, preferably on Edward Crawley. The screen door didn't appear to be latched, but I wasn't ready to try to actually enter the house until I knew a little more about what was happening inside.

So I listened at windows. Not much luck at the first three, but at the fourth I heard a man's voice, deep, angry. It was Joseph Crawley.

"We'll just have to make the best of the situation. But I'd hoped you would have removed the element of uncertainty."

"It's likely that he's dead." That was Edward, but the self-satisfied tone was missing. "Even if he missed the rocks. And even if he somehow survived, what could he possibly do? No one would believe his word against ours, particularly if Turner and Weathers corroborate our story that he and the girl had been fighting. We can be sure they won't find her."

"She's secured below?"

"Of course. Both of them are."

"Don't sulk, Edward. It doesn't become you."

"I just don't understand why you're so angry.

What does it matter now anyway, when we're so close?'

"It's precisely because we are so close that I'm perturbed. We'll be particularly vulnerable for the next several months."

"I don't see why. The Children are beginning to come through now."

"Three of Them have joined us. A fourth will arrive tonight. That's hardly enough of a vanguard to ensure success. We need more time, Edward, perhaps as much as a year before we'll be in a position to act with impunity. Even the Children can die."

"But if the Summoning works in Providence, we'll be ready to move within days."

"I have less confidence in the efficacy of that ceremony than you, Edward. The people here are conditioned to follow our lead, and have proven themselves capable of opening the gateway. In a strange environment, with minds unprepared and unaware of what they're really doing, too many things could go wrong. It's a chance worth taking, I'll grant you, but we must continue to act as though that option is closed to us, so that we can still move forward if it fails."

They moved out of earshot at that point, still talking but inaudibly insofar as I was concerned. I considered my options. They'd referred to Alyson as having been taken "below." That might mean a basement, but it was more likely that Crawley had referred to the structure down at the shoreline, which I'd only seen from a distance.

The front door slammed shut and I peered around the side of the building just in time to see the two Crawleys crossing the road. There was a good chance that the house was empty. I decided it was worth the risk to explore the interior. I might find something that would help, some clue as to what was really going on in Crayport. I eased the screen door open and slipped inside, gently shutting it behind me.

The house felt empty. Somewhere a fan was humming. I was standing in a large, old-fashioned kitchen that was spotlessly clean and organized with military precision. I crossed to the interior door, which revealed a corridor stretching in both directions, the left branch of which ended at a staircase to the second floor. There was no sign of life, so I did a hasty search of the ground-floor rooms. The living room was exactly as I remembered it. A large dining room was dominated by a row of curio cabinets and an oversized oak table, but it had the feel of a stage setting. I suspected that people rarely if ever ate in this room. There was a small library as well, which displayed considerably more character. The deep shag rug showed evidence of heavy wear, the leather armchair beside the window was shiny with use, and the shelves themselves were filled with old books, all heavily bound and heavily used, and most in languages other than English. The titles I could read seemed to deal mostly with metaphysics, comparative religion, and physics, although I did notice a modern atlas. One particularly ancient-looking volume lay on a small table in the center of the room. The cover identified it as the *Necronomicon*, which I had never heard of but which even sounded repulsive.

There was a small handgun lying on the desk. It was loaded, so I slipped it into my pocket, but a cursory search of the drawers and shelves uncovered no additional ammunition. I still had my crude cudgel as well as I headed for the stairs.

I paused on the landing halfway up, listening intently. There was no sound from above except the ticking of an elaborate grandfather clock at the head of the stairs. The air smelled musty, filled with molds rather than dust, with a bittersweet scent. The silence persisted, but I had the uncanny sense that the house was listening, that something was about to happen.

It took a conscious effort of will to mount those last few steps, but I couldn't miss the chance that there might be some clue to be found that would tell me what was going on. I reached the top and found myself staring at a row of closed doors. I tried the first one, which was not locked, and looked into a perfectly ordinary bedroom, currently untenanted. The bed was bare, the curtains drawn, the other furniture orderly, but overall there was an atmosphere of complete emptiness and disuse. I closed the door and moved to the next.

This was a different story. It was a man's bedroom, presumably one or the other of the Crawleys. The bed was neatly made, but once again the curtains were drawn. A small safe stood in one corner, but it was closed and, when I tried the door, securely locked. There was a large desk in one corner of the room, but the papers were mostly bills and circulars. I noticed that two of them were utility bills for a warehouse in Providence, noted the name, and left them there. There was another tattered book of considerable age, but it wasn't written in English and all that I could determine was that it was written by someone named Prin.

Impatiently, I tossed the book back where I'd found it. This was getting me nowhere, and for all I knew, Alyson and Jennifer were in imminent danger. I decided to forego searching the rest of the rooms and quickly returned to the hall, planning to leave the house. But as I stepped through the door, some subliminal sense warned me and I turned to my left, just in time to see the silent housekeeper charging directly at me with outstretched hands.

Her fingers were unnaturally thick.

Chapter Eight

She was an elderly woman, and if I'd had a chance to think about what I was doing, that would probably have been the end of my story right then and there. But she didn't give me the opportunity to think, and I swung up my arm defensively and instinctively, without realizing that I was still holding my makeshift cudgel. Her arms were deflected to one side and as they swung past my face I noticed something peculiar about the tips of her fingers. Then I was twisting away as she fell against the wall, set off balance by my own exertions.

My first inclination was to apologize and offer to help her up, but she recovered and was moving again faster than I. Her expression still unnaturally placid, she raised her hands again, and this time I saw clearly that there was something wrong with her fingertips. At the end of each, a shiny black filament protruded from under the nail, a filament that visibly elongated and swelled as she approached. Abruptly I remembered how Jennifer had been caught the previous evening even though she seemed to be out of reach. Something was emerging from the woman's fingers, something dark and wirelike and clearly animate. Instinct told me to avoid its touch at all costs.

This time I had no qualms about using the cudgel. I struck deliberately and with enough force to break bones. There was a satisfyingly loud crack as it landed. Her left arm dropped, forearm shattered, and began to jerk about spastically, but she continued to approach. I retreated hastily to the top of the stairs, unwilling to turn my back. "Stop right there!" I shouted ineffectually. Instead she rushed forward even faster, and I leaped to one side in a desperate move I feared would be too slow. She staggered past me, came to an abrupt and nearly impossible halt at the top of the stairway, and began to turn.

I stood up, and swung the cudgel backhanded at the rear of her skull, so overcome with terror that I no longer cared what damage I might do. She tried to dodge and her uninjured arm windmilled for balance just as the blow struck, but it was too little and too late, and she toppled forward, somersaulting down the short flight of stairs to the landing.

Breathing heavily, I leaned back against the wall until my legs stopped shaking, then pushed away and began to descend the stairs. The woman lay in a totally unnatural position, her neck quite obviously broken, along with her arm and possibly one of her legs. I was two steps above her when the body began to twitch. I hesitated and, as I did so, it began to rise, impossibly, the head slumped to one side, the broken arm dangling uselessly and twitching constantly as though an electric current was running through it. As she stood, she began to turn in my direction, awkwardly because her right leg was not functioning properly.

When I saw her face, I almost stopped breathing.

The fall had smashed her nose to one side and dislocated her jaw. There was some blood, though not as much as I would have expected, and it seemed to have stopped flowing already. Something thick and black was extruding itself from her mouth, her tongue I thought at first, but it twitched and moved more like the fangs of a serpent, seemingly with a life of its own.

Awkwardly but relentlessly, she began to mount the stairs.

I think for the next few seconds I was quite mad. The thought of having her touch me was more than I could bear and I raised the cudgel and brought it down with all my strength on the top of her skull. It connected with such force that it was nearly jarred from my grasp and the woman shuddered, still silently, but paused only a split second before lifting her bad leg toward the next step. I swung again and again, shattering her good forearm, breaking her collarbone, and smashing her dislocated jar to one side. Finally she reared back, lost her balance, and crashed down to the landing a second time. This time she didn't rise.

But it wasn't over yet.

Her eyes were closed now, but her limbs continued to move galvanically, first in small jumps, then more energetically. I stood frozen, unable to summon the courage to slip past. Her torso began to heave as well, a movement that quickly became a frenzied thrashing that caused her body to topple and slide down the lower half of the staircase into the main hall. Gripping the length of wood so tightly that my fingers hurt, I cautiously followed.

Just as I reached the lowest step, her body began to split open. I had just a second to register that before I was fighting for my life once again, because from inside what I now perceived to be a ruined, nearly bloodless shell, there erupted a creature like nothing I had ever imagined even in my darkest nightmares. It was as though a coil of rubber-coated wire had been fashioned into an elaborate and ever-changing stick figure. There seemed to be no central body but rather a series of nodules scattered randomly throughout the writhing mass of blackness. The individual strands whipped back and forth, blindly I think, slapping against the floor and nearby wall.

I stood back, taking a position I believed was safely out of reach. I was wrong. One of the strands shot out in my direction. Although I flinched back, the tip slashed across my left cheek for just a split second before it fell away. It was as though someone had thrown acid in my face. I screamed and fell back onto the steps, clawing at my face. Fortunately the pain stopped almost immediately, but it left me soaked with sweat and even more terrified than I had been already.

Below me, the creature was thrashing with increasing fervor, and seemed to have completely extricated itself from the now motionless body of the housekeeper. To my great relief, it appeared to be blind, because its movements did not indicate that it knew my location. Gathered together, I imagine it would have been about the size of a basketball, but its filamentary limbs now covered a rough circle of the floor fully two meters in diameter. Dispersed throughout its body were a half dozen of the round nodes, but there were no other distinguishing features, no signs of sensory organs. Situated as it was, I could not possibly descend from the stairway without touching it, an experience I was not eager to repeat.

I retreated up the stairs, hoping to find another exit, but a quick examination of the remaining rooms provided no solution. The house lacked a fire escape and the drop from any of the windows, while probably not fatal, could quite easily have resulted in a twisted or sprained ankle. It would be my last resort. I returned to the stairway and glanced down. The creature had changed position slightly, but my situation had only worsened. Now its tendrils slapped at the bottom steps, and the bulk of its body was directly under the railing. Any chance of climbing down that way was now lost to me.

Or was it?

It took some effort, but I managed at last to push the oversized grandfather clock to the railing. Then I knelt, slipped both hands under the bottom casing, and lifted with all my strength. It tilted slowly, then more quickly. The railing disintegrated, and both it and the clock fell away from me, striking with a crash so loud that I expected the Crawleys to rush in to find out what was happening. Even now the creature was still alive, thrashing wildly about in its blind search for me. But most of its longer tendrils had been drawn close, were exploring the object that pinned it to the floor. When I saw that the stairs were now unencumbered, I descended at a run, edged around the squirming mass, and ran to the back door.

To my considerable surprise there was no evidence that any alarm had been raised. There was no one visible from the backyard, no shouts from beyond the road, and when I worked my way cautiously around the house, there was no one in sight in that direction either. That small

relief caused the last of my strength to evaporate
for the moment, and I sank to the ground, sitting
with my back against the side of the house, forcing myself to breathe deeply and regularly. What
I had just seen was so strange and unbelievable
that I was shaking with reaction.

What was going on here? Invasion from another planet? This clearly was Crayport's secret,
or part of it. From wherever it came, this bizarre
parasite hid inside the bodies of its victims, animating them or at least manipulating their minds.
But if that was the case, if all the people I'd seen
with frog fingers were no longer human, then
how explain the Crawleys and Jared Turner and
presumably Ralph Weathers? Why were they cooperating with them? Fear? It seemed unlikely.
Turner might be susceptible to that kind of pressure, but both Crawleys struck me as men of considerable self-composure. What's more, Edward
had clearly been in charge of the party that captured us in the cemetery, and my experience of
what Sean called Those Who Serve led me to
believe they were of limited intelligence.

I needed more information, and I wasn't going
to get it by sitting on my butt. With an effort of
will I struggled to my feet and began to cross the
road.

Although I couldn't see anyone moving about either at the top or bottom of the slope, I cautiously
chose to descend a few meters away from the
buildings, taking advantage of the gnarled trees

and jagged fingers of rock that protruded from the hillside. The footing was precarious and I fell twice on my way, once sliding uncontrollably down a steep slope. Happily, no one appeared to have heard my less than graceful stealthiness. When I had nearly reached the narrow strip of rocky shore—no beach here—I started back toward the large building that huddled near the shoreline, just this side of the Crawleys' private pier. The launch was tied neatly in place and unattended. There was a large crate sitting on a small level space, similar to the one we'd seen being conveyed up the hill on our first visit, but one end had been pried off and lay flat on the ground and it was clearly empty.

Other than a small pile of rusted metal trash and what appeared to be the housing for the motors that powered the lift, there was nothing remarkable except for the building, which was painted a dark brown, had no windows, and was in excellent repair. It was considerably larger than it had appeared from the water, accidentally or cleverly camouflaged by the hillside against which it had been placed. I emerged from my cover and ran to the rear wall, pressing up against it while I gathered my nerve. The silence was unsettling. Except for the lapping of water around the rocks, it was utterly quiet. No voices or movement from inside the building, not even an inquisitive seagull poking around for a handout. The water lapped at the shore with little enthusiasm, and even the usual sea breeze had dropped to a murmur.

I edged around the corner and walked quickly the length of the building, hesitating again when I reached the next corner. A peek around told me that the door was closed but unguarded, at least from the outside. I felt in my pocket for the revolver I'd stolen. It was only mildly reassuring to find it there, and I'd lost my cudgel on the trip down the hillside. Still, my only choices were to cut and run, with dubious results, or press forward with no more certainty but at least a chance to rescue Alyson and Jennifer. It occurred to me to wonder about Sean as well, but he'd managed to survive for a considerable time on his own, and I suspected he was better off than the rest of us.

With my weapon gripped in one hand, I tried the doorknob. It wasn't locked. Slowly, ready to bolt at the first shout of alarm, I opened the door just far enough to slip inside, easing it shut behind me.

Although there were at least two overhead lights, they were low voltage, distant, and didn't do much to dispel the interior gloom. I stood motionless for a few seconds while my eyes slowly adjusted to the dimness. Shapes began to emerge from the shadows, enormous wooden crates next to the overhead, garage-style door adjacent to the one through which I'd entered, and an electric motor, presently silent. A few chairs and tables were scattered about, along with several dozen corrugated boxes. And in the center of the floor an oblong shape that I first took to be an oversize table, but eventually realized was a small but clearly recognizable railroad flatcar. What's more, it was mounted on well-maintained metal tracks.

As far as I could tell I was alone in the building, which made even less sense. I could see the opposite wall clearly, and although it was remotely possible that someone could hide by crouching behind one of the cartons or crates, it seemed unlikely. At least four men had descended this hill less than an hour earlier, and I had assumed that Alyson and Jennifer were down here somewhere as well. Had I been mistaken? The launch was at the pier. Had there been a second boat that I hadn't seen before, one that carried the Crawleys and their henchmen off to some other location?

I was confused and discouraged as well as frightened now, but I was also starting to get actively angry. Drawing upon that, I found the strength to move and began exploring the interior, moving counterclockwise around the outer walls. The intervening debris was not, I was happy to discover, concealing an ambush, although I was still perplexed by the apparent disappearance of my enemies. Some of the cartons were open, and several of them were clearly labeled. I discovered that the Crawleys had purchased an assortment of electrical equipment, piping, instrumentation, and other building materials, including an extraordinary number of floodlights. There was a bulky pile of lumber in one corner, along with an extensive array of tools and other hardware.

I had completed three-quarters of my circumnavigation before I noticed the darker patch at the foot of the fourth wall, covering quite a large area of the floor. Curious, I approached it, and almost stumbled when my foot struck the casing of something embedded in the floor. Kneeling, I examined the obstruction and discovered that it was an enormous hatch cover, much too heavy to be operated manually. More significantly, the railroad tracks disappeared beneath it. I cursed myself for my stupidity. Of course the tracks must lead someplace, apparently into a tunnel of some kind. But a tunnel to where?

At first I could find no evidence of a control device, but then I remembered the motor I'd noticed earlier. There was a three-button console attached, OPEN, CLOSE, and STOP. Once again, I wondered if I was about to betray my presence, but I could see no alternative. Fortunately the mechanism operated very quietly, the hatch retracting smoothly into a raised portion of the floor. As soon as the gap was large enough for me to slip through, I pressed the STOP button and cautiously approached the opening.

It was more than a hole; it was in fact a broad sloping ramp that led down into the murky darkness. In the distance an emergency light was mounted on the wall and illuminated, and once my eyes had adjusted I was able to descend without tripping over the rail bed. The tunnel expanded slightly within a hundred steps, at which point it was about five meters wide and almost as high. The slope was steep for that distance, then began to level off gradually. I proceeded through the featureless earthen tunnel for another few minutes before I realized that I must be underwater by now. The passageway had been gradually turning to my left, but very gently, pointing directly out into the harbor and the ocean beyond. I began to perspire heavily, partly because it was hot and damp, partly because the thought of a collapse, however unlikely, stirred some primal fear I'd never experienced before. I've never particularly cared to drive through the tunnel to Logan Airport in Boston, although I've done so on several occasions. It invariably makes me irritable and sweaty.

A low-wattage lamp was mounted approximately every fifty meters, providing barely enough light to see by. Other than the wires running along them, the walls were unadorned. The rails seemed to be in good repair despite the dampness, and the ground around them was covered with loose gravel. Except for an occasional ominous dripping that I told myself was just condensation, my footsteps were the only sound.

I continued in this fashion for what seemed ages, but by my watch was only another ten minutes. Although the tunnel still sloped downward, it was a very gentle decline by this time, and the slow curve had achieved its purpose, for the track had been absolutely straight for the last nine lamps. I became more cautious at this point, because I could see brighter, more numerous lights up ahead. The tunnel was opening into a much larger cavern, although whether natural or artificial I was never able to determine. It was probably a little of both. There was also a sound from ahead, an almost subliminal thrumming that grew so gradually that it was a while before I realized that I was listening to the sound of machinery.

Abandoning the tracks, I pressed close to the left wall, for the lamps were mounted on the right. Staying within the inadequate shadows as much as possible, I continued forward until I was able to better see what lay before me. The interior walls of the cavern, at least as much as I could see from my vantage point, were decked with catwalks and ladders, from many of which lights had been strung, though only a few of these were presently lit. A handful of small, roughly made buildings were scattered across the cavern floor on either side of the tracks, which extended beyond my line of sight. I saw at least one human figure moving in the distance and crouched low, waiting until he was out of sight before approaching the entrance.

It was even larger than I had first surmised, and the construction inside more elaborate. I spotted a small holding area filled with cartons and boxes of various sizes, piles of two-by-fours and plywood, and sections of metal piping that looked like giant Tinkertoy parts. I ran quickly across an exposed stretch and concealed myself behind a wooden crate, peering around to reconnoiter.

At first it felt as though I had walked into an airplane hangar, but if so, it was an awfully crowded one. Fortunately for me, the several people visible from my location were all gathered at the far end, around what appeared to be a depression or perhaps another tunnel leading even deeper into the earth. An elaborate spiral staircase stood to one side of an enormous pillar, the only indication I could see of any kind of internal support. The pillar and the staircase reached all the way to the ceiling far above, and there was a concentration of the overhead lighting in that area. The people beneath moved slowly but methodically, several of them clustered around a railcar that seemed to be the twin of the one I'd seen earlier. Two figures stood a short distance away, relatively motionless, and although I couldn't see any details I thought I recognized Joseph Crawley's ramrod straight posture.

Somewhat closer to me was a good-sized generator, the source of most of the noise that had penetrated into the tunnel. A double row of fifty-five gallon drums separated it from a small metal building, which probably housed sensitive electrical equipment, judging by the number of cables that sprang from its roof and rear wall. On my side of the building but across the tracks was a relatively open area that was covered with miscellaneous debris, broken lengths of wood, rusted pipes, crumpled cardboard cartons, the remains of some wooden crates, and other less identifiable detritus. On this side of the tracks I could see at least three buildings between myself and the far wall, as well as a series of incongruous picnic tables. I had a bad moment when someone I hadn't noticed and didn't recognize stood up from one of these latter and started in my direction, and I ducked back behind my shelter, but there was no cry of alarm, no one came to roust me from my lair, and I concluded that I hadn't been seen.

The catwalk was tempting. There was a ladder quite close at hand, and from above I would have a much better view of the cavern and could plan more reasonably. Although I had seen no sign of Jennifer or Alyson, I was more convinced than ever that they were here somewhere. I was less confident about the state of their health. No one else was using the catwalks at present, and they provided access to almost any place I might want to go. Unfortunately for the most part they provided very little cover in the event that anyone glanced upward at an inopportune moment. It was possible that I might be mistaken for one of the conspirators, but I couldn't count on it. I wasn't at all confident that the Crawleys would be that lax in their attentiveness. Reluctantly I discarded the idea, at least for the time being, and instead started to work my way through the storage area.

I progressed past the first two buildings without incident. Beyond the third were the picnic tables, unoccupied at the moment but displaying evidence of regular use. Scattered across several of them were loaves of bread, blocks of cheese, packages of crackers and cookies and other foodstuffs. My stomach grumbled sympathetically and I realized I hadn't eaten anything more substantial than berries for several hours. A glance at my watch told me that it was already late morning. Suddenly the need to fill the aching void in my stomach transcended all other concerns. Crouching low, I scuttled across to the nearest table, snagged an oval loaf of bread, then returned to my meager cover in the same fashion, where I devoured a good portion of it, even though it was stale.

From my present position I could hear voices, male, at least two and perhaps more, although they were too indistinct for me to make out the words. My options weren't the rosiest. Although the picnic tables provided some cover, there was considerable open ground before I could reach the shelter of the last building, and I would be directly in the line of sight of the men working at the railcar if any of them happened to look in my direction at the wrong time. I might brazen it out and simply walk across the gap with my face averted, and possibly I would get away with it. Somehow I couldn't gather much enthusiasm for this idea, however, so instead I scuttled around the tables in a fairly wide arc, keeping as much distance as possible between myself and the work crew. This added to the distance I would have to cover in the open but allowed me to take advantage of the shadows that were puddled around the fringe of the cavern.

I reached my new shelter with a sigh of relief and remained motionless until my legs started shaking. Heroism is not my strong suit, obviously, but I'm stubborn, and I was determined to see this through, at least until the odds against me grew too large. I had a bad moment when two men walked over to the picnic tables, sidling around the nearest corner in time to avoid being spotted. They sat down and began to eat without speaking a word.

At the far corner of the building I crouched and peered cautiously around the side. I was very near the back end of the cavern now and the far wall towered above me and above what appeared to be an enormous pit in the floor, ringed by smaller ones. I wasn't close enough to see whether one or all of them led to another, lower chamber, but I did notice a sharp increase in the bitter smell that had teased my senses ever since arriving in Crayport. To my right the wrought-iron staircase spiraling up to the ceiling was an impressive bit of construction, and the column next to it, although capped with stone, was clearly artificial, its sides far too regular to be natural unless, I suppose, it had been chiseled and polished to near perfection. The cluster of men had moved away from me and were out of sight, but I could still hear the distant rumble of their voices.

I edged cautiously forward into the open, shuffling my feet sideways so that I could concentrate on watching to see whether anyone had remained behind where they might spot me. The area seemed completely clear, however, and the voices were growing noticeably fainter. I was almost all the way to one of the smaller pits before I risked taking a look around.

That quick glance almost cost me everything. I gasped and froze where I stood, and if one of the Crawleys or their henchmen had appeared in the next few seconds I would have been captured as easily as an invalid. The pit was only about six meters at its greatest diameter and almost equally deep, at least as far as I could tell. The interior writhed and twisted in a continuous seething motion that tricked my eye for a few seconds until I realized that what I was looking at was an entire nest of black wire creatures like the one that had emerged from the Crawleys' housekeeper. There must have been at least a dozen of them, their unnatural limbs intertwining in an elaborate dance of . . . what? Affection? Competition? Even as I wondered, a score of strands whipped into the air and reached for the edge of the pit where I stood.

Chapter Nine

When my body once again condescended to obey my orders, I retreated from the lip of the pit, not stopping until I was back in concealment behind the near building. There I crouched and waited until a wave of the shivers passed and I felt once more in control of myself. I was beginning to believe that I finally understood what was happening in Crayport. As incredible as it might be, we seemed to be dealing with a parasite of some sort. I wasn't ready to speculate about their origin yet; it might be outer space, it might be some unexplored ocean deepness or a government experiment gone awry. The result was the same. Apparently the parasites could seize control of a human body, animating it like a puppet but absorbing at least some of the knowledge of

151

the former host intelligence. Either the Crawleys were actively cooperating for reasons of their own, or they too had been invaded, but more successfully. I wondered if there was some physical or mental attribute that made the parasite's effectiveness vary so drastically. It wasn't the most reassuring theory, but I felt better anyway now that I believed I understood what was happening.

As it turned out, I was only partially correct, and the whole truth was far worse.

With a quite irrational surge of self-confidence I ran silently past the picnic area and sidled along the wall of the building opposite, determined to find out where the Crawleys had gone. I was startled to discover how close they were, less than a dozen meters away, and for the first time I could hear them distinctly.

"You're certain we shouldn't wait until another evening?" That was Edward, sounding less confident than usual.

"Yes, I'm certain. Even if he's still alive, it's unlikely that he presents any real threat to us. He didn't strike me as quixotic enough to come riding in to rescue the fair maidens, and even if he were so inclined, he'd never find them here in the temple." I felt a rush of hope when I heard that. Not only did it sound as though Jennifer and Alyson were still alive, but they were apparently close at hand, probably locked up in one of the buildings. I might have passed within reach of them without realizing it.

"And even if he was a potential source of trouble, that would only underline the need to move quickly. With each transition we become better attuned. It took years to bring the first of the Children across. The fourth one required only three callings. If all goes well, I expect to succeed with each gathering henceforth."

"That would accelerate our plans dramatically."

"It would also make it unnecessary for us to rely on the riskier Summoning. A disciplined congregation provides better control over the shaping of the gateway. With the uninitiated, there's also the chance that something will happen to disturb the equilibrium at a critical moment. Even here, the longer we wait, the greater the chance that something will miscarry. It is very important to maintain control. We're dealing with immensely powerful forces. This troublesome business with the outsiders can probably be delayed for at least several months, and even after they've started building their facility we might still be able to proceed with circumspection, although it would certainly be a troublesome situation. The time when we can expect to remain free of interference is growing ever shorter. If we can rely on a successful crossing with each ceremony, we could reach the critical point by the end of the year."

One of the other men in the party said something inaudible.

"Yes, it's possible we could arrange something

like that to discourage the outsiders. But institutions are often more resilient than individuals. Once they're determined to do something, it becomes difficult to discourage them without acting in a way that would attract more attention than would be convenient." He changed the subject abruptly, as though tired of it. "Let's get back to the house, Edward. I would be happier if I learned that the body had shown up. You do have someone responsible supervising Those Who Serve, I assume?"

"Jared is taking care of it. He's taken a rather personal dislike to the young man. I think he might actually manage a brief smile if he could be assured Canfort is dead."

Their voices began to fade and I peeked again. Virtually the entire party was trudging back along the tracks toward the tunnel. Virtually. One man stood by the door to the building next to which I was standing, fortunately with his face averted. I ducked back quickly to consider my options.

That didn't take very long; it was a very short list. I needed more information in order to make a decision. With the revolver I could presumably overwhelm a single guard, but what if there were more waiting unseen in the area? Once I was sure that the main party had left the cavern, I retraced my path to the entrance, moving quietly but as quickly as I could manage. A glance at my watch told me it was already early afternoon, and I was amazed at how rapidly the time had passed. It still appeared that only one man had been left behind, but I was taking no chances and ran across the short open passageway, concealed myself behind a pile of trash on the opposite side of the cavern. The catwalks and other structures were even more elaborate here, and a gentle air current stirred the sheets of canvas that dangled above so that it made a constant low murmur as the rough fabric rubbed against the wooden framework.

There were human remains scattered within the trash. At least two bodies. I had a bad moment before realizing that they were too far deteriorated to be Jennifer and Alyson. Even the smell had been muted by the passage of time. I felt no inclination to look more closely and quickly moved to the opposite side of the mound of debris, taking advantage of whatever cover offered itself. A large open shed contained more building materials, lumber and piping, a barrel of nails, rolls of canvas and heavy, textured paper, and a wide variety of tools. I selected a small crowbar from among these to supplement the pistol in my pocket. The shed was only partially enclosed and I studied the guard for a few moments. He stood exactly where I'd first seen him, directly adjacent to the door of the small, windowless building. His posture hadn't changed; he didn't lean against the building, or move about. I watched for several minutes and not once did he scratch an itch or yawn or shift his weight from one leg to another or do any of those small things that would mark him as human.

That single observation gave me a fresh attack of the shivers and it was some time before I was able to proceed.

Adjacent to the tool shed was a fuel dump. There were numerous fifty-five-gallon drums and one very large metal tank that I hadn't noticed earlier. Several fuel lines lay on the floor, some connected to drums, others apparently spares or discards. I could also see the elaborate web of power lines reaching from the rear of the generator to the building beside it, as well as to the nearest support column for the catwalks. The lines then dispersed in every direction, providing power to what I estimated must be several hundred floodlights, only a small fraction of which were currently in use. In fact there were more than seemed necessary. Either the Crawleys believed in multiple layers of backup, or periodically the interior of the cavern was illuminated to the level of a bright summer day.

There was one more building beyond the generator, and after that the stone column and the spiral stairway, but I couldn't advance any farther at ground level without being seen. The large open space between the generator and the building was directly opposite the motionless man guarding the area. There was no possible way he could miss me if I ventured forward. So I chose an alternate route.

Although some sections of the catwalk were open, others were covered by the canvas or sheets of heavy brown paper. I couldn't figure out

what purpose these served unless they were designed to keep falling dirt and other debris from
the cavern walls from landing in inconvenient
places or to reduce the amount of dust in the air.
They provided enough concealment that I risked
climbing up a ladder to the lowermost level, from
which point I had several choices. By backtrack-
ing a few meters I was able to climb higher without exposing myself to view, and then worked
my way past the generator and the open space
to the rear of the last building.

The far side was an open work area with a rail
spur that ended at a raised platform, apparently
a loading dock. One of the large crates that I had
seen earlier was resting on the platform, its door
open, but that side faced away and I could not
tell if there was anything inside. More perplexing
was the large oval tank mounted alongside,
clearly marked as liquid nitrogen. I could see the
sheen of ice on some of the piping. I tried to get
closer, but the catwalk ended abruptly on this
level and I was forced to backtrack and then
climb three levels higher before I could advance
that far. I was now halfway between floor and
ceiling. Not fond of heights under the best of circumstances, I felt distinctly uneasy when looking
down. The catwalk began to seem dangerously
frail, although it barely trembled under my
weight and had clearly been built for heavy use.

The scaffolding was exposed for several meters
on this level, but I was well above the guard now,
and even if he glanced in my direction, the pip-

ing from the generator was dense enough to conceal me. At least so I hoped. The catwalk briefly shook under my feet and I had a bad moment when I was certain it was going to collapse, but then I was over the long, unsupported section and behind a concealing fall of canvas. From my new position I could see that the crate was empty.

The stone column was only a few meters away. Beyond that I could see the lip of the pit full of creatures I'd encountered earlier. I could also see a portion of the larger declivity that I had thought might be the passageway to a lower chamber. On the near side a ramp had been cut into the stone floor, leading from the far end of the platform to the rim of the depression. By advancing to the very end of the catwalk I could look down directly into what seemed to be a cauldron of fog. I crouched for several minutes but could make out no features within the swirling mist and dancing shadows below me. Nevertheless I sensed that there was something lying there in concealment, something that restlessly agitated the shrouding fog so that it moved in patterns that repeated themselves, a gigantic unholy kaleidoscope.

I was still trying to make my eyes focus on what lay within when the gun was pressed into my back.

"Put the crowbar down very slowly, Mr. Canfort."

I did as I was told without turning. The voice

was very familiar. I didn't need to see his face to know that it was Ralph Weathers standing behind me. I hadn't felt his step on the walkway, so he must have come up from directly below me on another ladder, his approach concealed by the flooring.

The pressure against the small of my back went away, but probably not very far. "You can turn around now, but please do it very slowly."

Weathers was standing just beyond my reach, holding the service revolver just above his hip. I wet my lips but couldn't for the life of me think of a snappy comeback. Something in his expression suggested that was probably just as well. He crouched without letting his eyes drift from my face and retrieved the crowbar.

"I must compliment you on your resourcefulness. For nearly a century we've managed to conceal all of this from the outside world except when we chose to bring newcomers into the fold. You're the very first to have entered uninvited. I'll be very interested to hear how you managed to accomplish that." It didn't sound much like a compliment.

I still lacked a rejoinder. My mind was busily considering and discarding a variety of rash acts designed to overcome Weathers, all of which most likely would end with my dead or dying body falling to the rock floor below.

"Nothing to say, Mr. Canfort? Aren't you supposed to be threatening me with exposure, assuring me that we'll never get away with all of this?" He gestured broadly with his free hand. "Not quite cut out for the hero role, I see." His mock smile slipped away. "Let's climb down now, shall we? You first, and very carefully. I wouldn't want you to do something rash and fall." He stepped to one side so I could pass.

I had indeed thought about lunging for his weapon, but not for very long. His eyes were alert and he was a heavy, muscular man. I walked as slowly as possible, desperately trying to think of something to do or say that would alter the situation.

"You don't have a clue, do you?" Unlike the Crawleys, Weathers seemed inclined to gloat. And talk. "We're going to change the world, Mr. Canfort. We've worked for years, as did our fathers and grandfathers before us, and it's finally beginning to happen. And now it looks like you'll play a part in that change. Not a pleasant part, perhaps, but a necessary one. Great achievements require their little sacrifices."

"I don't see anything great about helping alien parasites take over human bodies."

"Parasites?" Weathers seemed honestly puzzled for a moment, then recovered. "Oh, you mean the Passengers. They're simply a means to an end. Certain of our neighbors were rather troubled by what is taking place here, and it was necessary to apply some form of control. They're not very bright, but they do follow instructions, and as an interim measure they were far better, and more humane, than simply eliminating the dissident element."

"Then you don't have one inside you?"

He laughed, but I thought there was an uneasy undertone. "Certainly not. I serve the Children and their Sire willingly and gladly. The Passengers are a temporary measure for disruptive people such as you, Mr. Canfort. Only Turner took one into himself willingly, and then only because of the cancer that was eating him up inside. The Passenger repaired the damage, and Jared retained more of himself than did the others, perhaps because he didn't fight the change. You may soon understand at first hand, Mr. Canfort, although it's quite possible you might receive an even greater honor, the chance to become one of the Children yourself."

I didn't like the sound of that.

We descended by way of a much more direct route than that which I'd used before, reaching ground level not far from the base of the spiral staircase. "What is all this?" I asked, hoping to keep Weathers talking.

"This is the Vault of the Gods, the Temple of Time, the gateway to worlds beyond. Did you know, Mr. Canfort, that in the ancient past real gods walked this Earth? Not your pallid Jesus myth or the similar pathetic delusions of primitive minds, but real, living immortal beings. They were—they are—majestic creatures who command the elements, dispense power and longevity the way you'd scatter loose change among the poor. They've been gone for a very long time now, but they haven't forgotten us, and now they have sent their Children among us to help restore the old ways."

This metaphysical nonsense seemed ludicrous coming from Ralph Weathers, who looked very much the hard-bitten, pragmatic officer of the law. I was facing him now, conscious of the pistol in my pocket. I had lowered my arms at the foot of the ladder, and now I wondered if I could casually place them in my pocket, or if that gesture would draw Weathers's attention to the suspicious bulge.

"What kind of a god needs human help?" I temporized.

A brief look of annoyance came and went on his face. "Not even the gods are omniscient, nor are they immune to treachery. They were betrayed by others of their kind, cast out from this universe into another, and the way back obscured and concealed. The passage of centuries here is but a blink of the eye to them, and now it is time for them to return."

"And you and the Crawleys are going to make all this possible, I suppose?"

He nodded. "A few have been honored with that task, yes. We will help the Children to enter our world and prepare it for the return of their Sire and his brethren."

"And I suppose you'll all be rewarded for your efforts on their behalf?" My hand was close to my pocket now.

"It is honor enough just to serve," he answered, "and if by so doing I deserve a higher place in the order that shall come, I shall continue to serve my masters in whatever capacity they feel appropriate." Weathers raised the weapon and was suddenly more alert. "I think it would be better if you raised your arms and turned around, Mr. Canfort. I'm sure you have too much sense to contemplate resisting, but I wouldn't want you to give in to impulse simply because I was less than professional."

I hesitated, but only for a second. Weathers was careless, probably because Crayport was virtually crime free, thanks to the alien parasites and the Crawleys' reign of terror. But he wasn't so careless that I was ready to try anything without first reducing the odds against me.

Fortunately my luck changed at that moment.

There was loose gravel and sawdust where we were walking, and the rock floor was uneven. There was a natural ridge not far away, atop which the foundation of the loading dock building had been laid, a crosshatch of timbers. To my right I could actually look down beneath the building into a crawlspace that I automatically identified as a potential hiding place. It would serve that purpose even sooner than I expected. I heard a grunt of surprise and a thud behind me, and when I glanced back over my shoulder saw that Weathers had fallen to his knees, apparently having slipped on the uncertain surface. If I had stopped to think about it, my advantage would have been gone, but once again my instincts took over and I turned and lunged toward him, hit him square in the chest with my right shoulder. The impact seemed to stun the burly police chief temporarily, and I wasn't feeling great myself, but I grappled with him despite the pain, terrified that he might turn the gun in my direction.

I managed to get my arms wrapped around his, but it was only a temporary respite. Once he regained his full wits he'd be able to overpower me easily in a simple test of strength. I belatedly remembered my own pistol, but when I tried to disengage my arm, Weathers moved with such obvious purpose that I knew I'd lose that race. But I had to do something. Already my opponent's greater strength was beginning to tell. He broke one arm free despite my efforts and struck a glancing blow along the side of my head. I fell to one side and my hand struck something cold and hard. The crowbar! I grabbed it and swung desperately as Weathers jerked his other arm free and started to bring up his own weapon.

The crowbar struck him in the center of the forearm and he cried out in pain but didn't drop the gun. I tried to strike again, but now it was Weathers who was intent upon closing with me. Our arms became entwined and in my effort to pull free I tangled my legs with his. We both lost our footing and fell onto our sides, then rolled over twice as we struggled. I managed to pull the pistol from my pocket, but either by chance or intent Weathers struck my elbow and I dropped it. We came to a stop at the lip of the drop with Weathers sprawled across my legs. I was almost out of breath, but when I saw his gun hand coming up I summoned the energy for one last swing of the crowbar.

It missed his arm but caught him just above the left ear. The blow landed with enough force that it should have knocked him unconscious, but somehow Weathers managed to retain just enough of his senses to grab my collar as he fell away. Although I tried to pull free, I could get no purchase on the gravelly surface. Weathers toppled over the lip, dragging me with him.

It was a full meter drop and I didn't have time to shield my head fully before the impact.

I woke to blazing pain. My head hurt, and when I tried to move it a shower of sparks burst against my eyelids. My right shoulder complained as well, and so did my left knee. I shifted slowly into a more comfortable position and for those first few minutes I could barely remember my name, let alone what had happened to me. Eventually the pain dulled a bit, or I became used to it, and I started to remember. Then came fear. I was lying in shadow and near silence, cold stone beneath my body. A cursory glance around told me that I remained where we had fallen, beneath the loading dock building. I also had a moment of alarm when I realized I wasn't alone, but Weathers was motionless and, when I finally found the courage to check, I discovered that he was no longer breathing. His head lay at a peculiar angle and I assumed he had broken his neck in our fall. I felt as though I had done the same.

I found the crowbar protruding from under his body and reclaimed it, and a few seconds later my groping fingers located the small pistol I'd been carrying. I tried to find his revolver as well but without success. Either it was trapped beneath his body or had ended up in some peculiar hiding place of its own. In any case I didn't have time to spare to search for it. There was a good chance that Weathers's corpse would go undiscovered for a while, unless his absence resulted in a thorough search. That meant I still had time to effect a rescue, if I could figure out where Jennifer and Alyson were being held. I was pretty certain that it was in the building with the guard; I couldn't imagine any other reason for him to be posted there. But supposition was not certainty.

I considered trying to sneak up and brain the guard with the crowbar or, failing that, shoot him and take the risk that the noise would attract attention. But then I remembered the housekeeper and what had emerged from her body and realized that I needed a better plan. The hum of the generator provided one and I climbed out of the pit and hobbled around to the fuel dump. There were half a dozen five-gallon cans filled with gasoline and I found one about half full, enough to do the job and light enough to carry. I would incapacitate the human shell, either with bludg-

eon or bullets, and use the gasoline and my cig-
arette lighter to dispose of the creature wearing
it. Then I'd use the crowbar to open the door, set
Alyson and Jennifer free, and lead them out
through the tunnel. There might be another
guard back in the small warehouse, but I had the
pistol and the element of surprise, and once we
were out in the open we'd steal a car, at gunpoint
if necessary, and get out of Crayport one way or
another. Enter the cavalry, the marines, or whoever the authorities used in situations like this.

It was as good a plan as I was likely to be able
to devise on the spur of the moment, but I never
got to put it to the test.

I hadn't carried the gas can more than a few
meters before I heard distant voices. Several of
them. I placed the can down in an inconspicuous
spot and retreated behind the generator. At least
a half dozen people were entering the cavern,
judging by the sounds, although I couldn't see
them. Cursing under my breath, I retreated to the
base of the scaffolding and concealed myself behind a double fold of the heavy paper draping.
It was then that I glanced at my watch and discovered that I'd been lying unconscious for
much longer than I had originally thought. It was
almost seven o'clock in the evening. No wonder
I was so stiff and sore. I must have been unconscious for at least four hours, wasting what should
have been more than enough time to carry out
my planned rescue. And now it appeared to be
too late.

Chapter Ten

Using the hanging paper as a shield, I moved parallel to the chamber wall until I could see the oncoming party. Edward Crawley was among them, readily identifiable even from a distance, although I didn't see his father this time. There were eight people in total, two of them women, although I could identify none of the others. Crawley was speaking to two of the men, but the rest of the party remained silent, and I suspected that if I was closer I would have seen at least five pairs of frog fingers. There was something quite subtle but quite wrong about the way some of them walked, as though their bodies were unable to relax and must remain rigidly upright at all times. I hadn't noticed it before, so perhaps they took more care with their mimicry above ground.

Or perhaps it had been there all along, and I just hadn't been observant enough to see it until I was looking for features that marked them as inhuman.

I waited in hiding to discover where they were going and was somewhat heartened when they passed the guarded building without pausing. Unfortunately the guard remained at his station. I was trying to develop a new rescue plan when a second group of people entered the cavern, six more silent ones led by Joseph Crawley and Jared Turner. Crawley was doing most of the talking and he sounded angry, although his voice was too low for me to make out individual words. I figured that by now the dead housekeeper had been discovered. They almost certainly knew that I was still alive, although I didn't think they suspected I'd penetrated into their underwater inner sanctum since there was no indication that they were planning a search. That might change when they realized that Weathers was missing. I would have to act quickly as my chances of success were rapidly dwindling.

The second group split up into three distinct parties. Crawley and Turner proceeded alone along the same path Edward had followed minutes earlier. To my dismay, two of the men entered the guarded building, closing the door behind them. And to cap off the list of minor disasters, the remaining two, a man and a woman, were headed almost directly toward me. I waited, hoping they'd turn to one side, but they showed no sign of doing so. Trying to make as little noise as possible, I edged over to the nearest ladder and began to climb up onto the catwalk.

I was two levels up before I felt reasonably safe from immediate discovery. Although the canvas almost certainly would cover my movements from those standing below, I dropped to all fours and crawled to a spot from which I could look out over the cavern. There was considerable activity at the loading dock in the vicinity of the empty crate, and another cluster of people at what I took to be an electrical control panel near the base of the stone column. What really attracted my attention however was the makeshift jail, whose nature was confirmed for me at that moment. The two newcomers emerged from the building along with a third figure, whom I immediately recognized as Jennifer Blackley. There was no sign of Alyson. They were holding Jennifer's arms, so I assumed she was in good enough condition to run if given the opportunity. But how was I going to provide one?

Advancing on all fours, I paralleled their course until I reached an open section free of canvas. That forced me to backtrack and climb up two more levels, where I was high enough that I felt justified in walking erect behind the screen of dark paper. If someone had looked in my direction, they might possibly have seen a shadowy movement through the gaps between sheets, but sooner or later I was going to have to take some chances, and right now I desperately needed to

Join the Leisure Horror Book Club and
GET 2 FREE BOOKS NOW—
An $11.98 value!

— Yes! I want to subscribe to — the Leisure Horror Book Club.

Please send me my **2 FREE BOOKS**. I have enclosed $2.00 for shipping/handling. Each month I'll receive the two newest Leisure Horror selections to preview for 10 days. If I decide to keep them, I will pay the Special Members Only discounted price of just $4.25 each, a total of $8.50, plus $2.00 shipping/handling. This is a **SAVINGS OF AT LEAST $3.48** off the bookstore price. There is no minimum number of books I must buy and I may cancel the program at any time. In any case, the **2 FREE BOOKS** are mine to keep.

Not available in Canada.

NAME: _____

ADDRESS: _____

CITY: _____ STATE: _____

COUNTRY: _____ ZIP: _____

TELEPHONE: _____

E-MAIL: _____

SIGNATURE: _____

If under 18, Parent or Guardian must sign. Terms, prices, and conditions subject to change. Subscription subject to acceptance. Dorchester Publishing reserves the right to reject any order or cancel any subscription.

know what was happening. I still had the pistol, but chances were that at least some of the people below me were armed, and they were likely to be far more proficient than I, as well as outnumbering me. I needed an edge.

There was a sudden whine as an electric motor began to throb somewhere below me. A few seconds later a shower of sand and small debris fell from the cavern roof, raining down all around the stone column. The motor changed pitch at the same time and then, incredibly, I realized that the column was beginning to move. A cloud of dust rose from around its base and more light debris fell from above as it slowly began to withdraw into the stone floor. There were similar stirrings and slippages all around the cavern, confirming my suspicion that the canvas and paper shields were meant to reduce the dust level. Within a minute I could see open sky above my head, a disc that I estimated to be nearly five meters across. At first I was totally disoriented, because I was absolutely certain that the tunnel had led us out under Crayport Harbor, but then I realized the truth: The cavern was directly beneath Crawley Island; in fact, I suspected that the top of the column was the stone plate Alyson and I had discovered during our visit. No wonder the Crawleys had been unwilling to consider selling or leasing the property. Any excavation would certainly have ruptured the roof.

Most of Crawley's followers had gathered near the descending column by the time it had diminished to a mere half dozen meters in height. Two men rolled out a portable staircase from behind the building and positioned it so that Joseph Crawley could climb to the top. The last of the disturbed sand drifted down from overhead and I could see a patch of lightness that I realized was the sky, already turning dark. There were hints of starlight. The crowd below me swelled to approximately twenty, another party having entered the cavern unobserved. I could no longer see Jennifer anywhere. I moved forward cautiously, inching my way along the catwalk in a crouch, trying to find a position that would give me as wide-ranging a view as possible of whatever was about to take place below.

Crawley stood in the exact center of the stone platform for several minutes without speaking or moving. There was a brief flurry of activity among the group standing beside the ramp to the large pit, but my view of that area was obstructed by the stone column. I was considering climbing up to the next level, which extended farther toward the rear of the cavern, when Crawley abruptly threw both of his arms straight up into the air and shouted loud enough that his voice echoed throughout the vast emptiness.

"Are you prepared to serve?"

The people assembled around him shouted their affirmatives, followed almost immediately by a fainter echo from above. I glanced up and saw a fringe of faces around the disc of sky, and realized that Crawley Island was not, for the moment at least, the deserted landscape I'd seen earlier. They were too indistinct for me to recognize them, but I assumed these were more of the citizens of Crayport. And then I remembered the one time I'd seen a fishing boat leave the wharf, and wondered if it was gone again, anchored instead just off the coast of the island above us. The column continued to rise, carrying Crawley up toward the sky, but he was speaking through a public address system now and his words must have been as clear to the audience above as they were to those of us below.

Just what was going on here?

"Long ago, it was considered an honor to serve. Are you worthy of that distinction?"

There was another affirmative chorus, but in general it lacked enthusiasm, sounded like the ritual replies I remembered from my churchgoing days. That was what this ceremony reminded me of—an old-fashioned revival meeting.

"We serve the Children of those who once ruled this world, and who will one day rule again." Crawley let his arms fall and half turned on the elevated dais. *"Through their Children shall they find their way back to us,"* he declaimed, *"And by serving those Children shall we receive our rewards."*

There was a rustling sound as the assembly below me responded to some cue. From the group whom I could not see clearly came three figures, one of whom struggled briefly as she was dragged to the center of the trough I had noted earlier. It was Jennifer, caught between two men whom I could not identify from this distance.

"Their Children shall precede them, and we shall be their instruments, the blood for their hearts, the air for their lungs, the bones for their bodies!"

Jennifer's captors forced her to kneel on the grooved rock, and I realized that they were securing her ankles with chains anchored by steel pins driven into the stone. She began struggling once again, and I realized to my horror that the two men were methodically removing her clothing, one holding Jennifer's arms while the other used a knife to cut through the fabric of her jeans. They managed the entire thing so easily that I suspected this wasn't the first time they'd been called upon to do so, and within a minute or two Jennifer was standing naked, her arms crossed protectively across her hips and breasts. The two men retreated without haste to a point out of my line of sight.

"This, the least of us, shall serve as the key to the lock while through your devotion you light the way." Crawley gestured toward the cringing girl, but his face was turned up to the heads that hovered above us. *"Behold the hand that turns the key!"*

I jumped back instinctively as an enormous bank of overhead lights illuminated as one, arranged so that their brilliant glow fell upon the swirling mists in the pit beyond. And as though the mist itself had felt that touch, the agitation grew instantly more violent and the strands of fog

174

began to shed their opaque quality, growing first translucent, then nearly transparent, then burning away entirely, revealing what lay concealed within.

I looked down into chaos.

It took several seconds before my mind could interpret, partially at least, the information provided by my eyes. The pit contained, or perhaps provided a glimpse of, an enormous creature whose nature I suspect was beyond the capacity of the human mind to perceive in its entirety. What I saw I will never be able to describe adequately. In some ways it resembled a gigantic coral reef, an intricate series of body parts that moved independently of one another. Some resembled tentacles, others the limbs of gigantic crustaceans, still others were draped in what seemed to be matted fur, although the coat moved with a life of its own. There were throbbing, tumescent structures that might have been internal organs and jet black threads of flesh that appeared and disappeared as they moved from one place to another. Its color was predominantly shades of red and purple, although I suspected that other portions of its body were beyond the spectrum visible to human beings. Still others were pale, sometimes translucent. The total effect reduced me to shocked paralysis, which was perhaps fortunate. If I had retained the ability to move during the first minute or two, I might have betrayed my presence by running screaming from the scene.

By the time I was able to tear my eyes away, the shock had subsided somewhat, but I avoided looking back at the thing in the pit. Some of its limbs were multiply jointed, and sometimes those joints twisted in a direction that my eyes could not follow, as though they extended into another dimension of space. The human eye tried to trace the line of those forms and failed, and that failure was unsettling and nauseating.

My aversion did not seem to be shared by Crawley and his followers, for they all stood in rapt awe as this horrid manifestation heaved itself upright. A fleshy orifice twice the height of a man was thrust onto the base of the ramp, a sickly green organ that pulsed with increasing rapidity for several seconds before opening with a squelching sound audible even to me at my considerable distance. From the dark interior thus revealed came a movement at first tentative, then more assured, and yet another nightmare began to reveal itself.

Initially I thought the greater creature was merely expelling some waste product from its body. A mass of almost completely transparent jelly poured out, formless and featureless. But almost immediately a misshapen glob rose from the main mass and other extrusions gathered themselves very loosely into unbalanced but recognizable limbs. It came clumsily erect then, its stance canted to one side, and began to advance, although the two lower limbs—I hesitate to call them legs—weren't entirely differentiated from one another, causing it to shuffle rather than walk. The upper limbs hung loosely, although the one on its left twitched periodically, as though the nerve endings were misfiring. Its head began to refine itself into an elongated, almost canine shape. Most horrible of all, however, was the fact that I could see completely through its body and was quite certain that it had no skeleton at all.

A thin scream wakened me from my reverie and I remembered that Jennifer was tethered in its path. Although she was facing toward my position and away from the approaching horror, she had looked back over her shoulder and clearly was aware of its presence. I am ashamed to say that it never even occurred to me to draw my weapon and attempt to rescue her. Against even the human enemies assembled here, I would have had little if any chance. Against that unearthly creature and its repellent spawn any such effort would have proven suicidal. Logically, even in retrospect, I acted correctly, but in truth I was simply too terrified to think of intervening while it was happening.

The amorphous creature lumbered forward until it was directly behind Jennifer, hesitated a moment, then advanced again. From a distance I could see little detail, but it appeared that its body flowed around Jennifer's struggling form as though it were made of water. Her cries cut off abruptly as she became completely encased, but I could still see her desperate struggles. The creature stopped then, but did not become motionless. Rather, its body began to reshape itself more closely to the proportions of its captive, though without reducing its immense size. I blinked and rubbed my eyes because instead it appeared that Jennifer was growing larger, and in a sense she was.

Small dark clouds began to appear within the transparent form as Jennifer's skin began to rupture. I thought at first that her limbs were being torn from her sockets, but the truth was even more incredible. Her body, even her bones, was stretching to impossible lengths, and her flesh was literally bursting under the strain. Although it was impossible to tear my eyes away, I was mercifully spared the worst of it as the billowing blood rapidly filled the interior, masking the final stages of the process. The creature, what Crawley had called a "Child," grew completely opaque, an angry dark red that verged on black. The unbalanced limbs now matched each other, and I saw that each arm was tipped with what I hesitate to call a clawed hand, since the talons were arranged in a circular pattern around its palm rather than in the fashion of human limbs or animal paws. The feet appeared more conventional, though disproportionately large.

It raised an oversized head that appeared to have neither eyes nor ears, just a tubular snout with insectlike mandibles that were constantly snapping open and shut, almost a full meter wide when fully extended. From between them, a long, bifurcated tongue flicked about from time to time as it moved its ponderous head back and forth. But what unnerved me most was that with its head raised, I could see the Child's chest, marked by a small, pale circle which I eventually realized was Jennifer Blackley's face. I prayed that she was dead, but something told me my hope was in vain.

"Behold the Child!" I had almost forgotten Crawley, but he returned to his harangue with renewed vigor. *"The Children shall prepare this world for the coming of the great ones, and those who serve the Children will be rewarded for their devotion."* He paused and slowly turned in a circle, somehow managing to encompass those above and below. *"And those who oppose the Children shall be punished for their iniquity."*

As he was speaking, two men had appeared bearing oversized hoses. They waited a few meters away from the Child, which was flexing its arms and turning its head from side to side, as though practicing the use of its new body. Crawley let the moment drag on and the tension was a physical pain in my chest. Then he nodded to the two men and a second later some gas billowed out of the hoses. My eyes glanced at the nitrogen tank and I realized what it must be even before I noticed the sparkling frost forming beneath their feet. They flanked the Child now, and using the streams of cryogenically cold gas as prods, urged it farther down the rocky declivity, up a short ramp and into the open crate. A third man slammed the door shut and helped the other two fasten the hoses to fixtures at either side of the door, so that the stream of supercold gas flowed into the insulated walls of the crate.

"The Child sleeps now until it is needed. So must we all abide patiently until the appointed hour." Crawley had turned and quite deliberately looked at his son while saying this last, and the younger man dropped his eyes to the ground.

Now that the Child was no longer visible I was released from the paralysis that had gripped me throughout its appearance. A wave of quite uncharacteristic courage gave me renewed strength as I silently vowed that I would not allow Alyson to suffer the same fate as had overtaken Jennifer. Fortunately I didn't allow my outrage to overwhelm my caution. I had descended two levels before a movement below caught my attention, and I froze in place while a pair of men passed beneath me. I was close enough to see that each of them had frog fingers. They joined the fringes of the larger crowd and I retreated several meters to the next ladder before descending to ground level, concealed from the assembly by the generator and fuel dump. I heard the cough of a gasoline engine starting somewhere out of my line of sight. It was irregular for the first few seconds, then settled down to a muted thrumming.

Crawley's voice boomed out one last time. *"Go now until you are needed again. Take heart from the knowledge that the time of our elevation grows ever closer."*

I had no specific plan in mind except to somehow rescue Alyson and get her out of this horrid place. Any compunctions I might have had about shooting someone had long since vanished, and I was fully prepared to gun down the guard and anyone else who got in my way. As it turned out I was once more denied the opportunity to indulge my bloodthirsty emotions. By the time I was in sight of the building where I believed her to be held, the railcar carrying the Child had advanced onto the main track, powered by a gasoline engine mounted at one end. Most of Crawley's flock were following along on either side, and as the procession passed between me and my destination I took cover behind a row of fuel drums and waited impatiently as it chugged past.

I was watching the last few stragglers when the situation changed again. Peering between two drums, I saw the familiar face of Edward Crawley and a moment later his father, accompanied by perhaps half a dozen others. To my consternation, they stopped right in front of me, talking in voices so low that I could only make out random words, not enough to follow the conversation. Beyond them I saw the metal door of the informal jail open and seconds later an angry cry of protest. Instantly I had my weapon in hand, the safety off, and was estimating my chances. Alyson's distinctive voice, still raised in anger, had on the one hand given me a surge of hope, because it confirmed that she was alive and within reach. But it was a mixed blessing as well. There were too many people around, some of whom were undoubtedly armed and better prepared to use deadly force. I had fired handguns before, but never other than on a practice range.

I waited, hoping that Alyson would be returned to her cell, but when her voice fell silent I risked another peek and saw that she was being led out of the cavern within a group of close to a dozen people. Even then I considered brazening it out, but the odds were just too long. I figured Crawley would have no compunction about sacrificing some of his parasitically controlled followers in order to stop us. Frustrated, raging inwardly, I lay in hiding until their voices and footsteps had faded away, taking some comfort from the fact that at least she seemed to be in no immediate danger.

Once again I climbed the latticework of catwalks to perform a reconnaissance. After Crawley had been allowed to descend, the stone column had risen about halfway on its way back to plug the hole in the ceiling, but it went up much more slowly than it had come down. At least two men were standing near the control panel, and a third was moving around near the loading ramp. Beyond them the pit was once again obscured in fog, a development for which I was profoundly grateful. I moved circumspectly back the length of the cavern and saw no evidence of any other living being, and even as I was doing so one of the last three men passed me on his way out.

I would have to leave, and quickly, if I was to

discover where Alyson was being taken, but I was loathe to do so without first striking at least a symbolic blow against this place and everything it implied. And perhaps it could be more than symbolic.

There were several five-gallon cans of fuel behind the generator. I could only manage one of them at a time without making noise that might give me away, so it took longer than I would have liked to carry them to strategic spots around the perimeter of the cavern and lay them on their sides. Of the final three I positioned two adjacent to buildings, and the last as close to the loading dock as I felt I could go without risking exposing myself to the two remaining men. By the time I had finished, the stone column was very near the roof of the cavern and already obstructed my view of the sky.

Satisfied that everything was arranged as best I could manage, I retraced my route and opened each of the containers, allowing the gasoline to run out onto the floor. Finally I opened the petcocks on the generator's main fuel tank, stepping back quickly to avoid splashing the flammable liquid on my clothing. Retreating to the far wall, I waited until there'd been time for a considerable amount to spill out, then used a match to ignite the nearest pool.

Flames rushed away in both directions with startling speed, and then the metal container five meters away exploded with such force that I was thrown from my feet. I lay stunned for several seconds before staggering erect, then ducked reflexively as another explosion came from my right, followed almost immediately by a third. My sabotage had gone only too well, it seemed, because already the catwalks above me were draped in flaming streamers.

In a near panic, I retreated toward the center of the cavern. Someone shouted in the distance, but the roar of the flames soon made it impossible to hear anything else. The generator faltered, then blew up so violently that the metal building adjacent to it went flying through the air and the ground shook under my feet. Somehow I managed not to fall, but I was nearly deafened and briefly disoriented as well. Flaming debris from the explosion ignited the fuel I'd spilled on the opposite wall, and several lesser explosions threw burning liquid in great arcs that set the rest of the catwalks alight.

Unfortunately I'd underestimated the speed with which the fire would spread. The stores of supplies near the cavern entrance had apparently included a considerable quantity of paint. My exit was cut off by a wall of fire within which individual paint cans were exploding like hand grenades. The heat was a palpable force that drove me back into the narrow peninsula of ground that had not yet been overwhelmed by flames.

It appeared that I had trapped myself.

Chapter Eleven

For several priceless seconds I was incapable of movement, almost of thought. The growing heat finally forced me to abandon my position, and that set my mind working once again. The fire was spreading rapidly, and even if it spared a portion of the cavern, the oxygen would be depleted before it burned out. The air was already stirring violently, and that made me realize that the opening above had turned the entire place into a gigantic flue. I made a tentative move toward the tunnel, but even as I did so a wall of flaming wreckage fell in my path, cutting off that avenue of retreat.

I drew back from the flames, raising my arms to shield my face, cursing myself for not planning things better. But there would be time for regrets later. If there was going to be a later. I ran back toward the stone column, which still slowly climbed toward the roof. The platform was out of reach already. My only chance was to use the spiral staircase and escape up onto the island above.

Running parallel to the railroad tracks and no longer bothering to conceal myself, I raced quickly in that direction, detouring only twice to avoid rivulets of fire. The catwalks were collapsing in great sections, and the sound of their impact was the only punctuation to the steady roar of the fire. One enormous segment leaned away from the wall and came crashing down on my left, and I noted with brief satisfaction that the flaming debris covered the small pit full of alien parasites I'd spotted earlier. I assumed that they were vulnerable to fire. I had no time to waste determining whether or not I was right.

One of the men was waiting for me at the base of the staircase, or perhaps he was just too stupefied to react in any other fashion. I saw the swollen fingers just before I raised my weapon and shot him through the chest. The body fell and began to thrash about, but I simply leaped over it and continued toward the bottom steps, leaping the first few.

The metal railing was already warm to the touch and I began to cough as smoke and ash drifted through the air.

Ignoring a painful stitch in my side, I began running up the stairs, two and sometimes three at a time. Because of its spiral construction, I was not able to move as quickly as I might have ordinarily, but terror gave me strength and I concentrated on not wasting a second. Once a nearby remnant of the catwalk system exploded in a shower of sparks, some of which stung my face and hands, but then I was above the worst of it and still climbing.

I was perhaps two thirds of the way to the top when an enormous section of the catwalk began to break up, buckled near its base, and then fell to pieces in a downpour of flaming debris. A significant portion of this fell across the large, mist-filled cavern, and as it struck the swirling fog erupted in a boiling frenzy that was so violent I froze in my tracks, fully expecting to see that gigantic horror burst forth into the cavern. I braced myself for the sight but was totally unprepared for what actually happened. The cavern reverberated with an unearthly sound that was felt as much as heard, loud enough to drown out the still growing fire, shrill enough that my teeth ached. It was a cry of consummate rage and hatred so intense that I would have thrown myself into the fire rather than face its author. The mist seemed to withdraw rather than expand, and the surrounding rock pulsed and began to swell. Then, so quickly that I doubted the evidence of my own eyes, it literally closed, leaving a bare expanse of stone with no indication that the pit had ever existed except a faint scarring of the surface. Of its unholy occupant there was, I am happy to say, no sign at all.

I resumed my climb in a mild daze, overwhelmed by everything that had happened in the last several hours. The stone column ceased to move when the generator exploded, leaving a narrow gap between itself and the roof. If I had hesitated another moment or two in setting the fire, I might have trapped myself, this exit as thoroughly blocked as the other. As it was I managed to squeeze through the narrow aperture with difficulty while choking on the growing volume of smoke that rose from below.

But I was through at last, stumbled to my feet on the sand and managed to run a few steps before my strength finally ran out and I fell, gasping for air, coughing and retching while the muscles in my legs spasmed painfully. I might have lain there even longer except that a smoldering spark in my hair began to burn. I beat it out with my fists, then ran down to the beach and ducked my entire head. The cold chill of the saltwater helped me to regain my composure.

Crawley Island was deserted. I could see one of the fishing boats getting under way just offshore, the last of its passengers climbing aboard from a small launch that lay alongside. There were several lights above the decks and I estimated that there were at least a hundred people aboard, crowded uncomfortably close together. The sky was clear and a nearly full moon dominated the sky. Nearer at hand a column of smoke was boiling out of the hole through which I'd just exited, the darkness broken by tiny airborne sparks and occasional pieces of flaming wreckage that grew visibly more numerous as I watched. Nothing could possibly have survived down below in what was now the interior of an oversized furnace.

My own situation was less than ideal. I was stranded without a boat and had to assume that everyone in Crayport was the enemy, at least passively. Sean excepted, of course—but I had no time to wonder what had become of him. A quick scan of the horizon offered no suggestions except the obvious one. I would have to swim for shore.

The closest land was the Crawley wharf, which meant swimming back into the frying pan from the fire, but that was also where Alyson had been taken, and I still had no intention of abandoning her. Hopefully the fire would cause enough confusion to allow me to come ashore unobserved, and then I would have to improvise based on what I discovered there. Unfortunately a brisk swim wouldn't be good for my revolver, so regretfully I prepared to leave it there on the beach.

I had already stepped into the water when a sound behind me caused me to turn.

Leviathan towered above.

Sea serpents are something of a hobby with me. I must have read Jules Verne's *20,000 Leagues Under the Sea* twenty times when I was a kid, and *It Came From Beneath the Sea* was one of my favorite movies even as an adult. My fondness for sea monsters, giant squid, and other mysteries of the deep was what had led me to apply for a job at the institute in the first place. I didn't really believe in sea monsters, of course, although I like to think I had an open mind. And, frankly, some of the verified reports of oversized versions of known sea creatures were sufficiently scary that I never felt the need to believe in any of the legendary creatures of folklore.

Nothing in reality or even in legend prepared me for what I saw now.

The tentacle closest to me reached easily thirty meters above the waves, and two similar ones hovered over the fishing boat. They hesitated for a few seconds, then all three came crashing down in unison. The one that hit the island knocked me from my feet. The other two slammed into the hapless fishing boat, one shaving off a small section of the stern, the other landing directly on top of the cabin. Both impacts resulted in explosions of wooden splinters that riddled the passengers, who were too tightly packed to take any kind of evasive action even if they'd had time to become aware of the danger.

I lay on my stomach only a few meters from the tentacle, which withdrew quickly toward the water, leaving behind a shallow indentation that I knew I had seen before, down on the beach near where I had parked the trailer. I realized as well that this wasn't a true tentacle—at least not like one I'd ever seen before. There were no suckers or hooks, in fact no distinguishing marks at all, nor did it seem to taper toward the end.

The massive limb disappeared back into the ocean, but when I rose onto my hands and knees I saw that others had broken the surface, at least half a dozen now. Three of them lay athwart the fishing boat, which was listing to one side. People were screaming and jumping over the railing, and others lay motionless on the deck, some of them missing limbs or heads. The power of the thing, or perhaps things, paralyzed me. The entire scene became a surreal dream, and I found it hard to recognize that the tiny dolls crushed under the blows of this behemoth were actually human beings. Some of them, anyway. I still had no idea how many of the citizens of Crayport were infested with the alien parasites.

A fresh plume of fire burst from the cavern below, sending sparks flying in every direction and illuminating the terrifying scene. More tentacles emerged and wrapped themselves around the middle of the fishing boat. Metal screamed as it was torn like paper. The small mast flew through the air and landed on the beach only a few meters from where I cowered. The air seemed to vibrate around me and I felt so numbed that it was several seconds before I recognized that the irritating sound in my ears was that of people screaming. More bodies hurtled from the fishing boat's deck, some jumping into the water, others thrown into the air as the hull of the vessel literally imploded under the pressure of the tentacles. In less than a minute there was nothing but debris in the water, with several dozen heads bobbing up and down among the waves. The tentacles flailed about, and each time they slapped the surface there were fewer survivors.

The plume of smoke thickened and darkened and I retreated as far as I could without actually entering the water. The rain of sparks weakened and died away fairly quickly after that, and with it the last of the screaming. The light wasn't enough to allow me to visually search the area thoroughly, but I had a horrible feeling there'd been no survivors from the fishing boat. The night was suddenly too quiet. I felt a pang of conscience then, for I was quite certain that I'd precipitated the disaster by enraging the creature in the cavern, which had somehow communicated its displeasure to the sea beast. But on the whole I felt no regret at all in acting against the Crawleys and their allies, human or otherwise.

The moonlight was still bright enough to allow me to see that the tumult had not entirely subsided, although the creature's flailing was considerably more deliberate and restrained now. After a brief hiatus the creature began systematically smashing the floating debris into even smaller pieces, then began exploring the far shore of the island, probably searching for survivors. I took that as my cue to exit, turned and launched myself into the water without a moment's hesitation. The shore was barely visible and looked impossibly far away, but I tried not to think about the distance, instead concentrating on the steady rhythm of my arms and legs. I'd been a strong swimmer all my life, an ability that had never seemed as valuable as it did now.

The gentle sound of the surf striking the shore became audible eventually, and that confirmation that I was making progress gave me a burst of additional strength. A moment later I had an even greater incentive, because something struck the water behind me with an ear-splitting crash and I was lifted by a sudden, unnatural wave. I fought down a surge of panic, forcing myself to concentrate on what I was doing and to ignore what followed blindly—I hoped—behind. Twice I mistimed my breathing and once inhaled water, but I recovered each time and returned quickly to a regular cycle of stroking and kicking.

When something large and painfully hard struck a grazing blow across my right side I feared that all my efforts had gone for naught, but then I realized it was not the sea beast but the outermost support of the Crawley wharf that had struck me. I swam under it and continued forward in its shadow until the water was shallow enough for me to stand and stagger up onto the sand.

I had barely reached dry land when the far end of the wharf exploded in a fury of shattered wood. Fragments fell all over the beach, and if I hadn't been sitting under cover, I might well have died then. Standing at one corner of the now mostly ruined pier, I was considering running up into the woods when something struck the ground to my right with such a powerful impact that I was thrown from my feet. A huge tentacle had fallen heavily and was now withdrawing very slowly back toward the water. In the distance I caught a glimpse of another wavering in the air; then it also descended with a crash somewhere out of my line of sight.

Shaking with fear, I managed to get to my feet and began running straight up the hill, ignoring the trees and brush to either side. It appeared to me that the creature was striking indiscriminately and that any effort to take advantage of cover would just extend the time necessary to get out of range. The incline increased dramatically and I began clambering up with hands as well as feet, breathing heavily and consciously choosing not to look back. To my left I heard the sound of tearing metal, and that drew my attention just as an enormous piece of machinery came crashing down the hillside in a tangle of cable and rope. The sea beast had apparently caught hold of the Crawleys' elaborate winch system and literally ripped it off the hillside.

My foot slipped and I banged my knee painfully, fell onto my side gasping for breath. I could hear people shouting above me. For the first time. I looked back at the bay, far below me now, and what I saw there was in some ways even more incredible than the bizarre creature in the cavern.

I had assumed from the outset that the sea beast was a variety of giant squid, though one of unprecedented size, and that perhaps it was indeed a cousin of those rare but known creatures of the deepest parts of the ocean. But even in the darkness I could tell that this was no species with which I was familiar. For one thing the tentacles were far too long and thick, nor were they the proper shape. These were three sided, absolutely smooth, and they didn't taper appreciably until the very tip. Even in my near panic I was mentally calculating the size of the body that would be required to manipulate these monstrous appendages, and I didn't like the results. Something in its appearance seemed alien to everything I knew about marine life. I think its kind is unknown to our science because it is not of this world, any more than the creature in the pit, or the Children, or the Passengers.

I fell twice more on the way up the hill, and my sodden clothing was caked with dirt. I felt like an ant rushing from a nest disturbed by the footsteps of a human being. When I finally reached the crest of the hill I dropped into a crouch, trying to draw adequate breath into my laboring lungs. I was in that position when the impossible happened. One of the oversized tentacles soared over my head and crashed down on the small building a few meters away from me. It collapsed immediately, the roof broken in two, the walls exploding outward. Then the tentacle was withdrawn, dragging with it several crates similar to the one into which Jennifer Blackley and the Child had been loaded earlier in the evening.

Below me, its immense body wreathed in shadows, a creature I could only believe was not of this Earth lay sprawled on the narrow beach. There could be no doubt now that this was not some monstrous but perfectly natural denizen of the deep. There were superficial similarities; even the mantle that protected its body appeared vaguely familiar. But beneath that was a visage every bit as hideous as the creature of the cavern. Long white filaments danced around a central cavity that was probably a mouth, each one seeming to move with an independent will. They had the girth of a man's forearm and discernible joints, although far too many of them. And they literally glowed with an inner light that was brighter than the moon as they explored the underbrush and the wreckage of the chainlift. Above them, three distinct eyes stared unblinkingly about, eyes far too large in proportion to its face. This was a deep dweller, but of depths not found on our world.

"Hurry up, damn it!" A familiar voice came from somewhere to my right. The younger Crawley was on the road, directing a handful of men as they finished loading one of the crates into a truck. I rose to my feet, and two automobiles drove up on either side of the truck, each filled with passengers. Crawley approached one of them and spoke in tones too low for me to hear, but I took advantage of the situation to make my

way forward until I was within a few steps of the
vehicles, although still concealed behind a thick
mat of brush.

Behind me a tree was torn out of the ground.
The sea beast might not be able to climb the hillside, but it was certainly doing its best to destroy
everything on it. I glanced back nervously, not
entirely convinced that I was even yet out of
range of its tentacles.

Crawley straightened up and the two vehicles
drove off, both headed toward Crayport. He
watched as two men closed and secured the
back of the truck, then walked around to the passenger side and climbed into the cab. I hovered
indecisively as the engine started, then burst from
my cover and ran forward just as it started to
move.

The twosome noticed me, but they hesitated
just long enough for me to rush past them, although one reached out for me with what I feared
were frog fingers and I shied away, almost giving
up my chance by doing so. With a final burst of
speed I managed to catch hold of the door latch
and jumped up onto the rear bumper, flattening
myself against the cold metal. My left hand found
the seam between the door and the truck, but I
was unable to reach anything with my right to
help secure my position. Even over an absolutely
smooth road I would not have been able to remain there indefinitely. My fingers began to
cramp within seconds and this road was hardly
smooth. We were less than halfway to the town

when I lost my grip and fell off, banging my shoulder and skinning both palms and one knee, escaping greater injury only because the truck was unable to travel quickly over the convoluted road.

When I picked myself up I could see the cemetery fence in the distance, and beyond it the suppressed but helpful lights of Crayport. I started in that direction, wanting to run but only capable of an unsteady trot.

Had I known what was waiting for me, I might have slowed to a walk, or turned around and gone in an entirely different direction.

Clouds were obscuring the moon now, and when I glanced out over the water I could see no sign of the creature, nor were there any sounds of continuing destruction. In fact the night now seemed unnaturally quiet. There was the gentle shushing of water breaking gently on the beach, and a mild sighing of the wind, but otherwise nothing seemed to stir. I could no longer hear the truck's engine, and downtown Crayport had never been a haven of activity even during the daylight, let alone the night. Even the insect population was silent, and my own unsteady footsteps seemed unnaturally loud.

Twice I had to stop and sit for a few moments while waves of uncontrollable shaking surged through my body. I suspected that I was suffering from mild shock as well as exhaustion. My clothes were still damp and matted to my skin, and my sneakers squeaked with every step. I was bleeding in several places, but all my injuries were superficial and I was still too numb to feel real pain. Nevertheless if it hadn't been for Alyson I would have found a hiding place in the woods, curled up, and slept until dawn if not later. My watch had been broken somewhere along the way, but I guessed it must be at least midnight by now. It felt as though I had first entered that unholy cavern days, not hours earlier, and my time in Crayport seemed to stretch back endlessly.

I limped into town by a somewhat circuitous route, using the same overgrown path that we'd followed earlier to enter the cemetery. As I rounded the corner of the first row of buildings I saw a car start up from where it stood in front of Turner House, but it moved off toward the center of town rather than in my direction. There was no evidence of any other vehicle or pedestrian, and there were no lights in any of the windows that I could see, although there was still a diffused glow from the main road.

With extreme caution I made my way forward, running across the short open spaces, lurking in the shadows at each intersection for long seconds until I was reasonably sure that no one waited in ambush. Eventually I reached Main Street.

There were no working streetlights, but the closed-up store that I had thought empty and abandoned was now extremely well lit, and a small group of men and women were carrying parcels from within it to a row of vehicles. I counted six cars, two vans, and four pickup trucks, as well as one much larger vehicle that I recognized as the panel truck from the Crawley place. There was no sign of either Crawley, although I thought I caught a brief glimpse of Jared Turner at one point. No sign of Alyson either.

I was trying to decide whether I dared get any closer when someone touched me on the back, and I barely controlled a scream that had been crouching unsuspected in the back of my throat.

"Are you all right, mister?"

It was Sean Caspar, self-possessed as ever. I suppressed the urge to hug him.

"Sean! Thank God!" I whispered urgently, then led him back around the side of the building. "Do you have any idea what's happening?"

"I guess they're leaving. The *New Dawn* is gone, and they came tearing into town like the devil was chasing them." It took me a second to realize that the *New Dawn* must be the name of the fishing boat. Its name seemed terribly ominous.

"Do you have any idea where the Crawleys have gone? They still have Alyson." I hesitated, then decided he deserved to know the truth. "Jennifer's dead." At the time I assumed that was the truth. Later I was to find out otherwise.

Sean shook his head. "I saw them go inside, but there was a crowd and I couldn't tell who was with them."

200

"Inside where?" I glanced back toward Main Street.

"C'mon. I'll show you. There's a way we can sneak up on them."

I followed the boy to the rear of the block. We climbed down through a broken basement window into a place that smelled of earth and decay. It was too dark to make out any details, and I suspect I'm better off not having seen what we stepped on before we found the staircase to the ground floor. There were lots of insects and cobwebs, and I was still brushing them off my face when we emerged into the showroom of a small hardware store. A single security light burned near the front door, but it was enough to guide us to a service exit that revealed another staircase.

We climbed as quietly as possible to the third floor, then used a filthy, debris-cluttered corridor to cross to the opposite side of the building. Sean eased a window open and slipped outside onto a fire escape with such practiced ease that I was certain he'd been this way several times previously. It was a tighter fit for me and I tore my shirt getting through, but then I was outside. Down and to my left the systematic loading process was still under way.

"Across here. But be careful." Sean crouched, then effortlessly leaped across a narrow gap to a matching fire escape on the building opposite. I hesitated and glanced down, which was a mistake, then let anger wash away my fear. I followed him, landed awkwardly, and felt a moment of dizziness in which I was certain I was going to fall. Then it passed and I was following him through yet another window, this time into a small, very dusty bedroom.

"Mr. Burton used to live here, above his store," whispered Sean. "We have to be real quiet now, or they'll hear us."

And then he led me out into the hallway and I heard from somewhere below us the unmistakable voice of Joseph Crawley. And he wasn't happy.

Chapter Twelve

"Get hold of yourself, Edward. If you show your weakness, you'll lose control of the others!"

Edward's voice crackled with tension and, surprisingly, fear. It brought a smile to my face. "That's the least of our problems. The Old One is angry with us and has sent the kraken to destroy us all!" He was close to panicking.

The two men were on the ground floor, two flights down, but their voices were quite distinct. There was a sharp, sudden sound that I suspected was a face being slapped.

"Don't speak of that about which you do not know! He has withdrawn His face from us for the moment, but we are still the ones who serve the Children. For the moment we are denied His grace, and in His absence those of His creatures that lack true minds of their own may lash out blindly. Once the gateway has been reopened He will reassert His control and the danger will pass."

"But the chamber has been destroyed." Edward sounded as though he had regained some self-control, but his doubts were clear. "And much of our work is undone."

"Nonsense. We still have four of the Children and the means to welcome more of them. We knew that sooner or later we would have to abandon this place and move to a more heavily populated area. The kraken will leave nothing behind that might expose our purpose. You urged me once to trust in the Summoning, but apparently you didn't trust in your own advice. The ancient knowledge is ours now, the ceremonies have been refined, and our plans are well laid. This will at worst delay us slightly, and may actually advance things if the Summoning is as successful as we hope. There is risk in moving forward precipitously, but recent events have shown that there may be even greater risk in being too deliberate in our course."

"But we've lost so much . . ."

"We've lost nothing of consequence. A few buildings and some of the lesser Servants. Those Who Serve were always expendable, and more can be transformed if the need arises. The tool that is no longer adequate to the task should be readily discarded."

Joseph's calm demeanor was taking effect, for

Edward's voice regained some of its usual confidence. "We can't take more than a dozen or so with us."

"You and Jared should choose the strongest. The rest will cease to function shortly after we leave even if the kraken spare them, and the evidence of their transformation will disappear shortly after the hosts are dead. Without a fleshy home or the near presence of their Master, the Passengers will soon revert to their own plane."

I suddenly realized what he was talking about and gasped so loudly that Sean gave me a warning look. The Crawleys were abandoning Crayport with a few of their followers and the rest, at least those carrying the alien parasites, were to be sacrificed without a qualm.

"I don't suppose our chief of police has surfaced anywhere?" Joseph's voice sounded more distant, and I realized they were on the move. Edward replied, but I couldn't make out the words. I had taken a tentative step toward the stairs when an enormous crash from somewhere on the harbor side of the building made the windows jump in their frames and raised a cloud of dust from our surroundings. Someone shouted something, then came a scream, followed by the sound of metal tearing.

"Come on!" Sean whispered urgently, grabbing my arm. "We have to get out of here."

He led me back to the window through which we'd entered, but two more concussions shook the building during those few seconds, and the

cloud of dust had us both sneezing uncontrollably, the sound thankfully masked by whatever
was happening outside. We slipped out onto the
fire escape, and I saw the dancing light of flames
from the waterfront, but not the fire itself.

Sean was preparing to leap back across the
gap between the buildings when I caught a
glimpse of something large and dark moving
across the night sky. I froze, stunned momentarily
by the size of the thing, which seemed to hover
directly over our heads. Then it fell, fortunately
far short of where we stood, although the end of
what I belatedly recognized as an oversized tentacle smashed down through the roof of one of
the houses on the street nearest the pier. Not content with destroying the Crawleys' facility, the enraged beast had turned upon the town.

The impact shook the ground and Sean almost
fell from his perch on the railing. I heard more
shouting from below and the sound of automobile engines starting up.

"This way!" I shouted, pointing at the metal
steps that led down to the ground. There was no
point in remaining furtive now. We were all on
the run, friend and foe alike. After only the
slightest hesitation Sean nodded and started
down. I was right behind him.

The next few minutes are still disjointed and
almost feverishly unreal in my memory. By the
time we reached the street the caravan of vehicles was vanishing in the distance, including the
freezer truck and, hopefully, Alyson. If they had

left her behind, she was almost certainly dead, so my only hope was that they still had some reason to keep her alive. I shied away from considering what that reason might be, though Jennifer's horrible fate was a vivid image I would bear to the grave.

Sean and I ran quickly to Main Street, and from there I could see the monstrous creature that had pulled itself up onto the shore, completely demolishing the town wharf in the process. One of the fishing boats had overturned and the others were bobbing agitatedly in the surf churned up by the sea beast's flailing limbs. I froze, awestruck, and watched as two more buildings exploded into a blizzard of shattered wood and shingle. Sean tugged at my arm and I allowed him to lead me away toward the south end of town. But we were not to escape so easily.

Ahead of us something vast and living was moving ashore between Troll Rock and the Jenson property. It was another of the oversized sea beasts, every bit as large as its fellow, and already a half dozen tentacles lay along the shore, the tip of one extending into the roadway. It appeared less agitated than the first, but that hadn't prevented it from destroying at least two buildings, from whose wreckage flames were springing up. Behind us a good portion of the downtown area was on fire as well, and the kraken, its tentacles still furiously lashing at the frail buildings, had raised much of its body onto dry land.

It looked even less like a giant squid now that

I could see more detail by the light of the fires. The central body was roughly barrel shaped and rose about twenty meters above the water level like a giant cactus. The tentacles were not fixed; that is, their bases were mobile and slid around the bulk of the body as though its outer skin was laid over an elaborate system of cams and tracks that covered all but a dark ovoid on the side facing the shore. There I could dimly see a concavity that might have been a mouth, except that from it came forth comparatively fragile, fibrous limbs the size of my thigh, but immensely long and multiply jointed. These last glowed with a cool blue light that made their progress through the ruins of Crayport starkly visible.

I counted six of these strange appendages and watched as they advanced rapidly. One of them encountered a human body lying in the street, half buried by debris from the adjacent building, which had collapsed onto its foundations. The body stirred at the contact and I thought it might be with life, but then the appendage began to draw back and I saw that the corpse was somehow affixed to it, as if cemented there. It vanished into the dark maw and almost immediately the blue white limb emerged again. The body was gone.

"Come on! We have to get to my car!"

I broke into a run, pounding along the blacktop on a path that would lead perilously close to the towering creature that had interposed itself between us and my campsite. Sean hesitated for only a moment before following, and then the two of us were side by side, not speaking, watching as the tentacles furled and unfurled nearby. We saw one of them lash out and shatter a tree on the shore side of the road, and I thought we might be cut off, but then it thrashed about in the empty lot behind and quickly withdrew, having found nothing further upon which to vent its wrath. We barely broke our stride, actually passing under one of the oversized limbs as it drew back to deliver another blow, and then we were past it.

By the time we reached the trailer I was out of breath and my head was spinning. Too much had happened in too short a period of time, and my physical reserves were threatening to run out. I noticed without emotion that the trailer had been thoroughly ransacked. The culprits had been looking for something, and most of its contents had been thrown outside onto the sand and thoroughly examined. Even the bed cushions had been torn apart. Somewhere in the litter I might have eventually found my key ring, but I only glanced in that direction, then led Sean to the car.

"Get in!" I slipped into the driver's seat and leaned to the side, retrieving the spare key from the glove compartment. Yeah, I know, lousy security. But my car is so beat up, I can't imagine anyone actually wanting to steal it.

We were back on the road sixty seconds later. I proceeded cautiously and with the lights off, watching for signs of the kraken, but the nearer one appeared to have abandoned Troll Rock. The other one was still picking Crayport apart; one of the larger buildings collapsed noisily as I coasted to a stop to consider our options. The fires were spreading through the downtown, casting enough light to illuminate the entire area. The blocky center of the creature was still firmly ensconced on the beach, and the powerful tentacles were reaching toward the as yet untouched portion of the town, apparently completely oblivious to the flames through which they passed. The smaller white appendages were busily exploring the wreckage, and we saw two more bodies dragged free as we watched.

I started to turn to the left, hoping to bypass the chaos ahead of us.

"This is a dead end," Sean told me quietly.

"I know." The street ended at a small house sitting forlornly beside an open field. I eased up on the gas, squinting to try to see clearly. There was plenty of light from the fire, but the wind was blowing an increasing volume of dark smoke in our direction, and it was like a great porous wall spreading across the field. We ran out of asphalt and I slowed even further as we left the road surface and started across the field.

It was bumpy and we had to run up the windows to keep the smoke out. I nearly ended our trip prematurely by running into a large rock that sat in the middle of the field, but it was a glancing blow, we weren't moving all that fast, and the car managed to shake it off. Then we were on a slight downslope and the worst of the smoke was behind us. I rolled up onto the asphalt when we reached the main road, turned left, flicked on the lights, and pressed down on the accelerator. Ahead of us was the bridge and escape inland.

As we picked up speed I began to breathe more easily. If I had remained alert, I might have anticipated what was to come. I wonder about that sometimes even now. It's unlikely, however, that I could have done much different. To remain where we were was clearly unwise; the tentacles hadn't reached that far inland yet, but they were still on the move. Our only hope was to get out of their reach for once and for all.

I saw the outline of the bridge ahead of us and eased up slightly on the accelerator. Just as I did so there was a brilliant flash from the right, and two more from the left. The windshield exploded into a million pieces, something clanged metallically as it caromed off the hood of the car, and our left front tire blew out. I felt the car swerve to the side, fought with the wheel, thought I had managed to maintain control but ultimately failed. The untouched front wheel hit the ditch that ran alongside the road and we canted up at an impossible angle. We teetered there for a breathtakingly long second, then rolled completely over, still moving forward at a pretty good clip. I lost my grip on the wheel, preoccupied by the inane thought that my insurance company would be upset because I hadn't been wearing my seat belt.

We rolled completely over at least twice. I hit my head against the roof and was stunned for a few seconds, so I might have missed another revolution or two. When it was all over we were upright; the lights were still on, but the engine had died.

"Sean? Are you all right?" He was slumped against the door and I gently lifted him away, then let him fall back. I thought at first that the bullet that took out the windshield had struck him, but there was no evidence of that. But his head dropped forward with a terrible limpness impossible for a living human being. I felt a wave of despair even greater than my anger. I was tired of watching children die without being able to do something about it. And then cold fury began to build again and I realized I could hear a voice somewhere near at hand.

The door wouldn't open so I climbed out through the broken windshield, ignoring the badly bruised thigh that had been added to my growing list of injuries. Limping slightly, I jogged down the gulley for several meters, then climbed back up to the roadway under the cover of a thicket of wild roses. From the top of the rise I saw one man standing above the spot where we'd crashed. He was fanning a flashlight over the area, and down below at least two more were thrashing around in the brush, presumably searching for survivors.

I picked up a large stone in one hand. It felt good and solid and I kept squeezing it for reassurance as I emerged into the open, approaching at an angle that would keep me out of his line of sight. The small sounds of my advance were masked by the roaring of the nearby fire. At the very last minute something must have warned him, because the man with the flashlight started to turn in my direction and I saw that he was Jared Turner, the first person I'd met in this demented, doomed town. Then my arm was swinging and the stone smacked against the side of his head with a satisfyingly solid thud and he fell to his knees, wavering there for the second or two it took for me to raise my arm again. This time the rock slammed down onto the bridge of his nose. There was a brief spurt of blood as he fell away from me, dropping the flashlight and letting out a gasping whistle of breath. It was the last sound he ever made.

He wasn't armed, but there were keys in his pocket. I found the car farther up the road, just before the bridge. There was a shotgun on the front seat but no passengers. The engine started on the first try and then I was crossing the bridge, leaving Crayport—or what remained of it— behind me forever.

For all that, Turner had the last laugh. Less than ten minutes later the engine began to cough. I eased up on the gas—I'd been driving entirely too fast for that twisting, unlighted road in any case—but it didn't help, and three miles later I coasted to a stop adjacent to a stand of dense woods and turned off the ignition. I let it sit for a while and gathered my wits, then tried to restart the engine. It sputtered several times but never caught.

Weariness overwhelmed me, along with too many bumps and bruises to count. I searched the glove compartment and found only a packet of maps and some candy bars, no shells for the shotgun. It was loaded, however, so I took it with me and started walking along the roadbed. My strength deserted me almost immediately, and I made less than half a mile before I surrendered to the inevitable, concealed myself in a patch of blueberries, and fell asleep.

The chattering of squirrels woke me the next morning. I blinked away my disorientation and tried to sit up, failing on the first attempt because I hurt in so many places that my body refused to be cooperative. With considerably more care I made a second effort and this time managed to succeed, although my head was swimming and my stomach rebellious. I was a mess, my clothing torn and stained with blood and dirt and smoke, my body bruised and cut and abraded. Fortunately there was a narrow, fast-moving brook nearby, and I washed as best I could manage and drank enough to aggravate my growing hunger. While I was crouched there I heard sirens in the distance—a lot of sirens—and then they were racing past me headed into Crayport. I hesitated, wondering if I should attempt to flag one of them down, but I was so unsteady on my feet that I sat down instead, struggling to overcome a very bad case of the shakes.

At this point I didn't know how best to proceed. Clearly the authorities knew that something had happened in Crayport. I'd seen police cars as well as fire and emergency vehicles roaring past, at least a score of them. Were the kraken still attacking the town? In the light of day the previous evening's events seemed like a particularly unlikely nightmare. Then I remembered Sean and Jennifer and Alyson and the feel of Jared Turner's skull cracking when I struck him and I knew it was all real. What I didn't know was how much of the truth would be believed. I had no intention of ending up in jail or a mental hospital, so I decided my best bet would be to say as little as possible before it was necessary.

So resolved, I stumbled down to the highway and waited, and a few minutes later I managed to flag down a police car. It swerved to the side and began coasting to a stop and I started to walk unsteadily forward to meet them, but the world began to swim around me and I never made it.

I have a vague memory of waking up in an ambulance. There was a paramedic hovering over me and I think I tried to say something about Alyson, and maybe I was trying to get up because she was pushing down on my shoulders and telling me that everything was under control and I should just rest and that she was sure my friends were all right. They weren't, of course; two of them were dead and the other had been abducted, but apparently I didn't convince her, or if I did, there was nothing she could do about it.

I definitely remember the emergency room, but by then I was either in shock or someone had administered a drug that left me completely out of it. The walls seemed to be moving around of their own volition and everyone was talking in slow motion and using strange words I couldn't comprehend. For some period of time I drifted in and out of awareness, once noticing that I'd been moved to another room, and sometime later still another. Then I must have slept for a long time, because when I woke up I was lying in bed in a hospital room that I shared with three other people, and it was nighttime. Although I managed to rise up onto my elbows without passing out, I still felt dizzy enough that I didn't dare try to get up. Instead I slowly reviewed everything I could remember from the previous forty-eight hours, hoping to uncover some clue that would help me find Alyson. To my great satisfaction I did think of something, but then I was drifting away again and fell back against the pillow and dropped back to sleep.

My neighbors in the hospital ward were eager to discuss the excitement from the previous day's news, so I pretended to be asleep and listened intently while they talked so that I'd be properly prepared for the questions I knew would come.

They provided tantalizing hints but nothing more.

"Did they bring in anyone else last night?" asked one.

"Didn't hear nobody. Things quieted down right after they brought in our neighbor there. The nurse said the ambulances were all coming back empty."

"That's a good sign, isn't it? Means people weren't hurt."

"I dunno. I heard a doctor talking last night out in the corridor when I went to take a pee, and he was talking like the whole town got wiped out. Some kind of freak storm."

A few minutes later a nurse showed up, and I opened my eyes and admitted I was conscious.

"How are you feeling this morning?"

"Pretty rocky."

"You weren't in great shape when they brought you in last night, although there's apparently nothing seriously wrong with you. The doctor will be right in to talk to you about your case."

My stomach growled ominously. "Do you suppose I could have something to eat? Or maybe some coffee?"

Her lips pursed. "I'll see what the doctor says." And then she was gone.

The doctor showed up about fifteen minutes later. She found me sitting up on the bed. Except for a variety of aches and pains that all seemed reasonably bearable I felt surprisingly good, though light-headed, probably because I'd eaten so little in the last forty-eight hours. Her name tag said THYNNE and she was.

"It appears you had quite an adventure yesterday, Mr. Canfort." She never met my eyes, instead bending to examine a particularly livid bruise on my left arm. I wondered how she knew my name, then realized that I was wearing a hospital johnny. Presumably they had checked my wallet.

"I don't remember much about it," I said slowly. My first inclination, to tell the truth, was clearly impossible. *Well, Doctor, you see this bizarre cult was worshipping some superhuman creature from another dimension, and when I destroyed their temple two giant squids from another world destroyed the town. I managed to escape, but naturally I had to kill a man in the process, and now I need to rescue my friend from a man who is preparing to destroy the entire world.* Sure. Not only would they believe me and let me go, they'd award me the Congressional Medal of Honor.

"The police will want to talk to you. Do you remember the storm at all?"

"The storm?" I squinched my features as though trying to remember something that wouldn't quite come into focus.

Dr. Thynne clucked disapprovingly and gave me back my arm. "You're the only survivor so far, Mr. Canfort. I hope you can help us figure out what happened."

"All I can remember is this roaring sound and seeing a building collapse. And there was a fire. What happened?"

She crossed her arms and glared at me disapprovingly. "Apparently there was some kind of freak local storm in Crayport. A tornado is believed to have struck the center of town, possibly two of them. There were numerous fires, and with all those old buildings packed so tightly together . . ." She shrugged, as if the rest was self-evident. "They've brought in half a dozen bodies, but you're the only one alive. The rest may have been blown out to sea by the storm."

Later that morning the hospital admitted that none of my injuries prevented my releasing myself from their custody. I had a short, unpleasant interview with two police officers whose names I immediately forgot. They had already received an account from another survivor, they told me, so they knew about the tornado's having struck just as most of the people in Crayport were celebrating a town festival aboard one of the local fishing boats. They didn't appear to specifically suspect any foul play, but they treated me as if I were a serial killer anyway.

"We'd like to ask you about the shotgun you were carrying, Mr. Canfort. It seems a bit strange under the circumstances."

I shook my head in pretended confusion. "Seems strange to me as well. I remember grabbing one of the local kids and trying to get out of town, and then I lost control of the car and went into a ditch. Everything after that's pretty vague. I think I remember finding a car with the keys in the ignition, but I hit my head pretty hard in the crash and that's about it until I woke up here. Maybe the shotgun was in the car."

"We didn't find any trace of a kid." But they had, I suspected, found the commandeered car. I had already decided to stick as close to the truth as possible.

"Who else survived?"

The two policemen exchanged looks before one of them answered. "Two guys named Crawley, father and son. They told us the whole story."

Chapter Thirteen

The hospital seemed reluctant to let me go, but I was even more determined not to remain. I called Jane at the institute, who flattered me by being uncharacteristically emotional when she found out I was still alive. When I explained that I was without transportation she told me she would drive out personally to pick me up, a gesture that left me with moist eyes, although it was perhaps as much a reaction to everything that had happened recently as to her generosity.

I watched CNN's account of the disaster on one of the hospital televisions. The incident was now believed to be a freak storm that had spawned at least two tornadoes and possibly a waterspout, and that struck just as most Crayporters were partying aboard a fishing boat. A subsequent fire had destroyed more than 90 percent of the local structures. Less than a dozen people had survived, including what was described as "several emotionally disturbed individuals," although various state agencies were still searching the ruins in hope of finding others. It was considered extremely unfortunate that most of the dead had been lost at sea. Sixteen charred bodies had been found among the ruins, along with a child who "apparently perished in an automobile accident while trying to flee the fire with an unknown companion." With one exception, none of the survivors were interviewed on camera, and most were described as suffering from "intense shock" and other injuries.

Joseph Crawley was quoted briefly in the newspapers, as well as in the CNN coverage, which consisted mostly of aerial footage of the wreckage. Crayport had effectively ceased to exist. The town pier and the entire fishing fleet were gone. One broken hulk lay on the beach, one overturned hull floated in the harbor; the rest had been smashed to kindling.

Nor had the town fared any better. What hadn't been destroyed outright fell prey to the fire. A few outlying buildings had escaped, but the downtown was a gutted ruin that looked like a firebombed city from World War II. Three more charred bodies had been recovered, but none had been successfully identified. Neither had Sean. Only four survivors had been named, of which I was one, identified incorrectly as a vacationing camper. Presumably this meant the Crawleys would know that I was still a threat to them, however ineffectual. They were also identified, and later someone named Josiah Walton, an elderly man listed in critical condition with burns over most of the surface of his body. His prognosis was not good.

Joseph Crawley was interviewed again briefly early in the afternoon. He appeared very solemn and indicated that he and his son had been returning to Crayport after a business trip when they spotted the twin storms and the fires. He expressed shock at the great loss of life, a sentiment that seemed transparently false to me; but then, I was prejudiced.

"Then you weren't actually present when the disaster occurred?"

"No. No, I wasn't. Most of the damage had already been done by the time we arrived. But we've had waterspouts in the harbor on occasion in the past. They've always drifted just offshore until now. It's a terrible tragedy. I've lost a great many good friends today, and it appears we will be denied even the solace of laying their bodies to rest."

Jane arrived about half an hour later. I discharged myself, listened to some perfunctory admonitions about taking care of my various wounds, accepted a small pharmacy of medications, then climbed into Jane's Jeep.

"Want to talk about it?" She had waited until

we were on Interstate 95, headed south toward Providence.

I'd been thinking about what to say to her for most of the day. I respected Jane and felt that she had a high opinion of me, but I don't think it was high enough for her to accept anything other than a very watered down version of the truth. At the same time I didn't want to have to lie to her. I wasn't sure I could get away with it even if I did. "There isn't much to say," I opened cautiously. "The town is gone, along with almost everyone in it."

"Including Alyson?"

"She might have survived. I lost track of her." It wasn't hard to sound despondent.

"If she survived, wouldn't we have heard by now?"

"Not necessarily." I hesitated, then decided that I had to trust her. "There was something illegal going on in Crayport, Jane. Alyson and I sort of stumbled into it and they caught us. I got away, but everything got out of hand after that."

She frowned, and it was a while before she spoke again. "And you think she might still be alive?"

"Yes. I think there were quite a few survivors who haven't been identified or even located yet." A prolonged, awkward silence followed.

"You're not telling me everything." It was a statement, not a question, so I didn't answer. "I've never had reason to mistrust your judgment, Steve, so I won't press. Not yet, anyway. I assume you have a good reason to be reticent."

"It's complicated, Jane. And before you suggest it, I can't go to the authorities. Any proof I might have had was destroyed along with Crayport, and they wouldn't have any reason to believe me. There's something I need to look into, something that might help, but if the police get involved, Alyson will be in even graver danger than she is already. If she's still alive."

"All right." We drove several miles without talking. "I'm authorizing a week's paid leave effective immediately. If you need longer, give me a call and I'll see what I can do."

"Thanks. Thanks a lot." I thought about Alyson and then about Jennifer Blackley. "A week should be plenty, one way or another. And I promise to tell you the whole story, once I know the ending myself." Assuming I was still around to tell it.

Jane dropped me off at my apartment building. I thanked her again and rode the elevator to the third floor. Ordinarily I climb the stairs, but some of my bruises had tightened up during the ride, the painkillers were wearing off, and I was starting to feel light-headed again. My apartment was at the very end of the hall, which provided me with more privacy than my fellow tenants, most of whom I knew only by sight. I'm not the gregarious type, I guess. I let myself in and closed the door behind me, so tired and preoccupied that I never noticed that the inside lights were already on.

When I entered the small den someone rose from a chair and turned to face me.

"Beverly? What are you doing here?"

"Waiting for you." Alyson's sister had just turned eighteen but still looked three years younger, and she was capable of displaying such a wide range of maturity levels that I never knew what to expect from her. She was clearly far more responsible and thoughtful than Alyson when it mattered, but she also seemed to derive more pure joy from life that anyone I knew, and she didn't seem to share her sister's periodic spells of self-doubt and depression. There were times when she was outright silly and other times when she scared me a little. This was one of the latter. "Where's Alyson?"

"I don't know." I knew instantly that Beverly would not let me off as easily as had Jane. She would see through any lie, even one of omission, in an instant. It was a talent she'd demonstrated to me on previous occasions. "It's a long story."

She sat down on the arm of my favorite chair and crossed her arms. "I have lots of time."

I didn't answer immediately. Instead I crossed to the stack of orange crates that serves as my bar and found the bottle of expensive brandy I'd been saving for a special occasion. After a second's hesitation I took two glasses. Contributing to the delinquency of a minor was the least of a long string of crimes I had committed already or was contemplating in the future, and I had a feeling that, self-assured or not, Beverly was going to need a drink before our conversation was over.

She raised an eyebrow when I poured the second brandy, but she didn't turn it down. I sipped enough to burn a line down my throat before plopping down onto the small couch across from her.

"Alyson's in a lot of trouble," I said quietly. "And I don't know exactly how to do anything about it, and you're probably not going to believe most of it."

Beverly slid down into the chair and waited.

I started slowly, describing the first few odd things I'd noticed. As the story progressed I forgot about my audience, got lost in my own unlikely memories. I had meant to tone down the more grisly details, but instead found myself describing all too vividly my horrified reaction to the events of the previous two days—Jennifer's terrible death, the parasitic creatures operating human beings as puppets, even my indirect responsibility for several deaths including that of Jared Turner. It was the first time I'd ever confessed to murder, and I found the process emotionally and physically exhausting. When I was done I poured myself a second brandy. Beverly held out her own glass as well. At least she hadn't run screaming from the room.

"So what are we going to do about it?" I wasn't surprised that she was taking this so calmly. But I was surprised that she appeared to have accepted everything I said, however bizarre.

I sighed and leaned back, staring up at the ceiling. "I don't know yet. We can't go to the police with that story, obviously, not without some kind of proof."

"Maybe we could track down the Crawleys."

I had no idea how to do that and said so but almost immediately realized that I was lying. "I remember something. The trucks they hired were from a Providence company whose name I recognized. We might be able to trace them, find out where the crates were delivered. If we locate the crates, the Children and the Crawleys will be nearby."

"How much time do you think we have?" For the first time there was a hint of a tremor in her voice.

"I don't know, Beverly. Days, I hope. Weeks, I doubt." I hadn't mentioned my speculation that Alyson was fated to die as had Jennifer Blackley, but I knew Beverly had reached the same conclusion. Surely it would take a few days for the Crawleys to find a suitable location in which to reenact the ceremony. And it was entirely possible that not enough of their followers had survived to complete the invocation. That might work in our favor, because captive audiences weren't quite as easy to find in a city.

My head hurt. I stood up, intending to retrieve some aspirin from my desk, and the entire room began to swim. Two brandies should not have had this massive a reaction, so I guess the abuse my body had suffered recently was starting to catch up with me. I caught the arm of the couch and then Beverly had hold of my other arm, just in time as it happened, because my knees buckled and I would have fallen if she hadn't caught me. And so I found myself leaning on her shoulder as she led me into the bedroom, and then I just let everything slip away for a while.

I woke up feeling considerably better physically than mentally. The apartment was silent, empty. It was dark outside so I turned on the light, shed my bloodstained clothing, and took a long shower. Wearing just a bathrobe, I went to the small kitchen in search of food and found half of a small pizza sitting on the table. I had disposed of most of it when the front door lock clicked and the door opened.

I had a kitchen knife in my hand when I peered around the corner, but it was Beverly. I watched as she locked the door behind her.

"How did you get in here anyway?"

If I'd startled her, it didn't show. She turned easily and even sketched a smile. "I know where Alyson keeps her key." She raised her hand and displayed it. "How are you feeling?"

"Better," I admitted. "Only half dead."

"I found out something." She ignored my banter and pulled a spiral pad out of her hip pocket, flipped it open. "I made a few calls, but I used Alyson's phone so they couldn't trace it here. Just in case."

Alarm, not unmixed with anger, coarsened my voice. "Are you out of your mind? I don't want you taking any chances in this, Beverly. I already feel responsible for your sister," not to mention Jennifer and Sean, "and I don't want you taking any risks."

She ignored me completely, or at least my tone. "I called the trucking firm and told them my boss was interested in renting some of their trucks and needed some recent customers as references. They gave me three names."

I stepped forward and caught her by the arm. "I'm not kidding about this, Beverly. I don't want you involved. I'll take care of this myself."

This time she did react, but it was with a surge of anger that made my own seem like a trivial tantrum. "Don't you dare try to keep me out of this, Steven Canfort! I lost my boyfriend to cancer and couldn't do anything about it. I lost my parents in an automobile accident and couldn't do anything to help. Now I may lose my sister and I'm not about to sit on the sidelines and wait to see what happens." She glared at me, daring me to say something.

"These are very dangerous people, Beverly." And very dangerous not people as well, I thought quietly.

"I'm feeling pretty dangerous myself." Her voice broke a little and she visibly fought for self-control. "Now do you want to know what I found out or not?"

We sat around the kitchen table finishing the pizza while she read me the names she'd gleaned from the trucking firm.

"That's the one," I said when she mentioned

Temple Warehousing in Providence. "It has to be. The others are companies I never heard of and I saw a bill with that name on it in Crawley's room."

"All right." She flipped to the next page. "I have the address. They only have one location, on Republic Street down near the waterfront. Here, I'll show you." She pulled a Providence street map from her purse and opened it. Three locations had been marked in bright red, and she pointed to a rhomboidal block not far from Narragansett Bay. "Want to go take a look? I have my car outside."

I thought about it. "It's pretty dark. We won't be able to see much."

"Which also means that much won't be able to see us either. Just a drive-by."

I couldn't think of any good objection, and truthfully I was feeling considerable impatience myself. Just to be doing something, anything, would scratch the itch at least a little bit.

I let Beverly drive. No, that's not true; she never gave me the chance to do otherwise. We hadn't interacted a lot in the past, and to be honest she made me feel uneasy. Half the time I figured she thought me unworthy of her sister's affection, and half the time she seemed angry that I might come between them. Now she just struck me as a determined young woman with a commanding presence of which I'd only had hints in the past. My opinion of her had already changed radically in the past few hours, and it was to change even more in the days that followed.

The warehouse seemed larger in real life than it had on the map, although part of that might have been because of the blanket of inky darkness that covered the area. It was set in an area filled with similar buildings, some of them warehouses, others manufacturing plants, still others abandoned shells, predominantly sporting brick or cinderblock facades. Unlike most of the others it was poorly lighted, boasting just four low-wattage lamps, one at each corner, and an even dimmer one over a small door halfway along one side. On the other hand, the metal fence surrounding the property was brand new, eight feet high, surmounted with four strands of barbed wire, and had only a single gate, closed and securely locked. There was a small guard shack just inside, but we could see no indication that it was occupied. Beverly stopped the car immediately in front of it, but I convinced her to move on.

"We don't want them to suspect we've found them, if in fact this is where they've gone to ground. It still could be coincidence. The name, I mean. Or they might have abandoned this for some other hideaway."

She reached the far corner and turned right, following the property line. We circumnavigated the building without finding any other features worth mentioning. There were no vehicles on the property, but all twelve overhead doors were closed and they might have concealed a small fleet of trucks. And crates.

"Want me to go around again?"

I shook my head. "There's nothing we can do tonight. We'll come back in the morning. If they're here, we should see something."

"Do you have an Internet account?"

I shook my head. "No. I work with computers enough at the institute that I have no patience for them elsewhere. The only thing I use my PC for is games."

"Then we'll stop by the house."

Alyson and Beverly shared the fairly roomy suburban home they'd inherited from their parents. She parked around the back and led me inside. "Make yourself comfortable. There's beer in the fridge."

I passed on that and made coffee for both of us instead. Beverly had fired up her computer and was doing arcane things with screens full of symbols that I didn't recognize. "What are we doing?"

"We," she said quietly, "are hacking into the computer at the Better Business Bureau."

"And why are we doing that?"

"Because we want to know something about a certain warehousing company, and because the BBB has a very simpleminded security system."

I drank coffee and waited, but it didn't take long. "Nothing," she said at last.

"What did you expect? Complaints that they were transporting unlicensed monsters?"

"Very funny. No, I mean nothing at all. No complaints, not even a basic entry. Have some more coffee."

It took longer this time, and I think I even heard Beverly issue some very atypical Anglo-Saxon words under her breath before she sat back from the computer a second time. "Now that's peculiar. They paid very low taxes to the state for the past two years; unless they've cooked the books, their income level isn't much more than mine, and I only work part-time."

"How about before that?"

"There is no before that. The company was founded two years ago."

"Who owns it?"

"Something called the Old Masters Holding Company."

I laughed. Apparently Joseph Crawley had at least a mild sense of humor. It was nice to know he wasn't entirely inhuman. That fact made him seem more vulnerable. "That's the Crawleys. I'd be willing to bet on it."

"Then we've got them."

"Maybe."

It was well past midnight. Beverly suggested that I spend the night and overrode my objections. "It's not as though you haven't slept here before. In fact, I believe there are a couple of spare sets of your clothing in the back of Alyson's closet."

She had me there.

* * *

We ate breakfast silently and left the house just as the sun was coming up the following morning. Most of my bumps and bruises had subsided into quiet ongoing complaints, and I decided to forego the painkillers in favor of aspirin. Beverly seemed completely refreshed, and every bit as determined as she had been the night before. I offered to drive, but as before she ignored me. Twenty minutes later we were parked as unobtrusively as possible across the street and half a block away from the warehouse entrance. The gate was still closed and it remained that way as the time inched past eight o'clock to nine and then ten. There was no sign of life from the warehouse at all, except that the exterior lights had been extinguished, possibly by a timer.

"I've got an idea." Beverly started the engine.

"What?" We pulled away from the curb.

"Get down. I don't want anyone to see you." I was about to protest, but she pulled over and stopped the car directly opposite the guard post, so I hastily slid down out of sight. "Stay here. I'll be right back."

She was gone before I could answer. I waited a few seconds, wondering just what was going on, then lifted my head high enough to peer out over the rim of the driver's side window. Beverly was standing with her face pressed against the gate. A heavyset man wearing dark clothing, not a uniform, slowly walked out from the guard shack. He stopped just out of her reach and stood silently while she talked, her voice too low for me to hear it clearly over the busy morning traffic. Finally, he shook his head, paused, then shook it again. Beverly spoke some more, but he turned away and went back inside, out of sight, ignoring her. After a few seconds she came back to the car.

"That was a lot of help," she said short-temperedly. "I told him I was lost and asked for directions and he wouldn't even answer."

It was more help than she realized, though. Even from this distance I'd noticed something unusual about the guard. He had frog fingers. Any lingering doubt I might have entertained was gone now. This was the Crawleys' home away from home. There was a good chance that Alyson was inside. Even if she wasn't, this was a tangible link to those who held her.

"I'd give anything for a quick look inside that place," I told her as we drove off.

"I was just thinking the very same thing."

We cruised several blocks before finding the first pay telephone, and a good many more before we found one that worked. Beverly told me what she had in mind and I had reservations, but not strong ones. I finally convinced her that it would sound more plausible if I made the call, since her voice still sounded very much like that of a child. I don't think she liked my saying that, but she was sensible enough to accept its validity.

So I called the Providence Police and informed them that I had planted a bomb in a certain waterfront warehouse.

I didn't think it would be a good idea to park the car in the area; I suspected the police would routinely note the license-plate numbers of everyone within a block or two. Instead we left the car at a small supermarket several blocks away and walked back to the warehouse district. I bought a handful of random groceries from a curbside vendor for camouflage. We heard the sirens long before we were close enough to see anything, and by the time we arrived the front gate was open and the bomb squad was on the property. A small but growing crowd of spectators had gathered outside the fence and we joined them, moving away when a uniformed officer ordered us to, but only the minimal distance required.

As I had hoped, they rolled up some of the overhead doors. I spotted several crates that might have originated in Crayport, but they were stacked three and four high, and there were at least a score of them. Teams began searching the building, but most of them moved off into portions we couldn't see. They finished very quickly, too quickly to have been particularly thorough. The crowd was already thinning around us as the first emergency vehicle drove off, its siren silent. The officer in charge was talking animatedly to someone whose face I couldn't see initially, but then the officer turned away and I recognized Edward Crawley.

"Let's go!" I said quietly. The last of the overhead doors was closed again. "There's nothing more to see here."

We returned to the car and sat for several minutes without speaking. "We need to get inside," I said finally, unnecessarily. "Even if she's not there, it's the only lead we have."

"Any idea how we're supposed to do that?" For the first time Beverly sounded slightly frantic. We were both aware of the fact that time was not on our side, and that we had no idea how little we had left.

"Actually I do. But first we need a weapon and some burlap bags."

"I can help with the first. Dad belonged to a gun club. But you're on your own for the burlap."

"No problem. I know exactly where I can get some."

I chose a very nice handgun from the gun cabinet after Beverly unlocked it, and she took one herself. "Do you know how to use that?"

"Probably better than you. Dad used to take me target shooting. Alyson didn't like the noise. Where next?"

Next was a self-storage locker on the outskirts of Providence. The institute used it for storage of items that were of no immediate use, and I was usually the one called on to schlep things back and forth. The key was in my apartment. We loaded about two dozen empty burlap sacks into the trunk of Beverly's Toyota.

"I don't suppose you'd like to tell me what you have in mind?"

I couldn't think of any objection, so I did. Beverly thought about it for a minute or two, then nodded. "Sounds okay to me. But how do we get out afterward?"

I hadn't thought that far ahead. Getting into the warehouse seemed to me the immediate problem. The rest would have to work itself out later.

It did, but in a way I could not have predicted.

Chapter Fourteen

It was easier getting inside the grounds of the warehouse than I had anticipated. We parked the car near the darker of the rear corners of the property at nine o'clock and waited for half an hour before getting out. The area was moderately well lit, but there was no pedestrian traffic at all, and only three cars had driven past us during that period. Directly across the street on one side was an abandoned factory, slowly decaying into crumbling masonry and broken glass, and on the other was a similar warehouse in somewhat better shape, also showing no signs of life. The lot diagonally across was empty, heavily overgrown, and liberally sprinkled with trash.

I had no difficulty climbing the fence, and Beverly handed up the cloth bags so I could lay them over the barbed wire. When I was satisfied that they were adequately covered I swung myself up and across. Something snagged my pants leg in the process, but I pulled free without injury and dropped to the ground on the other side. Beverly swarmed up in my wake and was beside me in seconds.

We ran to the side of the building and edged our way around toward the front. The security light was on over the door, but the guard shack was dark and appeared deserted. A battered pickup truck was parked near the single door. There was a brief, bad moment when a pair of headlights picked us out, but they moved on as the vehicle turned into a side street and roared off. The door was locked, as I had expected, but I was prepared for that. Growing up the son of a locksmith has its advantages. I had my own set of tools and the skills to use them, although I wasn't nearly as fast or as elegant as my father. The warehouse lock didn't provide much of a challenge, though, and we were inside in less than five minutes.

There was a small, glass-fronted reception area just inside the door, dark except for a tiny night-light on the far wall. A ring of keys hung from a nail just below the bare bulb. A short corridor led to a cluster of three doors, all closed. The first of these was another office, this one showing little evidence of use. The cheap metal desk was bare; no tools, no papers, no personal items. No pictures on the walls, not even a calendar. There was a stack of flyers just inside the door that appeared to be of more recent vintage. I picked one up, but it was too dark to read, so I folded it and pocketed it to examine later. The second door was a utility closet.

The third opened onto another hallway that ran perpendicular to the first. The outside wall of the building was to our left, the receiving area behind the row of overhead doors to our right. There was a halogen light at the far end, barely enough to show us the humped forms of the stacked packing crates we'd seen during the daylight. There was no sign of life, no sound except for the faint buzz of the light fixtures and an almost subliminal mechanical thrumming that sounded like an electrical generator, or possibly an air conditioner.

It was Beverly who noticed another doorway, which revealed a steep, narrow staircase leading downward. The thrumming noise seemed to originate from the depths below. I drew the pistol before starting down, but Beverly left hers in her jacket pocket.

There was another door at the foot of the stairs and I opened this one very slowly and very carefully, just far enough that I could scout the territory beyond. This was much better lit, revealing a large open area directly in front of us, stretching off into the shadowy recesses of the building. I stuck out my head and looked to the right. A dark partition extended halfway across the floor, separating the open area from the rest of the basement level. In the distance I could see the doors of several large chambers whose exterior walls were decorated with insulated utility piping. The hum of the generator and a compressor was much louder now, originating from somewhere in that general area. A forklift truck was parked in the middle of the floor

"They wouldn't leave this all unguarded, would they?" whispered Beverly.

I'd been thinking the very same thing, but there was no evidence of any human presence. We slipped through the door and let it close gently behind us. Somewhere water was dripping. I experienced a wave of nervous anxiety that nearly paralyzed me. Despite the air of desertion, I knew on some primal level that we weren't alone in the building. I willed my hand to stop shaking as I raised my weapon and advanced cautiously toward the partition.

Once past the stairwell I could see the generator more clearly, and the liquid nitrogen tank that I'd been expecting. The large chambers at the far end of the building were almost certainly the refrigerated quarters of the Children. To our right a mound of boxes was piled up against the wall; to our left, as we neared the end of the partition, we could see smaller compartments, some with solid walls, others cages of wooden framing and wire mesh. I had just enough time to see that at least one of these had been turned into a makeshift cell with a bare mattress on the floor and a wooden chair in one corner before Jenson rushed us from out of the shadows.

He'd been concealed behind the pile of boxes. I had just enough time to recognize him before I was fighting for my life. He was a spindly man, and under ordinary circumstances I might have been a physical match for him, but as he charged he raised those frog-fingered hands of his and I saw the dark filaments extending from them and tried to throw myself out of the way. I was only partially successful; one of them grazed my arm and a burst of pain numbed it from elbow to fingertips. I lost my weapon along with my balance, stumbling to my knees. Jenson was off balance as well, and the second it took him to change direction probably saved my life.

"Shoot him!" I shouted, but a quick look told me Beverly hadn't even drawn her weapon. Then I was too busy to think about her again, avoiding another rush by ducking under Jenson's arm. I spotted my weapon, picked it up, and as Jenson turned to attack again, I fired two rounds into his chest.

The impact knocked him back, but he managed to stay on his feet until my third shot hit him in the face. That knocked him flat on his back, the human portion of him dead. I wasn't fooled, though. The body began to twitch almost immediately, as though something inside was trying to escape.

Beverly touched my arm. She had her weapon ready now. "Sorry," she said quietly. "I guess I wasn't really ready for any of this to be real."

"It's all right," I reassured her shakily. "It takes some getting used to."

"I'll be ready next time. I promise."

She sounded so much the little girl just then that I put my arm around her to try to reassure her. "Don't worry about it, Beverly. No one expects you to be Ellen Ripley."

She pulled away from me immediately, and her voice had hardened. "I said it won't happen again and I meant it."

I was spared the necessity of apologizing by the sound of a groan. Without another word we ran around the end of the partition and found what we were looking for. Alyson lay in one of the makeshift cells, sprawled across the mattress. She was conscious, but barely, and I'm not sure she recognized us for the first minute or two. My anger at the Crawleys and their associates, which had been simmering all day, reached the boiling point when I saw her condition. There was a bruise on her chin and another on her left cheek. The right sleeve of her blouse was a shredded ruin and her bare shoulder and arm displayed bright red streaks that provided mute evidence that she'd been struck by those black filaments. It wasn't until much later that I learned that more of those marks were to be found on her back and across both thighs.

Beverly shot the lock off the door while I stood frozen by rage. Then we were both inside, helping Alyson to sit up. She remained groggy even after we told her repeatedly that she was all right, and eventually she seemed to accept that she wasn't dreaming. It took three tries before she could stand up, and even then Beverly and I stood ready to catch her if she stumbled.

"Let's get her out of here." I couldn't escape the feeling that we were in imminent danger. Unfortunately my presentiment was absolutely correct. While we'd been preoccupied the Passenger had divested itself of the now inoperable host. The emergent creature had unfolded into a black web that writhed with unnatural life, and it stood between us and the only exit.

"Can you manage her by yourself?" I stepped away from my companions.

"Yes. Should we shoot it?"

"I don't think that'll help, but I've got an idea." The institute had a good-sized warehouse, and I'd spent many an hour helping move stock around. The forklift appeared to be in serviceable condition, and the engine started up on the very first try. My plan was to smash the creature flat. Perhaps if I destroyed all of its many nodes it would die. If not, I could at least pin it down beneath the weight of the forklift, just as I had crushed the housekeeper under the grandfather clock.

This Passenger was smarter than the other. My first run was successful, I think. When I backed away the appendages I'd traversed moved noticeably slower than before, but they continued to move. In fact, the bulk of the Passenger surged forward and several of the filaments flashed through the air, several slapping against the roll bar and one of them narrowly missing my face. These creatures might be blind, but they could track my movements in some fashion, perhaps by sound or smell or some sense entirely unknown to humans. I shifted and drove forward a second time, but this time all but one segment was withdrawn before I could crush them. In retaliation the Passenger flung at least a score of its filaments in my direction, and one of them slapped my left thigh.

I think I screamed that time, but an adrenaline rush gave me the strength to ignore the pain. I backed the forklift away, watching for another opening, then retreated again when the Passenger twisted and coiled, shifting its body mass across the floor. It still blocked our exit, but as it tried to cover more ground the intensity of its defense in any one area grew smaller. If Alyson had been in better shape, I think she and Beverly might have been able to run past, and for a second or two I thought Beverly was contemplating just such an attempt. But then she turned in my direction and shook her head, and I knew they couldn't proceed unless I gave them some more space.

I raised the forks, gunned the engine, and drove forward, just as the Passenger threw itself at me again.

More by luck than skill, I managed to get the forks within the densest concentration of the Passenger's body. That meant that I was also within range of too many of the filaments to stay where I was and I leaped from the seat, struck the floor, rolled across at least two of them without harm, then reached open floor space. I stood up immediately and backed away just as the Passenger convulsively wrapped itself around the forklift, which whined in protest as its forward progress was halted. The engine stuttered and died, leaving the Passenger pinned to the floor, its outlying tendrils thrashing madly.

I inched along the partition until I reached Beverly and Allison.

"I don't know if she can make it." Although her voice was strained, Beverly seemed perfectly composed. Alyson was blinking madly, as though her eyes couldn't quite focus, and occasionally she frowned and shook her head, as though listening to a conversation inaudible to the rest of us. I counted four filaments between us and the stairs, and one of those lay motionless, apparently out of action.

"She has to make it. Let me have one arm."

My plans were disrupted yet again, this time by the sound of a door opening. I had thought of the Passengers as no more than rather bright animals. Either this particular one was a comparative genius or our luck had just turned very, very bad, because somehow it had managed to release the locking mechanism on one of the refrigerated chambers at the far end of the room. Beverly and I both turned our heads at the sound of an almost serpentine hissing, and I found myself reunited with a nightmare I had hoped to forget.

A Child had emerged from the compartment, a hulking, vaguely human shape that seemed almost too big to be contained in the room. The misshapen head swung back and forth, as though attempting to pick up our scent, mandibles making a moist clicking sound as they opened and closed, and the oversized claws were spread wide. Worst of all, at least for me, was the sight of its broad chest, within which I easily recognized Jennifer Blackley's contorted face. It changed expression even as I watched, and for the first time I realized that those who were given to the Children to serve as the blueprints of their earthly existence did not die in the process.

I emptied my weapon into the head of the monster without consciously thinking about what I was going to do. I'm not sure that it even noticed. The bullets were absorbed by the flesh, but the wounds closed up instantly. I retreated a few steps as it advanced, still holding Alyson's arm, drawing her along with me. She slumped suddenly and I barely caught her before she fell. Beverly stepped past me, holding her weapon in both hands, raised to shoulder level. She fired two rounds and I started to tell her not to waste the ammunition, but before I opened my mouth I saw the Child stumble to a stop. Its body slowly began to lose shape.

She had fired both rounds at the creature's

chest, and one bullet had struck directly between Jennifer's eyes, ending her torment.

I couldn't tell whether or not it was dying, but with each second its body mass became less well defined, more amorphous. The massive head began to subside into the torso and the clawed limbs grew longer, thinner, and less distinct. It stumbled to one side as though disoriented and partially collapsed right on top of the mass of the Passenger.

The results were spectacular.

From all around the periphery of the sprawled mass the tendrils were withdrawn for an attack on the Child. It was like wrapping hot wires around a snowball. The flesh of the Child provided no resistance to the filaments when they contracted, but reformed, more or less, after its passage. Within that unnatural flesh I could see the darker strands of the Passenger thrashing back and forth, scything through tissues that reformed as soon as they were severed. The unearthly battle lasted for only a few seconds before the movement slowed noticeably, then stopped. The Passenger became completely inert, but the child's ruined and now completely featureless body continued to pulse for almost a full moment afterward. We remained motionless, unable to look away until there was one final surge of motion and the Child's surface tension collapsed. Where once had stood a fearsome creature was now an enormous puddle of filthy liquid interspersed with chunks of matter that continued to deteriorate toward slush.

We didn't wait around for the end.

Alyson remained semiconscious and it was difficult to lead her up the narrow staircase, but we managed at last, Beverly leading while I brought up the rear. We threaded our way through the office and Beverly cautiously opened the door. I was preoccupied with trying to figure out how we were going to get Alyson over the fence so when Beverly hissed a warning, I was slow to react.

"Get back before they see us!"

I had just a glimpse of the three men entering through the main gate before Beverly eased the door shut. A car was parked next to the guard shack with its lights off; it hadn't been there when we broke in. There was a small window embedded in the door and we pressed close, peering through the darkness.

"They're coming this way," Beverly whispered urgently.

I fumbled in my pocket for the extra ammunition I was carrying, but my hands were shaking so badly that I had trouble catching hold of them.

"Wait! They're turning away!"

I looked out again and saw that she was right; the three men had turned toward something to our left. "They've seen the burlap bags," I said quietly. The gate was closed behind them, and I suspected it was locked, barring us from escaping that way.

"Maybe we can hide in one of the spare offices and get out while they're downstairs searching." Beverly didn't sound as though she was convinced.

"We'll probably have to shoot them to get out." I had finally managed to load the pistol, but it only made me feel marginally better. The men were out of sight now, blocking our escape route. I wondered how quickly I could shoot off the lock and get the gate open. Not quickly enough, I suspected, particularly with Alyson staggering along like a zombie.

"I've got an idea." Beverly vanished into the small office and returned almost immediately, holding the ring of keys we'd seen earlier. "One of these is for a Ford," she whispered. "I think it's the truck."

Automatically I glanced outside. The cab of the pickup was barely visible. In the darkness it didn't look quite as bad as I remembered it. "We don't know if it will even start," I complained.

"We won't know if we don't try."

She had a point. "They'll be back any minute. If we're going to do it, we do it now."

"Can you manage Alyson?"

I nodded, then realized that meant she would have to drive. "I could run out and bring it back here to pick you both up."

"Don't be ridiculous. As soon as the engine starts, they're going to be coming right for us."

There was no time and no point in arguing. I eased the door open and pulled Alyson forward.

She managed two steps, then stumbled and went to one knee. Beverly was already outside, sprinting for the truck. There was no help for it. I squatted and maneuvered Alyson over my right shoulder, then stood up, adjusted her weight as best I could, and began a lumbering run toward the pickup.

Beverly was wrong. It wasn't the sound of the engine that alerted them. I heard running feet behind me even before I reached the truck. Beverly climbed up into the cab and I ran around the side, pulled open the door, and literally threw Alyson inside. For a moment I was convinced that we were trapped, that the engine wouldn't start and we'd be caught, but it fired up the second time Beverly turned the key, and we were in motion even before I pulled the door shut behind me.

Two of the men were nearly upon us and the squealing tires spewed gravel in their faces as Beverly pushed the pedal to the floor.

"The gate's closed," I said unnecessarily.

"I know that." Her sarcasm was oddly reassuring.

We were facing away from the gate initially and Beverly drove in a broad curve until she was headed directly toward it. One of the men was directly in our path, two others approaching fast from one side. Without a moment's hesitation she accelerated, passed the latter two, and bore down on the last man. She turned on the headlights and he looked vaguely familiar, although

253

his face bore no expression at all as we came at him. At the last moment he made an impossible leap, not out of the way but up onto the hood of the pickup. For perhaps a second or two he stood there, struggling to maintain his balance, then fell forward onto the windshield. We both recoiled instinctively, but the glass held and he slid up and over the roof. I was terrified that he'd end up in the cargo space behind us, but Bev swerved slightly and he rolled off and hit the ground.

Then we hit the gate. It held. No Hollywood exit for us.

I banged my head against the windshield and Alyson hit the dashboard and slid limply down off the seat. Beverly swore softly and pressed down on the gas pedal. The engine complained, the wheels spun, and the gate screeched in protest. I took out my weapon and was about to climb out of the truck when we lurched forward suddenly. The lock had snapped and the gate burst open as we rushed past it, so close that the side view mirror on my side was torn from its moorings.

But we were on the street and turning away from the warehouse.

"Where should I go?" Beverly had us headed toward the on ramp to the interstate.

"Take the highway. And hurry." I had just taken a look back. A car had come out of the warehouse lot and was turning in our direction. "They're coming."

"Maybe I should head for the police station."

I thought about it, but nor for long. "No good. At best they'd accuse us of breaking and entering, and they'd have plenty of evidence to back up the charges. Even if we get the police to go back to the warehouse, there's probably nothing left there to tell them what's really going on. At worse they'd kill us and/or the police. These are expendable soldiers we're dealing with. They don't care if they're caught as long as they take us out of the game."

"Where to, then?"

"See if you can lose them."

"In this?" She had a point, one which became more obvious as we started up the ramp. Our forward speed slowed noticeably even though Beverly leaned forward, trying to urge more speed out of the battered truck.

Traffic was light, as might be expected after midnight. Our pursuers got almost close enough for me to read the license plate on their late-model Honda before Beverly accelerated into traffic and left them temporarily behind. Within seconds they had closed on us again, and as we headed north through Providence it was obvious that we couldn't outrun them. I wasn't happy with our options. If I'd been a movie hero, I suppose I might have shot out their tires, and I even considered trying that tactic. But I was down to six rounds of ammunition, and I decided there was no point wasting them in an enterprise that was almost certainly beyond my abilities.

The Honda pulled into the extreme left lane

and started to draw alongside. Beverly swerved into their lane and cut them off, but the driver responded equally quickly, moving up on our right. Once again Beverly managed to cut them off, this time startling another driver into a chorus of angry horn blowing. She shifted right again almost immediately to avoid rear-ending the car in front of us. We flew past the new downtown mall and into a small cluster of slower-moving vehicles. The Honda changed lanes again, two lanes to our left now, and there was no way to intercept them this time. Once they got past the handful of cars blocking their way they could force us off the road.

"We're almost out of gas," Beverly said quietly.

Chapter Fifteen

The Honda pulled ahead of a Volkswagen and veered to its right. Beverly pulled down hard on the wheel and we swerved away, started for the state offices exit, then swung back onto the Route 146 connector. The sudden movement startled me, as I'd been in the process of moving Alyson into a more stable position between us. She had completely lost consciousness now and I was worried about her. I glanced back hastily and saw the Honda move to follow us, cutting across the lane divider in a cloud of smoke and sand. For a moment it looked like they wouldn't make it, but then they were past the barrier.

The chase continued north, and the traffic quickly thinned out. Alyson regained consciousness for a while, groggy but reasonably coherent.

Despite the violent movement of the truck she was asleep or unconscious again after only a few minutes. Beverly took advantage of every opportunity that offered itself, but it was obviously only a matter of time until we were forced off the road. If we didn't run out of gas first.

"I've got an idea," she said as we entered Lincoln. "Hold on!"

We exited onto Breakneck Hill Road, running up over the curb briefly as she struggled to maintain control. A horn blared at us at the foot of the exit, but Beverly ignored it and turned right, accelerating at the same time. The Honda was right behind us, but the third vehicle had passed the exit and was between us now, on a road so narrow and twisting, and soon declining so steeply, that it was impossible to pass. We gained a few car lengths, but I aged as many years in the process as we swung around a series of dangerous curves.

At the foot of the hill the engine sputtered for a second, and I thought we'd reached the bottom of the gas tank, but my concern was premature. We rushed off into a residential neighborhood while the Honda illegally passed and began to close the gap.

The next ten minutes were nerve-wracking. Beverly threaded her way through residential neighborhoods and past a couple of strip malls in a series of turns that left me completely disoriented. Although we were not able to lose our pursuers, neither were they able to catch up to us. I fretted about the fuel situation, though, and finally leaned over to look at the gauge. Where before it had hovered just above the E, now it was squarely in the middle of that letter.

"I know," Beverly said without looking away from the road. "We're almost there."

"Almost where?"

"Trust me. I used to hang with some friends up here. I know a trick."

The next turn took us into a narrow, winding, poorly lighted road that wound up into a series of low hills dotted with houses. It was exactly the kind of neighborhood I least wanted to be in right now and, even worse, there were no cross streets. The Honda began to close the gap. Beverly almost went off the road on the next turn, but she recovered quickly. Not quickly enough. They hit us at an angle and spun off. She fought the wheel and recovered, though not before we had used a tree to scrape the paint off my side of the truck. A few seconds later we turned into what I thought was an open field, but there was a just discernible gravel driveway here that ran off in the direction of a distant farmhouse.

"Where are we going?" I whispered urgently.

"Just do what I say." Tall grass and bushes grew all around us, brushing against both sides of the pickup. The Honda stayed right behind us, making no effort to force us off the road now. We appeared to have turned into a dead end and I didn't think they'd allow us the time to turn around, even if there'd been space to pass them, which there wasn't.

"I hope you know what you're doing."

She glanced at me for just a second and I swear she was grinning. "So do I."

"You know if we survive this, I might kill you myself."

Our speed dropped off quickly as we approached the house in a broad leftward curve. Abruptly Beverly took her foot off the gas and let us roll to a stop. She cut the lights just as I saw a narrow wooden bridge, platform only—no railings—that bridged a narrow stream. We rolled to a complete stop with their lights flooding through the rear window.

"Open your door for a few seconds, then slam it shut!" she whispered urgently.

I did what I was told. "Now what?"

"Tell me when the interior lights come on in their car." She had left the engine running and it was idling raggedly.

I craned my head around and looked. They'd stopped about ten meters back, and almost as soon as I sighted them, the dome light came on. "They're on."

The truck's wheels spun in the loose soil as we plunged forward, lights still off. I felt the change when we reached the narrow bridge, a hollow thrumming beneath our feet, gone almost as quickly as it came. Our headlights came on and then we were at an intersection of the gravel road and Beverly took the left fork, which swung abruptly back toward the paved road.

I looked out the back. The Honda's headlights were motionless, reached out at a strange angle. "They're not coming."

"Missed the bridge, probably. They thought we were getting out to run for cover." We reached the road and turned left, running back the way we'd come. "One night my date and I got chased by two guys who didn't like the way he was driving. He showed me the trick. This is his uncle's place."

We actually made it to a twenty-four-hour gas station and filled the tank. Beverly drove back to the house and I carried Alyson inside, then drove the truck back downtown and abandoned it a few blocks from the warehouse. Very carefully I scouted the area. The gate was closed and chained shut with a fresh lock, but there was no other sign of activity. The burlap bags were gone, but Beverly's car was right where we had left it. I watched it for a good long time, walked past it twice, then finally took the chance. It started up without exploding, there were no monsters hiding in the back seat, and I drove back to the house without incident.

Beverly opened the door before I could touch the bell.

"Where were you? I was getting worried."

"Being careful. How's Alyson?"

She glanced back over her shoulder. "Asleep. I checked her over. All I can find are a few bruises and scratches. She acts like she's been drugged."

"You look like you could use some sleep yourself." It was the truth. Her face was pale and drawn, her hair uncharacteristically unkempt, and her hands were shaking.

"Have you looked in a mirror lately?"

"Point taken." I glanced at my wristwatch; it was almost dawn. "I don't think we should stay here, though."

"Why not? They don't know . . ." She thought about it and nodded. "Your place is no good either. How about a motel room?"

"That might work." I wasn't comfortable with the idea.

"Wait! How stupid can I be?" She hit the side of her head with her knuckles. "I know just the place."

And so it was that I finished off the day by driving to their Aunt Grace's bungalow in Managansett, the town where I grew up. Aunt Grace was spending the summer in France this year, and Alyson and Beverly were supposed to look in every few days to make sure everything was all right. Beverly fell asleep on the drive over and barely woke up enough to guide me to the right house. Their aunt's car was blocking the driveway and I was nervous about advertising our presence by parking in front of the house, so I dropped the sisters off and left the car on a dead-end street a block away. A few minutes later all three of us were oblivious to the world and its problems, fully dressed, the sisters in the single bedroom, me on the couch.

It was afternoon when I finally woke up.

Beverly was in the kitchen, working over the stove. Her hair was wet and had obviously been recently washed. To my surprise Alyson was there as well, sitting at a table with both hands clasped around a coffee mug, looking relatively alert.

"How are you feeling?" I crossed the room and rested one hand on her shoulder.

She looked up and smiled weakly. "A bit light-headed, and sore around the edges. Thanks for last night. I don't remember any of it, but Beverly says you were quite the hero."

I glanced toward Beverly, who winked and turned away. "I couldn't have done it without your sister," I answered honestly, mentally adding another check to the scorecard of favors I owed little sister.

We had breakfast and coffee while Alyson told us what had happened to her since I'd seen her rushed out of Crayport, or at least as much of it as she remembered. The truck had gone straight to the warehouse in Providence, where it had been met by half a dozen men, none of whom were known to her. They'd held her in the up-stairs office for an hour or so before Edward Crawley arrived.

"He ignored me and talked to the others for a while. I tried to eavesdrop, but he must have noticed because he hit me"—she touched the side of her head—"and I was out of it for a while. What I did hear was something about getting things ready for the big event, whatever that is."

"The Summoning," I said almost under my breath. She looked at me questioningly, but I shook my head. "I heard them mention it, but I have no idea what it is."

"Anyway, after I woke up Crawley ordered the men to take me downstairs. There was only one of them, so I decided to try getting away. Didn't work. I lost my balance instead and fell down the stairs, and before I could get up he was hitting me with these . . . things . . . that came out of the ends of his fingers." She shuddered. "Then he locked me in the cage and went away without saying a word."

"You looked like you'd been drugged," I told her. "Maybe in something you ate or drank?"

She shook her head. "Crawley's jail doesn't come equipped with room service. But there was something else." Alyson paused then, unnaturally long, and I was getting ready to prompt her when she finally spoke.

"There was something else down there with me, something close, something obscene. I couldn't see it, couldn't hear it, but I could feel it nearby. It was absolutely loathesome and it somehow touched me inside." Her hand trailed across her breast, up one side of her neck and cheek, came to rest on her forehead. "I could feel its thoughts and it could feel mine. Not clearly, only bits and pieces, but it was real and it was terrifying."

"The Child," I suggested, then realized that she wouldn't recognize the term. But she did, instantly.

"That's it! That's how it thought of itself! And it was one of many. Thousands, I think. Maybe millions."

I shivered a little at the thought of thousands of these creatures. "There's only four of them, as far as I know. Three," I corrected myself.

Alyson was shaking her head. "There are more of them, countless numbers."

"The rest must be back wherever they come from," suggested Beverly.

Alyson seemed to accept that. "They don't think the way we do. That's probably why I understood so little. But I could feel its hunger and its hatred of me even while it was sharing my thoughts. More than anything else they want access to our world. When they think about it their thoughts get agitated and more intense than at any other time. They'll destroy us all if they can, all but a few favored ones."

"The Crawleys." I stood up and began to prowl around the room, restless. "And their followers."

"They have to be stopped, Steve."

"But we don't even know where they are or what they plan. Even if there's something at the warehouse that would help, it'll be too heavily guarded now." And then I remembered something. "Wait right here."

I found the jacket I'd worn the night before and searched the pockets. The flier was there, folded into an uneven packet. I was reading it as I returned to the kitchen. "Maybe we have a chance. Look at this."

It was straightforward enough. The Church of the Summoning invited the homeless to attend a "self-help" meeting at the Providence Performance Center. Those interested in attending were assured that they would be treated as adults, that they would not be preached at or made to feel foolish about their unfortunate situation. And they were enticed by the prominent notice that free food would be provided. "Before we can nourish your mind, we must first nourish your body." It even sounded like Joseph Crawley. The event was scheduled to take place the following night.

"So what do we do about it?" Alyson pushed her coffee cup to one side and leaned forward on both elbows, meeting my eyes unflinchingly.

"I don't know," I admitted. "I have to think for a while."

Despite her improved condition, Alyson was still unsteady on her feet, and we convinced her to nap for a while. Beverly made a fresh pot of coffee and we sipped at it in the front room while I thought. Inspiration had never seemed so far away, and I was desperate for an idea.

"You haven't said much today, kid."

She smiled gently. "I didn't want to get in the way."

"That never stopped you before."

"Yeah, well, I wasn't sure I liked you before yesterday."

I thought about that. "You didn't like me before I committed burglary and assault and murder? And now you do?"

She pressed her tongue against the inside of her cheek and looked away for a few seconds before answering. "Alyson's the only family I have, Steve. We're really close, you know? And even though she's older than me, sometimes it feels like it's the other way around and I have to protect her."

"From me?"

"From people who might hurt her or take her for granted. You haven't exactly committed yourself to her, have you?"

That wasn't an easy question to answer. "Sometimes I think we're in love, Beverly, and sometimes I don't. I know we're good friends, I know I enjoy her company, and I think she feels the same. I'm not sure if she's in love with me either. I can't honestly tell you where we're going, and I don't think Alyson is any more certain than I am."

"But you wouldn't hurt her unless it was absolutely necessary."

I nodded. "I think I can promise that much."

"Then it's okay." She deliberately picked up

her coffee and drank deeply. "So what do we do next?"

I accepted the change of subject gratefully, but I still didn't have any great ideas. We could wait for Crawley's Summoning, but I was afraid that if we waited that long, we'd be too late. Staking out the warehouse for a lead was dangerous, and probably a waste of time. They knew we knew about it.

As the day edged its inevitable way toward dusk I became increasingly frustrated and nervous. Alyson woke up in midafternoon, and although she remained pale and preoccupied, some of her quirky sense of humor came back, and she managed to walk without staggering. Beverly encouraged her to talk about a neutral subject and she grew more animated describing their childhood, much of it spent in this very house.

"We lived here until I was thirteen. Dad got a new job and we moved to Seekonk, and he sold the house to Aunt Grace. Gave it to her, actually. He took just enough money that she wouldn't feel like a charity case."

Beverly announced that we were out of coffee. "I'm going down to the corner store. I'll be right back."

I glanced worriedly out the front window, but the neighborhood was quiet except for a golden retriever that had been barking off and on all day, a woman weeding her garden, and a cable television crew working on a line half a block away. "Be careful."

"I'll be all right. I'll take Aunt Grace's car and gas it up while I'm at it. You never know; we might need a second set of wheels." She opened the side door from the kitchen to the driveway and disappeared with a cheery wave.

Alyson came and sat beside me on the couch a moment later and I put my arm around her. "How are you feeling?"

"Like I've had the flu for a month. My head is full of bad memories. They press against what I'm thinking all the time, and sometimes even when I'm awake I feel like I'm back in that basement."

"Do you remember anything that might be helpful? We don't know where the other three Children are, but I doubt they're far. Crawley isn't the type to split his forces too widely apart."

She shook her head. "I get fragments from what I saw, and what others around me were seeing. I have this really vivid image of myself lying on the mattress, like someone stood there looking down at me. Some*thing*, actually." She shivered and I pressed her closer.

"But nothing about the Children?"

She shook her head. "No. Just bits and pieces from around the warehouse. Someone sitting in the office, talking to another man I don't know. Can't hear the words. I remember that pickup being towed into the yard, and one of the guards walking around the fence line."

Something was odd about that, but it took me

a moment to catch on. "What do you mean, towed?"

Alyson blinked. "It was being pulled in by a big blue tow truck. I remember it coming through the gate, and the gate closing behind, and then the memory shuts off."

"But why would they have towed it in? It was working just fine when we stole it."

She shrugged her shoulders. "I don't know. Maybe they fixed it up later."

And then I had an epiphany. "Can you remember any details about the truck, Alyson? Are you sure it was the same one we escaped in?"

"Pretty sure. It was the same color, and I could see where the mirror was torn off. The metal was all ripped and jagged."

"Was it daytime?"

"Yes. I saw people moving on the street beyond the fence. It was very bright."

I hesitated, not certain how Alyson would react to what I was about to tell her. But there was no help for it. If we were to take advantage of this, she'd have to know. "Those aren't memories, Alyson, or at least not from your captivity. We did that damage last night. Somehow you're still linked, still sensitized to their thoughts."

She shivered and looked away. "That's really not what I needed to hear right now."

But I was already considering the possibilities. "There may be a way we can turn this to our advantage. If there's a link, we might be able to find out something about what they're planning, where they are. Can you remember anything else?"

It was our best chance. Unfortunately what I failed to take into consideration was that if we could use the mental link to find them, they might be equally able to use it to locate us.

Alyson made an effort to dredge through memories, half memories, and dreams. After several minutes she shook her head. "That's all I can remember. Not much to go on."

Practically nothing, actually. She'd had glimpses that might have been the inside of a dark, enclosed room seen from various angles, and the persistent sound of water lapping in the distance. "Someplace on the waterfront maybe," I suggested, but there was a lot of waterfront in Narragansett Bay, to say nothing of the banks of the Providence and Seekonk rivers.

She stretched and glanced around. "I need some more coffee. Shouldn't Beverly be back by now?"

I felt a stir of alarm and glanced at my watch. She'd been gone better than half an hour, double the time it should have taken. "Maybe there was a line." But I stood up and walked to the front window, glanced down the street toward the intersection where a convenience store was just visible from the house. There was no sign of the car along the way or in the small parking lot.

"Maybe I'll walk down and roust her out." I started toward the front door.

"You're not leaving me here alone." Alyson was on her feet. "I'm coming along."

I was a good enough general to realize it was a bad idea to further split our forces. "All right, but let's lock up the house first. I'll get the side door."

I moved quickly through the kitchen, growing more alarmed with each passing second. Beverly wouldn't have delayed unnecessarily without a very good reason, or unless she couldn't avoid it. She knew how little it would take to alarm us right now. My hand was on the lock when I glanced outside and my heart thudded to a stop.

The car was right where it had been when we'd arrived. And now that I thought about it, I couldn't remember hearing the engine start back when Beverly had set out on her errand. It was possible that she'd decided to walk after all, but I didn't believe it for a minute. She was far too sensible to take a needless risk for such a trivial reason.

Something was wrong.

I must have stood there for several seconds because I jumped when Alyson touched my shoulder from behind.

"What's the matter?" Then there was a sharp intake of breath and I knew she'd seen the car and come to the same conclusions.

"Check the phone," I said softly.

She crossed the kitchen and lifted the receiver off its hook, pressed it to her ear, then replaced it. "Dead."

"Did Beverly take her gun?" I stepped briskly

back into the front room and retrieved my own. It didn't do much to reassure me, but I'd take even a little bit right now.

"I don't know. We could check her room."

I was certain it was in her shoulder bag, wherever that was right now. "We have to get out of here." There were eight windows on the ground floor and I looked out through each of them as I made my way around the house. The cable television crew were putting things in the back of the truck and the gardener was gone. The dog was still barking. A couple of kids were playing a few houses away. I couldn't see any other signs of activity, but I knew someone, or something, was out there watching the house.

"I don't suppose there's a secret tunnel from your basement to a neighbor's house?"

Alyson gave me a look. "They wouldn't do anything in broad daylight, would they?"

"Do you think Beverly went with them voluntarily?"

"Oh, my God. We have to help her."

I nodded and tried to sound confident. "We will. But if we're going to do that, we have to get out of here first." I glanced out the front window. The cable men looked like they were nearly finished, but they were two houses away. If I opened the front door and shouted to them, would they respond? Could they help? I didn't like the idea of making our way on foot, but even forewarned I doubted that we'd be able to reach the car.

"Upstairs," I said quietly. "Let's see if we can spot them."

The bathroom window was directly over the driveway, and its single pane was a narrow, frosted slit that tilted forward, making it very difficult to look downward. I stood on the toilet seat and leaned precariously across. There was no obvious sign of any intruders, although the angle was such that a small army could have lurked just outside the limits of my vision. I had almost given up when I noticed just the slightest hint of movement. There was something lying concealed beneath the car, something dark and sinuous, coiled up like a garden hose. It was a Passenger.

"They're out there. I can see one of them. Let's check the front."

But Alyson had a better idea. "I should have thought of this sooner, but it's been years since I've done this." She led me into one of the rear bedrooms, the one she'd slept in as a child, although it was now a guest room. There were two small windows, but they were so encumbered by branches that it was impossible to use them to spy out our surroundings. I said as much, but Alyson ignored me.

"Help me get this open. The wood is warped and it sticks all the time."

It took more effort than I expected, but eventually the window slid up into the frame; the screen was much easier to manage. I stuck my head out cautiously. "Still can't see anything," I complained. Two tightly placed maple trees crowded against the rear of the house, and even though I could see where someone had trimmed away many of the branches, it was still impossible to see the ground.

"Let me." I stepped back, expecting Alyson to admit defeat, but to my surprise she made no effort to spy out the terrain. Instead she grasped the sides of the window frame and eased herself through, catching hold of a thick branch. It dipped alarmingly for a second but then stabilized. "I guess I'm a little heavier now than I used to be. This is how I used to sneak out when I was twelve. Come on. We can drop down behind the fence into Mrs. Dooley's yard."

It looked precarious to me, but I didn't have any better ideas. After making sure my pistol was snug in my pocket I crawled through the window.

Chapter Sixteen

The branch swayed alarmingly under me, even after Alyson had transferred to a higher one. She was surprisingly nimble, much more so than I, and I lost sight of her in the heavy foliage. The good news about that was that it meant it was even less likely that anyone watching below would be able to see us. The bad news was that I wasn't certain which way to go, and I didn't dare call out and attract unwanted attention.

I inched my way forward and eventually reached the main trunk, just in time to see Alyson threading her way back toward me. "Follow me," she whispered. "It's all clear at Mrs. Dooley's, I think."

If the first half of the trip had been scary, the second half was terrifying. I'm not afraid of heights. Not exactly, anyway. Well, okay, yes, I am. The constant swaying, particularly when both of us were moving at the same time, put my nerves on edge, and when we finally dropped to the ground in a small fenced yard that was so immaculate it looked like a still life, I felt almost giddy with relief.

From a vantage point near the fence we were able to peer back into the driveway where the car was parked. Our unwelcome visitor was invisible from this angle, but I had no doubt that it would wait patiently until it had an opportunity to attack. There was no sign of Beverly, and she had the ignition key with her, so even if some outside intervention drew the creature off, we would still be denied use of Aunt Grace's vehicle. On the other hand I had the keys to Beverly's car in my pocket.

I still didn't understand how we'd been located. There was no possible way that we'd been followed here the previous night. The traffic had been thin to nonexistent at that hour, particularly as we neared Managansett. It was almost as if someone had read our minds. And then I froze, suddenly suspecting that my metaphor was close to the truth. If in fact Alyson was receiving occasional glimpses of the surroundings of the Children, thanks to the affinity born of their time in close proximity, then why couldn't the link work both ways? The implications were chilling, but I didn't have time to consider them just then.

"I don't see any sign of Bev," Alyson whispered. "Where could she be?"

"Nearby, I hope." But I was wondering if they'd already taken her away. We hadn't heard a vehicle pass since Beverly's departure, but we hadn't really been listening for one either.

With the utmost care, we made our way through the neighbor's yard, eased open a side gate, and crossed another lot, this one considerably less well maintained. There was a set of child's swings, a gas grill, and some haphazardly weeded flower gardens, but no sign of life. Forsythia made up a formidable but penetrable border at the far end, and we pushed our way through to the sidewalk rather than walk around to the gate.

"We can't just leave her here."

"I know that." I had no intention of doing so, but I wasn't sure how to proceed. We advanced cautiously to the corner, concealing ourselves by crouching behind a dense privet hedge. The cable truck was still there, the back doors open, but there was no sign of the crew. A delivery van crossed the far intersection but didn't turn in our direction. A moment later, a mongrel dog ran out from between two houses and crossed the street, trotting toward us, its jowly head turning from side to side. It glanced at us without interest and continued forward.

I was considering a frontal assault, walking past the front of the house with my hand on my revolver; ready to attack or run depending upon what happened. That changed as the dog passed us, moved down in front of the house we'd just quitted, and came to an abrupt stop. Even from this distance I could see the way its hackles rose, the deep black lips curling away from its teeth. It advanced onto the sidewalk, staring malevolently at the cluster of rosebushes that dominated the front yard.

I raised my head for a better view, but I couldn't see anything crouched within or behind the roses, and nothing moved even when the dog began a stiff-legged approach, growling and occasionally giving a short, sharp bark that was repeated with emphasis by the golden retriever chained to a tree three houses away. Alyson must have realized what was coming a split second before it happened because I heard her draw in a sharp breath and her hand grabbed my arm in a painful squeeze.

Part of the rosebush uncoiled and flashed out toward the dog. Actually it was something that was not a rosebush at all but that had mimicked it well enough to fool me, although obviously the dog had seen through the ruse. Not that it did much good. The Passenger struck the animal with a deceptively gentle whiplash that cut it off in mid-bark. The poor mutt didn't even have a chance to fight back; the limp body collapsed and never stirred.

Forewarned is supposed to be forearmed, but I still had no idea how next to proceed. I hovered indecisively for several seconds and might have waited even longer if one of the cable repairmen hadn't suddenly appeared alongside the vehicle.

"Take these," I whispered urgently, handing the keys to Alyson and telling her where I'd left the car. "Bring it back to this corner and wait for me. I'm going to find out if either of these guys saw what happened to Beverly. And be careful." She hesitated only a second before nodding and running off. Satisfied that a quick getaway would soon be possible, I swiftly crossed the street and approached the repairman. His head was turned away, and that is probably the only thing that saved me from my own inattentiveness. As it happened I had almost reached him before I glanced down at the empty hand at his side and noticed the distinct shape of his fingers. Frog fingers.

I froze in my tracks, and a hint of movement to the right caught my attention. I had time enough to recognize the pattern of Beverly's blouse half buried in a mound of cable before the repairman suddenly became aware of me and spun around.

When I tried to draw the revolver it caught on the fabric of my pants. Panicking, I backpedaled as quickly as possible, but in the end it was blind luck that saved me. A neighbor woman had emerged from the adjacent house, unnoticed by either of us, and something in our attitude alarmed her because she was screaming even before I finally managed to draw the revolver. The bogus repairman froze for a second, as did his partner, who had emerged from concealment on the opposite side of the truck. Then she was back inside the house, almost certainly calling the police.

"Stop where you are!" I demanded melodramatically as they bolted for the cab of the truck, but despite all I'd been through, I found myself unable to fire on them in this setting. It was just too familiar, too mundane, too much a part of the normal life that had deserted me these past few days. It was as if I had suddenly become the villain, a crazed gunman menacing innocent people going about their everyday business. Yeah, every middle-income neighborhood came fitted with animated wire that coiled itself in bushes ready to gobble up stray animals.

Then the van was backing out into the street and I was running toward the corner where Alyson was waiting, the engine idling. She slid over instantly as I reached the driver's side door, her eyes asking a question I didn't have time to completely answer. "Bev's in the van," I said shortly as I accelerated away from the curb.

Our quarry was already out of sight, but when I reached the intersection I spotted them to our left, moving rapidly toward the town center. We rounded the corner without stopping, the tires squealing, and I almost hit a fire hydrant before regaining control. Alyson braced herself with a hand on the dashboard.

We halved the distance between us and the van after turning onto Main Street, and now people were stopping on the sidewalks and turning as we roared past. Another few blocks and we'd be out among the largely deserted farms on the east side of town. The road was relatively straight for the first two or three miles and I thought we had a good chance of overtaking the other vehicle before they reached the interstate. I wasn't sure what I'd do then, but I had no intention of abandoning Beverly.

As usual things didn't go quite the way I had them planned.

We were almost beyond the last buildings when the three youngsters came out of a side street, apparently racing their bicycles. One of the boys pulled up when he saw us, overturned, and crashed into a privet hedge. The second just made it across the street before the van roared through, although he was so startled that he side-swiped a tree and skidded to a stop. The third, who seemed disproportionately long in the leg, somehow managed to turn just before slamming into the side of the van, but the effort caused him to lose control and he wobbled precariously back and forth, struggling to stay upright, and then swerved abruptly right in front of me.

I pulled hard on the wheel and stamped down on the brakes, just barely missed him, and rode up onto the sidewalk. Unfortunately boy number one chose that moment to remount and pedal out from behind the hedge, and we were still going too fast. I swerved again, missed him, but tore out a sizable chunk of the well-manicured shrubbery. The engine stalled, and it took two tries to restart it, by which point a crowd was starting to gather. Ignoring angry shouts, I regained the street and started east, hoping that we hadn't lost too much time.

But we had. We never saw the cable van again.

Our problems seemed impossibly compounded now. The house in Managansett was lost to us, Beverly was gone, we had theories but no real proof about the Crawleys' intentions, and it was almost certain that someone had noticed our license plate. We would have to assume that the police would be looking for the reckless driver who almost ran down three kids, and that was a complication that could hamper us fatally. So we parked at the back end of the Foodworld shopping center just outside Managansett and Alyson kept watch while I swapped license plates with those from an aging Honda. It was at best a temporary respite, but we couldn't abandon the car without a replacement.

We rented a room at a motel in Seekonk, just a few minutes away from Providence, and I parked the car next to the Dumpster at the rear where I hoped it would be less noticeable. Once inside the room I found that I was shaking almost uncontrollably.

"I'm going to take a shower. Then we'll figure out what to do next."

Alyson was sitting on the bed and she just nodded without glancing in my direction, looking completely beaten. I wanted to say something reassuring, but the words wouldn't come, and my own exhaustion and anxiety had taken their toll. I turned the water up as hot as I could stand and stood under it for a long time before enough of the tension bled from my body that I was able to think clearly.

Wearing one towel and using the other to dry my hair, I returned to the bedroom to suggest that Alyson follow my example. I found her lying on her back, her arms folded across her eyes, obviously deeply asleep, so I left her undisturbed. We each deal with tension in our own ways. There was a sandwich shop across the street, so I wrote a note in case she woke up, and did a provision run, returning with a bag containing several cold sandwiches and a half dozen cans of soda. She hadn't moved.

Alyson woke about twenty minutes later, sitting up so abruptly that I choked on a mouthful of soda. "Steven, I know where she is!"

But it turned out she really didn't, although while she'd been sleeping the strange seepage between her mind and that of the Children had conveyed fragmentary images of their surroundings and a glimpse of Beverly slumped in a corner with her ankle chained to a post.

"Are you sure it wasn't just a dream?"

She shook her head vehemently. "I don't know how to explain, but there's a kind of texture to these images that isn't dreamlike at all. There's too much detail, for one thing. I can remember smelling salt in the air, and seeing Bev's arm move. Then I'm turning away and there are rough walls, painted dark I think, and dripping with condensation, and a window with cracked glass, small panes, and beyond that is an oil tank or something that looks like one."

"Are you seeing through the eyes of one of the Children?"

"No, I don't think so. Not exactly." She stood up and crossed the room, popped the top on a can of soda, and sipped at it. "I think the Child and I are both looking out through a third set of eyes."

I had a sudden unpleasant thought, and a moment later Alyson confirmed it.

"There's a vague sense of my body that comes through with the vision. And Steven, I think it's a man's body."

"Someone they've sacrificed," I suggested. "Or whatever you call it when you're absorbed into one of them."

"I suppose so."

"Can you remember anything more, anything that might help us figure out where she is? Is there writing anywhere? On the walls maybe?"

She concentrated for a while and pulled out a few more details. There were traffic noises, but they were intermittent, so the location was probably not close to the interstate that crawled down the west side of Narragansett Bay. Alyson thought that another of the Children was close by, hovering just outside her field of vision, but she couldn't be certain. Unless the Crawleys had managed to bring more through in the last few days there should only be three still alive, and it would simplify things if they were in close proximity. Assuming, of course, that we found a way to take advantage of the situation.

"I can hear water too, slapping against something. It must be right on the bay because I'm almost positive those are waves coming in."

The afternoon was already half gone and I was too anxious to wait around doing nothing any longer. Alyson wolfed down a sandwich and we drove back to Providence, spent the rest of the daylight hours working our way methodically along the waterfront from India Point all the way to Warwick, exploring every side street, stopping occasionally to walk where we couldn't drive, hoping Alyson would see or hear something that would resonate. At one point I spotted a heavily rusted car parked behind a badly maintained house. It had four flat tires and obviously hadn't been driven in a long time, but it had a set of license plates that I used to replace the ones we'd stolen earlier. I felt more confident now that at least we wouldn't be stopped by the police in the few hours remaining before the Crawleys did their worst. Or until we stopped them.

Our efforts proved to us that we had no future in the field of private investigation. There were a handful of buildings that Alyson said might be the place, but only because she couldn't definitely rule them out. We didn't find anything she could identify as the oil tank she'd seen through the broken window. I spent a lot of time looking at the people we passed, particularly their hands, but no one I saw had the distinctive frog fingers of our enemies.

Alyson was getting frantic by the time it became dark and responded angrily when I suggested that we continue once the sun came up. I think even then she knew that we were wasting our time, but like me she chafed at the idea of not doing something, however fruitless, to rescue her sister. After another hour or so, she suddenly lost heart and cried heavily but silently for several minutes, twisting angrily away when I tried to put my arm around her. We sat in the car until she was calmer.

"Let's go back to the room," she suggested in a small voice.

"We still have one lead to follow up on, you know—the dinner for the homeless tomorrow night. That has to be the big event they've been planning for, the Summoning."

"Bev might be dead by then. Or worse."

"I don't think so. If they were going to kill her out of hand, they could have done that back at the house."

"Why would they keep her alive?"

I thought of Jennifer Blackley's fate but didn't remind her of that. "We're probably the only real threat left to them. They'll want to keep her as a lever, at least until the Summoning is over."

"I don't feel very threatening just now," she objected, but her voice sounded stronger. "Although I'd love to have the chance. So what's next?"

"Sleep, I think. Tomorrow's the big day. If we're going to crash the party, we'll need to disguise ourselves somehow. They'll have people watching for us."

We were very close to the motel and I flicked the turn signals.

"No, keep going."

I hadn't seen anything, but I did as I was told. "What's up?"

"Just another couple of blocks. I thought I noticed one earlier today." And so it was that we spent a nervous few minutes sorting through a Salvation Army pickup box before stealing a few additions to our wardrobes.

Alyson was up before me, to my astonishment, and had our stolen garments spread out over the second bed. We'd chosen the most disreputable ones we could identify in the darkness, and Alyson had enhanced them by adding a few tears and some strategically placed dirt stains.

"I think that shirt's going to be a little bit big for me." I picked it up and matched it against my body. "The sleeves are way too long and the shoulders are too wide."

"Perfect. They'll look like you stole them from the Salvation Army."

"I don't suppose you saw anything else in your dreams last night."

"I didn't see Bev." There was an awkward silence and I knew she was holding something back. "Our minds touched, but it was too dark to identify anything. But I felt something. Hunger, an incredibly insatiable hunger, and not for food exactly, but for something else." She shivered a little and turned back to the clothing, using the sole of one of my shoes to add a dirty smear to the frayed jeans she'd chosen for herself.

"There's a diner across the street. How about breakfast?"

I thought she was going to refuse, but after a brief hesitation she tucked our costumes away in a drawer. A few minutes later she was devouring a pretty hefty breakfast, and the food seemed to revive her spirits as well.

"What time do we need to be there?"

"The circular says things start at seven P.M., but I figure we should show up earlier and check things out."

"Why don't we drive by now?"

It seemed pointless to me, but I couldn't think of anything else to do, and I suspected we'd both feel better if we were doing something other than just sitting around the motel room waiting for time to pass. We paid the check and took Route 95 back to Providence.

The city seemed unnaturally quiet, but that was probably our imaginations at work. I threaded my way through the narrow streets and cruised past the auditorium as slowly as I dared without looking suspicious. There was almost no traffic, vehicular or pedestrian. A right turn took us parallel to the building, and that's when we started to see the circulars posted on the walls, telephone poles, trash receptacles, and elsewhere, all advertising the gathering of the homeless and disadvantaged that evening. There was no picture of Joseph Crawley, but I felt a growing certainty that this would be the climax of our struggle. One way or another, things would change dramatically within the next few hours.

Another right turn took us past the front of the building. There were more pedestrians here, a few early shoppers, a man in an unseasonal overcoat who stared motionlessly at one of the posters, an aging black man who walked with a pronounced limp, and a middle-aged man dressed in corduroy who stood with folded arms near the auditorium entrance, calmly watching those who passed.

"Any ideas?" I felt a frustrating sense of powerlessness. We had no evidence to take to the authorities, and there seemed to be nothing we could do personally either.

"Pull over. Park someplace." Alyson swiveled her head to look back at the auditorium while I slowed and found an empty space at the curb.

"What's up? Did you see something?"

"No, not really. But I just have this feeling . . ."

I fed quarters into the parking meter and then we walked back the way we'd come, pausing to stare blindly into store windows so that we might be mistaken for shoppers. Personally I felt awkward and conspicuous and more nervous than

I'd been while we were running for our lives, perhaps because now I had time to think about what was happening. Breakfast was suddenly heavy in my stomach.

We passed the auditorium on the opposite side of the street, pretending to look at the musical instruments displayed at Tune Town, Inc. During one of my hopefully surreptitious glances across the street, I noticed a disreputably dressed man standing in front of the auditorium, making elaborate gestures with both hands. The man in corduroy was talking to him, but so softly we could barely hear his voice. We continued farther along the street, then crossed over higher up, working our way back with the same frustrating leisureliness. The gesticulating man had moved on, but Corduroy hadn't abandoned his station and was in fact speaking to two young women, one of whom seemed distinctly uncomfortable, although her companion was smiling and nodding her head.

"Down front or around back?" We were just across the side street from the auditorium block and needed to make a decision.

Alyson didn't hesitate for a second. "Straight ahead."

We were halfway across the street before I stiffened, grabbed Alyson by the arm, and forced her to follow me as I angled to the sidewalk beside the building and out of Corduroy's line of sight.

"What's going on?" There was a tremor of anger in Alyson's voice, but she kept it low and didn't resist.

"I know that man. Not his name, but he's from Crayport. One of Crawley's goons. He was part of the group of men who grabbed us in the cemetery."

Alyson shook her head and relaxed, following me more readily now. "I didn't recognize him. Do you think he saw us?"

"I don't know. Probably not. If he did, it's too late to worry about it now." At least we had further confirmation of a connection between Crayport and tonight's meeting.

We walked quickly around the back of the auditorium, then a further two blocks before cutting back to the main road and returning to our parked car. The city had changed dramatically since we'd arrived, and the streets and sidewalks were now filling rapidly. It took almost a full minute before I could pull into traffic, and while I was waiting Alyson stared back at the auditorium.

"He's walking away! Can we follow him?"

"Which way is he going?"

"Toward Johnson and Wales."

I swore under my breath. The exact opposite direction and we were on a one-way street. Typical of the way our luck had been running lately. I edged into traffic, turned right at the next intersection, then another right. The car ahead of me was inching along, either lost or looking for a parking space, and I pounded the wheel with the heel of my hand in frustration. Then the driver turned into a side street and I accelerated, covering three blocks quickly.

"I'm going to cut across. See if you can spot him while we're crossing."

The light was green, but I slowed anyway to give Alyson as much time as possible to find our quarry. A delivery truck behind us sounded his horn and I moved through the intersection.

"He's still headed south," Alyson informed me. "But he crossed to the opposite side of the street."

I took the next left meaning to cut right back, but the following cross street was blocked for sewer work and impassable. The one after that was a one-way, and beyond was the entrance ramp for the interstate. "We're screwed," I said angrily, then pulled over to the side of the road and killed the engine.

"There's no parking here."

"So we get a ticket. Let's go." I was already out of the car, and Alyson followed quickly. We half walked, half ran the block back to the main road, slowing as we reached the corner, trying to look casual again. At first we couldn't see Corduroy at all, but then a van pulled away just as he disappeared around the side of a building.

We shadowed him another three blocks and I felt painfully obvious throughout the process, although he never looked back and gave no indication that he knew we were there. Then he turned abruptly and entered a ruined building that had been partly demolished, ducking under the warning tape and ignoring the signs forbidding entry. He was out of sight by the time we reached the same spot.

"What do you think?" From where we stood I could see that most of the building was gone. The front wall, crumbling brick and decaying facade, was relatively intact, as was the wall abutting an adjacent building to our right. The rest of the structure, which ran all the way through the block, had been largely destroyed, except for the rear wall, which looked down over the highway. There were enormous piles of rubble strewn about the comparatively open interior—concrete, lumber, piping, old electrical conduits, and miscellaneous trash, including what appeared to be some ancient office furniture.

"Do you see him anywhere?" Alyson's whisper was tremulous and I suddenly realized that her fingers were pressed deeply into my arm.

"No, but I don't think he had time to reach the other side."

"There's something wrong here. I don't know what it is, but it doesn't feel right."

Ordinarily I'm not inclined to give much credence to precognition, but Alyson's tenuous mental link to the Children altered my feelings. On the other hand if we abandoned this lead, we were back to the waiting game.

"Let's be very careful, then." I ducked under the tape and Alyson followed, and a few seconds later we were inside what remained of the structure. Even in its diminished state the shell of the building held its own distinct atmosphere. Although the roof was gone, shadows lay thickly across the interior. The ground underfoot was treacherous, a layer of crumbled chalky concrete. We edged toward the right, staying close to the remaining wall, and spotted Corduroy almost immediately.

He was standing between two piles of rubble and his body was shivering as though he had St. Vitus's Dance. We froze where we were, afraid to approach more closely or even to retreat, since our footsteps were noisy and either action would be clearly audible. But he was paying no attention to us. Or more to the point, the creature that lived within his body was preoccupied with other considerations.

From several spots in the rubble things began to move. At first I thought they were more Passengers, but I was quickly disabused of that notion. They were rats, for the most part anyway. One scrawny cat also appeared from some hidden lair. There were about a dozen animals scattered through the debris, each advancing slowly—I thought reluctantly—toward the intruder. As they closed within two or three meters, Corduroy's gyrations became more violent and he raised his arms. From the fingertips, black fibrous claws extended themselves, growing steadily longer and waving through the air in an intricate dance that seemed random even though not once did any two intersect. I was almost used to this now, but Alyson shivered and moved closer to me.

The rats stood their ground, staring in apparent fascination at the ever more complex web of black fibers. With each passing second the Passengers' extrusions grew longer until they were within striking range. I almost called out a warning but held my silence at the last second, curious to see what would happen.

Then they struck.

It was a coordinated attack, the tip of each strand making contact with its intended prey simultaneously. Some of the latter had time to make a single startled outcry, but most remained silent as the strands fastened themselves to their bodies. What followed was almost indescribably horrible. Alyson turned away early on and I wanted to do the same, would have if I hadn't hoped to gain some advantage by learning more about our enemies. It was a wasted effort but left me more determined than ever to stop the Crawleys from achieving their goals.

The Passengers sucked the life out of them, cell by cell, and it started deep within their bodies and worked its way out. I'll spare you the details, but the captive animals literally turned themselves inside out in the process, and they appeared to remain alive almost to the very end. It was such over-the-top obscene grossness that I couldn't accept it as real, and that's probably why I managed to keep my breakfast down.

When it was all over Corduroy retraced his

steps and we were almost caught, just barely concealing ourselves behind another pile of rubble. We followed him back to his post in front of the auditorium, where he began greeting people once again. Alyson suggested that we were unlikely to gain anything further by watching him and I agreed, but I suspect both of us were dissuaded more by disgust than logic.

The good news was that we didn't get ticketed for illegal parking.

Chapter Seventeen

Neither of us said very much on the way to the motel, a new one where we took a room under a false name and ate a quick lunch at the diner next door. I don't know about Alyson, but I could barely taste mine, and I had trouble forcing it down. My stomach was queasy and it wasn't just nerves. Alyson managed to nap for part of the afternoon. I pretended to do the same, though I couldn't lie still for more than a few minutes at a stretch and finally abandoned the pretense because all I was doing was disturbing Alyson. I retrieved a couple of paperbacks from the trunk of the car and managed to read for a while but spent most of the afternoon running over various scenarios in my head. Things I should have done but hadn't, things I might still do, and their consequences. Jennifer and Sean still haunted me, two failures about which I could do nothing.

I intended to reverse that trend.

Alyson tossed and turned sporadically in her sleep, finally waking around four o'clock. She dredged additional vague images from her dreams that might have been from the Children, but apparently the connection was growing more tenuous with the passage of time.

We made a quick trip to the diner for another unsatisfying and untasted meal, then returned to the room to don our ill-fitting and badly worn disguises. I hadn't shaved in a couple of days and my hair should have been cut at least two weeks earlier. It didn't take much effort to turn it into an unruly mop. Dressed, I examined myself critically in a mirror and decided it also wouldn't take much effort to see through the disguise if someone was actually looking for me, but Alyson assured me that I only vaguely resembled my former self. "You look a lot older than you did a week ago."

I felt a lot older.

For her part, Alyson wrapped her hair in a stained scarf, scrubbed off all her makeup, and donned a baggy blouse that she filled out with some improvised padding. A pair of cheap sunglasses completed the transformation, which I thought far more effective than my own. She was decidedly unattractive for the first time since we'd met. We debated the wisdom of entering the building separately but finally decided that it was worth the risk to remain together. If either of us was identified the alarm would be raised, so there was really nothing to be gained by splitting up.

Just before six o'clock we parked on a remote side street half a mile from the auditorium and started walking casually downtown. I still had the handgun with five rounds in the clip, but otherwise we were armed only with our wits. What few of them hadn't been frightened out of us.

There were more people on the streets than I was accustomed to seeing, and judging by the number who were shabbily dressed, tonight's assembly might well draw a large crowd. Like most cities, Providence suffers from selective blindness. If we don't actually have to step over the homeless people sleeping on heating grates, if we don't read about dead bodies being discovered in Dumpsters, if we're not accosted by people begging for change on every corner, we assume that homelessness is not a problem where we live. Oh, there might be a few mentally retarded people sleeping in the open, or even an occasional bureaucratic oversight resulting in one small injustice or another, but basically everyone's all right and we shouldn't trouble ourselves with problems that aren't really serious. Yeah, right.

There were hundreds of occasional bureaucratic mistakes and small oversights on the streets of Providence that night, perhaps thousands. You could see it in their clothing, in the way they walked, in the way they refused to raise their eyes from the ground. But most of all you could tell that this was a different mix of people because of the sound. There was almost no conversation, even when the sidewalks became quite congested. Sometimes people walked together, though most seemed to be alone, but even those with companions spoke little if at all. And all of us were moving toward the same destination.

Though not for the same reason.

The area directly surrounding the auditorium was predictably heavily congested. That suited our purposes just fine, as we intended to enter only when the influx was at its greatest, to minimize the chance of being identified by one of the Crawley minions. I entertained no doubt at all that they'd be watching for us. Joseph Crawley struck me as an egotist, a megalomaniac in fact, and he would be utterly convinced of his own superiority. He'd dismiss us as no more than minor irritations, convinced that his cause would triumph. But I was equally certain that he would not allow his confidence to prevent him from taking elementary precautions, if for no other reason than that he would love to capture us and exact specific revenge for the trouble we had caused. Moreover, I suspected that his son Edward handled routine matters, and Edward was not nearly as convinced of their invulnerability as was his father.

I didn't think they'd openly kill us if we were

spotted, but they might well throw us out, or more likely provide some unwelcome company during the proceedings, at least until Crawley managed to open a gateway to the other realm, or whatever it was they planned to do. If things got that far, I suspected it wouldn't matter any longer whether we were spotted. I closed my hand around the revolver and hoped it wasn't shaking.

A large portion of the crowd consisted of obviously homeless people with worn, mismatched, and out-of-season clothing adorning worn, discouraged, and out-of-fashion people. There were others as well, curiosity seekers, fervent religious types hoping for a rousing revival meeting, even a handful of teenagers who seemed to have the Crawleys confused with rock stars. There was some conversation but less than you'd expect in a crowd this size, and almost no pushing and shoving. Alyson and I followed an indirect route toward the main doors, timing things so that we could blend in with a fairly large group as they passed through the central set of archways. A man stood off to our left, a stranger, but his demeanor convinced me he was one of Crawley's people. There was probably another to the right, but I couldn't see through the press of people.

Then we were inside, and the foyer was dark enough that it took a few seconds for my eyes to adjust. A woman stood halfway up the short flight of steps, gesturing for people to split into two streams, one to each side, gesturing with her two frog-fingered hands. I turned my head away and bent as though to talk to Alyson, hopefully concealing both of our faces until we had passed. We took the right fork, followed the crowd down the short walkway and into the main auditorium.

I'd spent a couple of summers working as a stagehand in the building so I knew it pretty well, but I was still disoriented when I looked around. The entire front stage was hidden from view by large curtains that had been strung overhead, not just the traditional ones but several new sets. The orchestra pit was draped and concealed as well, and so were all but one of the front balconies, although the rear ones were open. The farthest front on the right side had been spruced up with elaborate garlands and draping and had been fitted with a platform and a large podium so that from its upper level a speaker would be at the highest point in the entire auditorium. Even those in the highest balconies facing it would have to look up to see the performance. Although there were no crosses or other overt religious symbols, it was clearly designed to look like a pulpit.

Alyson and I edged out of the main traffic stream. "Any ideas?" I whispered.

She shook her head. "I can't see anything from here. Those curtains hide everything."

The same thought occurred to both of us and we craned our heads up to the seats above us. The stairs were nearby, but so far no one was making use of them. "Wait until the crowd starts up. We don't want to be too conspicuous." A good thought, not that it mattered in the long run.

The audience continued to file in without the usual buzz of conversation, and the constant shuffling of feet and squeaking of seat cushions masked the words of the few who did speak. After about ten minutes progress slowed, and a few at the back of the line headed for the stairs. As soon as they did so, Alyson and I followed. At the top we moved directly to the front row and leaned forward, craning to see those portions of the auditorium that had been concealed from ground level. Unfortunately we were little better off than we'd been before.

"We have to find a way to get backstage," I told her.

"How are we going to do that?"

I wasn't sure, but I was dredging through my memory, trying to remember the building's floor plan, when a too familiar voice made the exercise unnecessary.

"Well, if it isn't my dear friends Paul and Alyson. How nice of you to show up for our little gathering. But why the elaborate disguises?"

It was Edward Crawley and three frog-fingered Crayporters, and they pressed close so that we were trapped against the railing. Alyson glanced quickly over the side but I didn't bother. We would probably survive the jump, but we wouldn't be doing much walking after we landed.

"We weren't sure we'd be welcome after what

happened the last time," I responded weakly, hoping to get a rise out of him.

For a second I thought I'd succeeded. His forehead creased slightly and he hesitated just a bit too long before answering. But then he smiled and at least pretended to relax. "All is forgiven. After today all of the mistakes and misunderstandings of the past will be irrelevant. But let's not talk about the past right now, and by all means let me arrange for you to have better seats. You've seen so much, it would be a shame if you missed the climax."

I thought about resisting, but it didn't seem likely to accomplish much. They'd either overwhelm us, after which we'd be no better off, or we'd be forced to flee from the building, which would leave us helpless to affect the outcome. At least in their company we'd get closer to the center of things.

They stayed close as we descended the stairs, brushing through the moderately heavy group ascending from the now nearly filled main floor. During the descent one of the Crayporters forced me briefly against the side rail and deftly extracted the revolver from my pocket, handing it to Edward, who managed to make it disappear very efficiently. "I don't think you'll be needing that," he told me quietly.

The auditorium's geography had come back to me now, so I stayed oriented when we reached the lobby and passed through an EMPLOYEES ONLY door into a serviceway that ran back past the main floor toward the stage. We were closely watched and flanked at all times, but I was so thoroughly discouraged I'm not sure I'd have run even if an opening had offered itself. We reached a set of rough wooden steps that brought us up to stage level, but we were surrounded by the drapery and could see nothing except a narrow wedge of audience. Then we were mounting a spiral wrought-iron staircase that ended at the corridor that fed the private balconies. It reminded me of the one in the hidden cavern under Crayport Harbor, and I remembered once again that these people were powerful but could be defeated. As long as we remained alive there was still a chance we could disrupt their plans. Heartened, I began to pay more attention, and noticed that part of this corridor was blocked to prevent the audience from reaching this point, so we were alone as we climbed to the front balcony, directly under the elevated pulpit.

Joseph Crawley was standing there, a large antique book held in the crook of one arm. It was the one I'd seen back at his house, the *Necronomicon*. "So? They showed up after all. You were right this time, Edward."

The younger Crawley almost beamed. "I told you they wouldn't let it go once we had the girl."

"Ah, yes, the sister." He glanced toward the main stage distractedly. "Pointless, of course, but understandable."

"Where is Beverly?" Alyson took a half step toward Joseph, and one of the Crayporters caught hold of her arm. She winced, and I wondered if a Passenger had just nipped her; but perhaps not, because she retained her composure. "What have you done with her?"

"Don't fret, child. She hasn't been harmed. In fact she's occupying something of a place of honor." He smiled then, and it was the most loathesome expression I think I've ever seen. I don't know about Alyson, but I physically recoiled from him, sensing an evil, malevolent presence just as heartless and inhuman as that thing in the pit in the cavern in Crayport. Joseph turned to his son. "See that they have good seats, won't you, Edward? After all their efforts it would hardly be fair if they missed the climax."

And then he turned and began climbing to the pulpit, followed by two of the Crayporters.

"There's seating in front," Edward told us. "Why don't you make yourselves comfortable?" I turned in his direction and saw my revolver in his hand. The third Crayporter stood to one side, face expressionless, frog-fingered hands resting at his sides.

There were normally eight seats in the balcony, but four of them had been removed to accommodate the braces for the elevated staging. We took the center two of those remaining, and I took my first good look at the setting for Crawley's version of Armageddon.

The first thing I noticed was the audience. Most of the seats were filled now, with only an occasional figure moving in the aisle. But despite the nearly full house there was very little sound. I even spotted the group of teenagers we'd noticed on the way in, and they were sitting quietly in the front row. Then my eyes traveled back to the orchestra pit, concealed from the audience but perfectly visible from where we sat.

A ramp had been constructed from the lip of the pit to a point almost directly under us. At the far end, in the darkness where oboes and violins and trombones were normally concealed, there was now a deeper, richer lack of light, blackness filled with turbulence, a movement that was of space and time itself rather than matter, the confluence of chaos, the gateway to another world. The darkness was pregnant with possibility, and I knew that something waited there, waited to be summoned by its dark prophet, now climbing to a vantage point above us.

My eyes were caught by the swirling nothingness and I might have remained enraptured if Alyson hadn't cried out suddenly. "Beverly!"

She was so close that the side of the balcony had concealed her from me. Manacles had been attached to the near end of the ramp and she knelt there, nude, ankles and wrists secured by knotted cords. I caught hold of Alyson's arm because she seemed poised to leap down to the rescue.

"Your sister is about to be granted a great honor, Miss Branford. She will become one with the Children." Edward lacked the pious tones of his father and came across as merely snide.

The expression Alyson turned on him was one I hope never to see again. He actually flinched, then turned away. "You've been a source of considerable inconvenience to us, Canfort, but your interference is at an end. After tonight we'll be too powerful to oppose. My father's affinity with the Old Ones grows stronger with each Summoning. In a few minutes the gateway will open again and a Child shall come forth, and with its passage the bridge to our world will be secure. This time the cattle"—he gestured toward the audience—"will not wake from their trance but will remain locked in place, and the door will remain ajar."

I felt Alyson's muscles tense and, fearing that she planned a suicidal attack, I tightened my grip on her arm. "Why, Crawley? Why place yourself in service to these monsters?"

"Monsters?" He seemed actually offended. "You still don't understand, do you? These are the gods themselves, the ancient ones who lifted humankind above the animals. And in similar fashion They choose the best, the loyal, the most deserving from among us. We who serve Them will be raised and empowered once They return to Their rightful place. This world will have its rightful rulers restored."

"What kind of gods destroy children?" I would have gone on, but the lights dropped and the already quiet audience became even more attentive. A spotlight came on and focused somewhere above us, presumably upon the pulpit, and after a few seconds I heard the sonorous voice of Joseph Crawley, augmented by a state-of-the-art sound system.

"Welcome, my people. Welcome to the birth of a new age. I have come to lead you out of the darkness of ignorance and despair and into the light of a new reality. Within these walls all of us are of equal value. No one here is rich or poor, lucky or unlucky, handsome or ugly." He went on in that vein for several minutes, reassuring and confident words that were totally lacking in content. At first I was puzzled, because the speech seemed not only dissociated from what was actually happening but so bland that I expected the audience to be shifting restlessly. Instead they were completely silent and immobile, as though frozen in place. That's when I began to feel desperation on top of my fright, because I realized that this was the effect Crawley sought. His soothing tones were designed to lull his listeners into a suggestive state of mind.

I turned to Edward and was surprised to find him staring at us. "You see? They're already in his power. Do you really think that sheep like that"— he gestured broadly toward the audience again— "are worthy of consideration?" He moved to the railing, almost within reach, but the revolver was carefully pointed in our general direction. "Look out there and see the future."

Almost involuntarily we did look, and I saw something terribly familiar. A swarming mass of chaotic colors had formed within the orchestra pit. It was the same thing I had seen in the cavern back in Crayport, but it looked more intense now; the roiling nothingness exuded an aura of lecherous anticipation. I caught glimpses of a shape taking form within the blackness and then remembered Beverly, tethered below us.

She was using her teeth to gnaw at the ropes that held her left wrist.

Alyson turned in my direction, and it was almost as if I could read her thoughts. "I know," I whispered. We had to do something, even if it meant our deaths. The Crawleys certainly had no intention of letting us live, so we might as well make an effort to interfere with the ceremony. But what to do? There was so little time, and even less opportunity. And above us, Joseph Crawley continued his monotonous quasi-sermon, the words starting to blur and change now as he interjected what seemed to be foreign terms, or just nonsense. Words like *phtagn* and *thulhoo* and others even less pronounceable. It was almost like a litany, and I realized he must be reading from the *Necronomicon*.

A Child was forming at the far end of the runway.

The silent Crayporter stepped forward, leaning out over the railing. Crawley said something under his breath and the man nodded, then exited the booth, disappearing from sight. My spirits lifted, but so did Edward's arm, and now his weapon was pointed directly at my face. "Don't get any ideas. My father would prefer to deal with

311

you at some length after the Summoning, but he won't be greatly disappointed if I am forced to deprive him of that pleasure."

He was close enough that if Alyson and I co-ordinated our attack, he would probably only be able to shoot one of us. Edward was ruggedly built; I might be able to best him in a fight if he shot Alyson, but I doubted she'd stand a chance if I took the bullet, and the barrel was pointed directly at my face. Frustration was a physical force within my body now, a force that grew even more powerful when I glanced back toward the stage.

The Child had now fully emerged. Lacking a human tenant, it was more amorphous than the ones we had encountered beneath the ware-house. It humped forward in an awkward but no less purposeful fashion. Beverly was still working on the first wrist rope, but even if she managed to free her hand in the next few seconds it was unlikely she could remove the others before it reached her. And even if she did, the man who had just left us was now standing within a fold of the curtain a few meters from where she strug-gled, prepared to intervene if necessary.

I glanced out over the audience again, hoping against hope that there would be some sign that Crawley's mesmeric powers were failing, but I was largely disappointed. Almost without excep-tion the assembly remained motionless, com-pletely caught up in a stream of words that contained progressively less coherent English.

Here and there I saw a head bobbing, or an expression of puzzlement or inattention, but by and large the audience was sitting in the palm of his hand, unaware that the fingers were poised to close into a crushing fist.

Alyson drew in her breath sharply and I turned back. The Child was halfway down the ramp now. Beverly had turned to face the creature but still chewed at the ropes binding her. Even as I watched they parted and her right arm was free. Edward must have been watching as well because he turned and shouted down to the motionless Crayporter.

That's when I attacked.

I almost succeeded. By the time he realized the danger I was too close for him to fire at me. He swept his arm around anyway, and I was unable to block the blow, although I deflected it enough that I remained conscious when the pistol smashed into the side of my head. Conscious but stunned. I fell back against one of the seats, struggling to ignore the pain. Enraged, Edward raised his arm to strike again, but before the blow could fall, Alyson took two quick steps forward and kicked him squarely in the groin.

The expression on his face would have been comical under other circumstances. The revolver dropped to the floor as he staggered back against the railing, doubled over and gasping for breath. His head started to come up, and Alyson pivoted on one leg and kicked out with the other. The sole of her foot connected with his chin and he seemed to leap back across the railing. He just managed to avoid falling, tried to pull himself back, and Alyson rushed in his direction. I shook off the blackness that threatened to overwhelm me and began looking for the fallen weapon, found it under the nearest of the seats. Someone screamed behind me—not Alyson—and I stood up, armed, looking for a target, just in time to see Alyson free herself from Edward's grasp and push him the rest of the way over the railing.

The fall didn't kill him. He lay sprawled on the runway, close enough to Beverly that she could have touched him. One leg was folded back under his body, obviously broken, and there was quite a bit of blood, but his eyes were open and he moved one arm feebly, as though trying to signal for help. Towering over them both was the Child, which hesitated, trying to choose between the two potential victims. Both of Beverly's arms were free now, and she pivoted as far away as the bonds on her ankles would allow.

"Oh, God!" Alyson pointed to the silent Crayporter, who had started toward the injured man.

I didn't even have to think about it. I raised the revolver and fired twice. At least one of the rounds struck the man in the head, because I saw the top of his skull burst open as the bullet exited. But he didn't drop. Instead he staggered forward with his arms jerking spasmodically, and thin black wires began to emerge from his shattered head and wave around in the air.

Alyson climbed over the railing, and after a

second's hesitation I followed. Heavy curtains hung from the underside of the balcony. We caught hold of these and slid down, burning the palms of our hands in the process but arriving in better condition than had Edward Crawley. I touched the floor as the Child made its decision.

Crawley screamed just before the creature's substance flowed over his broken body. The sudden, awful silence when that sound ended was chilling. Joseph Crawley's powerful, measured cadence stopped at the very same moment, plunging the auditorium into near total silence. As Alyson helped Beverly remove the ropes from her ankles I looked up and saw him staring down at us, his rage visible even from this distance. Without making a conscious decision I raised the revolver and fired at him, twice, apparently with no effect other than to frighten him into drawing back out of sight.

Behind us the half-formed Child began to dissolve around the edges, as though the Summoning had not quite completed. There was a growing murmuring from the audience as they began to waken from Crawley's trance. The wounded Crayporter exploded in a flurry of black cables that lashed the air, the floor, and the side of the crippled Child. Its translucent flesh rose to the attack, but even I could tell it was fading fast. Within its depths the mangled form of Edward Crawley was horribly distorted as the Child attempted to match his skeleton to its mass, and his still living face was stretched into a mask of agony. For the first second or two I confess that I felt good about that. I remembered all the deaths for which he was at least collaterally responsible, including young Jennifer, who had been taken by a Child herself, and it seemed only justice that he share their fate. But then my revulsion for these creatures and the horrible fate of their victims overcame everything and I raised the weapon and fired two shots directly at that distorted face. The Child collapsed almost immediately.

I glanced at Alyson, who stood with her arms around Beverly. "Take care of her. I'm going after Crawley." I raised the revolver meaningfully. Then I was gone, searching for the base of the stairway.

Chapter Eighteen

At the first landing I glanced back down toward the orchestra pit and was gratified to see that the crawling chaos was fading back to normality. There was also growing unrest within the audience, which was collectively awakening from its trance state. A few people were already moving in the aisles, although they seemed disoriented. A few were shouting angrily; others cried quietly in their seats. At the next landing I almost literally ran into Joseph Crawley and two of his minions. The twosome launched themselves at me without waiting for orders and I fired into the face of the larger man. Then one or both of them crashed into me and we all went tumbling back down the staircase. I lost the revolver in the process, empty and therefore of no value to me, along with several patches of skin that were.

The man I had shot never got up when we hit the landing, but his body began jumping around as the Passenger tried to free itself. The second, smaller man rose into a crouch as I staggered to my feet, and I saw black fibers emerging from the tips of his frog fingers. Behind him, the elder Crawley disappeared through the doorway into the service corridor without even glancing in my direction. I thought about grappling with the Crayporter, but I remembered the sting of the Passenger's limbs and backed slowly down the stairs to the bottom level. He followed me, a youngish-looking man without much bulk; under ordinary circumstances I think even I could have physically overcome him. I reached the floor of the auditorium and risked a quick glance behind me. Alyson and Beverly were nowhere to be seen. A dripping, steaming mass of putrid flesh—the remains of the Child—lay in a nauseating pool of decay.

My opponent continued his slow advance and I had no choice but to retreat toward the orchestra pit. I glanced to either side, looking for something I could use as a weapon, but nothing suggested itself. There was evident turmoil beyond the curtain; I could hear more angry shouting and the rustle of feet. I was considering slipping under the curtain and running out into the audience when Alyson suddenly appeared behind the Crayporter, carrying a two-by-four. Her expression was grim but determined as she raised it high in the air and slammed it down against the back of the man's skull. He staggered forward, went to one knee, planted a hand on the ground, and began to rise almost immediately. Before he could do so I ran forward and drop kicked him right under the chin. I heard the loud snap as his neck broke but didn't wait around to watch the Passenger emerge.

"Where's Beverly?" I asked, but even as I spoke she emerged from the wings, now more or less dressed in an oversized sweatsuit that someone had obviously been wearing while painting sets.

"They went out through the rear exit." She gestured back the way she'd come. "The old man and two others."

"Come on," I said. "We have to catch him. If he gets away, we'll have it all to do over again." Alyson handed me her makeshift club and we were off and running.

Although we made our way as quickly as possible to the rear of the auditorium, we still wouldn't have been in time if the crowd hadn't begun to spill into the street. As it was, it was only Beverly's quick eye that spotted Crawley's unusual tall form on the far edge of the growing, unruly crowd, flanked by two smaller men. Tempers were short all around and a fight broke out very close to us. We tried to outflank the press of people, but it swelled so quickly that even though we could see Crawley, we couldn't get closer to him. Fortunately one of his companions was either too aggressive or pushed the wrong person, because he was quickly the center of a flurry of fists and feet that engulfed his mate as well as several bystanders. Crawley had no compunction about abandoning his allies, particularly when a swarm of police officers began moving in from both ends of the street. He disappeared into a narrow alley.

"We'll never find him now." Alyson sounded disconsolate, but I wasn't ready to give up yet. I knew where that alley led.

"Not necessarily. Come on. Hurry!"

We moved along the side of the building and away from the crowd. One of the advancing policemen took a half step in our direction but then stopped and nodded permission for us to leave. We sprinted for the next block and a half, then cut across a small quadrangle and into a side street. It was only later that I realized Beverly had been barefoot for the entire chase, but she showed no inclination to abandon the pursuit.

It started to rain about then, just a light spattering at first, quickly increasing to a punishing downpour. By the time we reached the next corner we were soaked to the skin. Once again luck lent a hand. Crawley had already passed through the intersection, but he'd apparently become disoriented because he reappeared on the opposite corner, then turned to his left, our right. Either he never looked in our direction or the rain gave us a cloak of anonymity, because he showed no particular haste, though he walked briskly and purposefully off toward the waterfront. I still carried the two-by-four, but even under these circumstances I seriously doubted I could consciously club the man to death. But what other choice did we have? I could just see us telling our story to the police, if we somehow managed to capture him. He'd roll his eyes and look fatherly and suggest that sometimes young people let their imaginations run away with them, even if not pharmaceutically enhanced, and it would be us, if anyone, who ended up in a prison cell.

Alyson seemed to sense my hesitation. "Let's follow him. Something will turn up." She caught hold of my free hand and squeezed it, and for a moment I felt that no challenge was too great.

My enthusiasm faded quickly during the next few minutes. Crawley led us several blocks through a relatively deserted section of the city. Only one car passed us before we reached the warehouse district. The rain increased in intensity and a rising wind sent stinging sheets of water down at us. Our clothes were matted to our bodies. Crawley must have been in the same state, but he never faltered. Twice we lost sight of our quarry and had to hasten to close up the distance. I had no idea where I was anymore. Even the lights on the taller buildings were completely hidden, and we could have reversed course completely and I wouldn't have known any better. It had started to thunder as well, and a few theatrically distinct spears of lightning split the sky, but the electrical show was over in less than five minutes, plunging us back into near total darkness.

We almost lost him a moment later. I hadn't even noticed the small alley until we were passing it, but Beverly's eyes must have been better than mine because she caught hold of my arm, rose on her toes, and shouted at me. "He went down there!"

I blinked and looked, and indeed there was a space between the adjacent buildings, but there was nothing moving in that direction except the rain. "Are you sure?"

"Yes." I must have looked dubious because she tugged on my arm. "I know this is where he went. I can feel it. They had me locked up near here, with those things. I can't explain how I know, but I'm sure of it."

There was such absolute certainty in her voice that I gave in. Truthfully, the pounding rain had beaten most of the energy out of me, and I was ready to follow the lead of anyone who was willing to assume that role. I glanced at Alyson, who hadn't been able to hear much of what we were saying, and she leaned over while Beverly repeated what she had already told me.

It was also Beverly who noticed the sliding door at the top of a short flight of steps. "In there."

She led the way, running up the stairs. I was suddenly terribly afraid that something would happen to her and I opened my mouth to say something, but I could think of nothing that was likely to convince her to step out of harm's way. When Alyson and I reached the top of the stairs she was leaning against the door, unable to move it until we added our weight to hers.

It slid back with a screech of protest, revealing a dimly lit interior.

We stepped inside cautiously, blinking to accustom ourselves to what was, comparatively speaking, a high level of illumination. Water streamed from our clothing and hair for several seconds after we were inside. There was a damp, fetid, rotten smell from within, but it wasn't strong. We were standing at the edge of an elevated platform that ran around the interior circumference of a large two-story storage area. There was an open-sided elevator to our left, a rickety staircase to our right, and ladders mounted on the walls. It reminded me unpleasantly of the cavern under Crawley's island and I shivered with the memory as much as from the sudden chill of my wet clothing. There was no sign of Crawley anywhere, but I was convinced that Beverly was right. This was where he'd come. The entire place reeked of the man and his unnatural companions.

"This way, I think." Beverly's voice seemed unusually loud now that we were out of the rain, but she spoke barely above a whisper. We followed as she led us to the right, marched single file along the elevated platform that ran the entire length of the building. There was a door in the far wall, and she opened it very carefully, only after glancing meaningfully at my wooden club.

The next room was set up similarly to the first but was smaller, and the far wall was largely glass windows, each consisting of many small panes. The windows looked out over the storm-tossed bay. A small, disreputable-looking wooden pier jutted out directly ahead of us, and two small boats rose and fell with each swell of the waves. We were halfway across the room when I saw something moving on the other side of the glass, something dark and indistinct that I thought might just be shimmering waves of rain until a brief ebbing of the torrent gave me a better view.

At least one of the sea creatures I'd encountered in Crayport was here in Narragansett Bay, riding the waves just offshore.

"Down here." Beverly was already a third of the way to ground level before I realized what she was up to, and Alyson was only a few steps behind her. The warehouse had been built into the side of an incline, so it was lower here than it had been back where we'd entered, below sea level in fact. A thick seawall had been erected to hold back the water. We reached the floor, and for the first time I noticed a trail of water drops across the cement floor. Obviously someone had been this way a minute or so before us, and that person could only have been Joseph Crawley.

We reached another door. "They're in here," said Beverly, and her voice had gone strange, almost unrecognizable, filled with such anger and loathing that it made me nervous.

Beyond the door might be Hell itself, or worse.

It was dark, so we didn't realize what we were walking into until it was too late to retreat. With Beverly in the lead, we negotiated our way across an uneven floor, around an enormous pile of rotting wooden crates. There were enough working overhead lights for us to find our way, but not enough to make the process entirely safe. We probably walked into trouble so easily because we were concentrating so intently on where we placed our feet.

I think I was the first to see the Children, two of them off to our left. I grabbed Alyson's arm and whispered Beverly's name sharply. She paused, glanced back at me, then followed my eyes and saw the creatures. One of them moved suddenly, not toward us but clearly positioning itself to cut off our escape.

"You people are becoming quite tiresome." I recognized Crawley's voice immediately, turned to see him emerge from behind a mound of rubbish. My hand tightened around the makeshift club, but I stood where I was. The third of the Children was right beside him, following like an obedient puppy in its owner's wake.

"You've lost, Crawley." I hoped I sounded as confident as I unfortunately did not feel. "Crayport is gone, the gateway is closed, Edward is dead, along with most of your followers. All that's left now is you and these three monstrosities."

His face had frozen when I mentioned his son, but it quickly relaxed. "All I've lost is a little time, Canfort. Their return is inevitable, and I am the chosen instrument of that return. You've seen what kind of power is working here. Do you really think you can change the outcome? Even I have the humility to accept that we're just footnotes to the destiny that is unfolding around us. If it doesn't happen here and now, it will be someplace else tomorrow. If it isn't my hand that turns the key, it will be some other's. The flood presses against the dam, Canfort, and the concrete is beginning to crumble."

"We can't let that happen. We'll stop you every time you try." Alyson spoke with such absolute conviction that even I was surprised. Crawley regarded her for a second or two with a raised eyebrow before responding.

"And how were you planning to stop me, young lady? Is Mr. Canfort going to bash in my brains with that length of wood he is clutching so tightly? Or are you planning to convince me of the error of my ways?"

"We'll take whatever steps are necessary." I found the courage to step forward, even though that brought me closer to the Child looming behind Crawley.

The situation changed so drastically in the next few seconds that I'm still not entirely certain of the sequence of events. Crawley's expression darkened and his hand disappeared inside his coat. I advanced another step and started to raise my club, but when I saw Crawley draw a handgun I knew I could not possibly close the gap quickly enough. I think I shouted a meaningless warning and I know I started to sprint across the remaining space. Crawley would have had more than enough time to fire at me if Beverly hadn't somehow managed to get close enough to distract him. In fact, he turned and swung his arm as she rushed forward. I heard rather than saw the pistol strike the side of her head and she fell limply.

At the time I thought she might be dead, and after the deaths of Jennifer and Sean I went nuts thinking we might have lost another. I charged in wildly but never reached him. The Children could move with surprising speed when they wanted to, and I slammed into a wall of hot, caustic jelly so hard that the piece of wood was torn from my grasp. It was a glancing blow, which probably saved my life. My feet went out from under me and I slid across the rough floor. Apparently Alyson managed to close with Crawley, even managed to knock the weapon out of his hand and scratch a bloody furrow across one cheek. But then he hit her in the face with his elbow and she fell to the floor, stunned and unaware of what was happening around her.

I hadn't realized how close the bond was between Crawley and the sea creatures. Although we didn't know it at the time, both of the kraken were in Narragansett Bay while we were battling in the abandoned warehouse. When we attacked

Crawley they sensed his anxiety and tried to come to his defense. Anything that happened to be in the way, which in this case included two piers, a pedestrian bridge, a power relay station, several trees, and a few assorted small outbuildings, was destroyed. Fortunately Crawley's lair was in a part of the city that was unpopulated at night; the only deaths during the next few seconds were two night watchmen who were crushed when a stack of crated electrical generators was overturned on them.

The entire left side of my body felt as though it was burning, but I forced myself to stand up. Crawley had turned away, searching for his weapon, and to stop him I would have to get past the Child. As if that weren't challenge enough, the other two were moving toward us, one of them tenanted by the waitress who'd served me back in Crayport. I felt a moment of helplessness and self-pity, but before I could actually accept defeat the situation changed again.

The outer wall of the warehouse exploded inward as one of the sea creatures slashed at it from the waterfront. The rain and wind rushed in furiously, and all of the loose debris on the floor quickly became airborne. Something hit me in the back of the head just hard enough to steal my balance and I fell to one knee. Crawley had been standing on an uneven surface and I saw him throw up his hands and fall back out of my line of sight. Even the Children seemed momentarily disconcerted. Two of them froze where they stood and the third, the one nearest me, appeared to be disoriented. It had been moving in my direction, but now it reversed course.

Something large and powerful pushed its way through the remnants of the exterior wall, the triangular tentacle of one of the sea creatures. It moved tentatively, brushing against the ceiling, apparently feeling its way along the inside of the building. I froze where I was, hoping not to be noticed. A quick glance showed me that Alyson was still dazed, sitting with her back against a more or less solid wooden crate. There was no sign of Beverly, or of Crawley for that matter, although a few seconds later he emerged from the rubble, looking considerably disheveled and bleeding slightly from a small wound on his forehead.

The nearest Child immediately started in his direction, but Crawley showed no alarm, confident in his ability to control the monstrosity. He was probably right about that, but I don't think he realized that neither the Children nor the sea creatures were particularly bright. Perhaps the Old Ones were super intelligent compared to mere humans; I don't know and I don't want to find out. But the lesser creatures over whom Crawley was able to assert his power were an entirely different story, no better than very bright animals. Just as a second massive tentacle began to probe inside the warehouse, the first somehow registered the Child's movement toward Crawley and apparently interpreted it as a threat.

Don D'Ammassa

The Child sensed its danger at the last possible second and swerved to one side, moving more quickly than I'd have thought possible, though not quickly enough. The tentacle slammed into the floor with such force that I found myself flying through the air. I slammed into a stack of rubbish and had the breath knocked out of me. When I picked myself up I recoiled at the sight of the Child, so close that I could almost reach out my hand and touch its side.

Then I saw what the sea creature had done to it. One third of its body had been smashed flat to the floor. The outer integument—I hesitate to call it skin—had ruptured, and the viscous, translucent internal fluids were bubbling out like hot lava. I didn't recognize the naked man who'd been embedded in this one, but it appeared that he'd lost his right leg and arm. The Child was clearly crippled and began to shrink visibly as its life stuff poured out through the wounds.

Crawley had recovered more quickly than I, and he had reasserted his influence. He stood on top of one of the crates, flanked by the two surviving Children, his arms thrust up into the air as he shouted a stream of unintelligible syllables just barely audible over the roaring of the wind. Above him, two enormous tentacles wove and danced wildly in the air, seemingly defying gravity, their movements synchronized with the patterns of Crawley's rhythmic speech. The gyrations were already beginning to diminish.

I knew that I had to act now. If I didn't, if I

waited until Crawley had reestablished full control, our last chance was lost and we would all die here in this decaying, rubble-strewn room. My first step betrayed me, however, because an intense pain shot up my leg and I cried out loudly enough that Crawley heard me.

"I'd admire your tenacity, Mr. Canfort, if it were somewhat more intelligently directed. The game is over, or at least your part in it."

"From where I'm standing it doesn't appear that you've done so well either." I managed to take a step forward with my good leg but winced as a shiver of pain raced through the bad one.

"No, my friend, no more talking. I'm not a movie villain and the cavalry is not on its way." He raised his head and began his weird chanting again.

I tried to ignore the pain and rush him, but my leg buckled when I put weight on it and I almost fell, saving myself only by grabbing hold of a stack of wooden pallets. One of the oversized tentacles was almost motionless now, and directly above me, and I had a flash of precognition, saw in my mind's eye how it would come crashing down to smash me into unrecognizable pulp. I turned back to Crawley, hoping desperately that something would happen, some intervention to save the day.

And it did.

His arms were raised again, but he turned to look at me, and his eyes betrayed a level of hatred that I hadn't seen before. And then he clenched his fists and I knew the end had come, and at that very moment there was a loud crack and the side of his head shattered. He stood for another second or two, staring with eyes that were already dead, and then he fell back out of sight.

I must have looked pretty stupid just then, because I didn't understand what had happened until Beverly emerged from behind another stack of pallets, holding in her hand the revolver that Crawley had dropped earlier. She stared at his body expressionlessly for a moment, then turned in my direction.

"Where's Alyson?" I gasped as another jolt of pain lanced through my leg. It didn't seem as severe. Either I was getting used to it or the nerves were overloaded.

She didn't get a chance to answer. Freed of their control, the sea creatures began to thrash around again. There was an enormous boom as a section of the ceiling flew apart, then collapsed inward, raining chunks of various sizes all around us. Beverly disappeared from sight and I was terrified that she was lying somewhere buried, but then she was at my side and Alyson was with her, looking stunned and filthy but at least in one piece. The torrential rain began to thunder down through the ruined ceiling. With the two of them to help, I managed to make progress toward the exit without more than an occasional whimper.

The building was coming down all around us. Beverly cried out once when a chunk of masonry struck her glancingly on the shoulder, but we kept moving. We were almost to the exit when the two remaining Children emerged from the murky shadows to block our retreat. Even without Crawley's control, or perhaps particularly without that influence, they were intent upon destroying us. The nearest was the waitress, the second a man I didn't recognize. Both of them were screaming soundlessly inside their fleshy prisons as they approached us.

At the very moment when I finally abandoned all hope of escaping alive, one of the flailing tentacles towered over us and crashed downward. The leading Child exploded like a balloon full of water, spraying its foul essence in every direction. The second suffered only a glancing blow, but the impact shattered the skull of the man inside, and bereft of that motivating force the Child altered course and we were able to slip past.

The rain was finally starting to ease up as we reached the street. Behind us, the abandoned warehouse imploded, one of the walls collapsing inward as the last of the roof gave way. The sea creatures belabored it for several minutes while we cowered in a doorway a block away, then retreated out to sea. Where they went after that is anyone's guess. Perhaps to wherever they'd come from originally.

The three of us had survived and Crawley was dead. That was all that mattered to me. That and the two people with me, who had suddenly become the most important parts of my life. I felt a sudden flood of emotion more intense than anything I had ever before experienced. I wanted to tell them both how I felt, that very moment, before the feeling had time to fade, but of course that's the point where the pain in my leg came back full force, and this time I quietly fainted away.

Epilogue

That's pretty much it.

My leg was badly broken and a nerve was pinched, but Alyson and Beverly managed to get all three of us to an emergency room somehow. There were enough other storm-related injuries that no one asked any awkward questions until after we'd had a chance to huddle and synchronize our stories.

For several weeks after the storm editorialists and politicians speculated about what really happened that night. There was some murky video-taped footage of dark, serpentine shapes hovering above the shoreline, but the most popular explanation appeared to be that a series of waterspouts had momentarily formed in Narragansett Bay, similar to the one that had helped destroy Crayport. Sure, there was no precedent for such a thing, but then the weather has been increasingly freakish the last few years, and no one could suggest a more plausible scenario. The waterfront damage was also blamed on the storm, which sprang up so suddenly that there had been no chance to raise the hurricane barrier.

For some reason we were never called to task for our various vehicular crimes. Apparently no one had managed to write down our license plate number, and I buried the "borrowed" plates where they weren't likely to be found. Even more fortunately, there were no witnesses to the deaths of Edward and Joseph Crawley. Six bodies were found in the aftermath of the riot at the auditorium, and several of them were never identified. Some of these may have been members of the unwitting audience, but I believe that most if not all were Crayporters who had been occupied by Passengers at the time of their death. Newscasters made fun of the scattered reports of monsters appearing during the assembly. The official explanation was that some variety of hallucinogen had been released, causing temporary stupor and delusions. The fact that the organization that had rented the auditorium turned out to be a shadow company whose owners could not be traced seemed to support this claim. Whether someone in authority knows more but is not talking is something I will never know, and I don't particularly care. There's been no indication of further disturbances in the eighteen months since, and while we can never be certain of these things, it at least seems unlikely that there is any imminent danger of another gateway being opened. If any of the Servants survived, they have not surfaced or troubled us since.

An abortive effort was made to rebuild Crayport, but the state abandoned the attempt when it became obvious that none of the handful of distant relatives who could be located were interested in relocating to the isolated town. Property values were so low that there was little interest in developing the area, and in fact the institute leased a fairly large parcel of coastland for a ridiculously low price and built an observation station. I've never been back, and the preliminary data suggests that the unusual conditions that brought me there in the first place no longer prevail, another sign that the threat to our world has faded.

Our lives changed nevertheless. Beverly appeared to shake off the effects of her ordeal almost immediately. She still has occasional nightmares, particularly on stormy nights, but otherwise she seems to have made a complete recovery. Alyson was more deeply affected, particularly for the first six months. Her nerves were continually on edge, she had trouble sleeping, and random events or sights that reminded her of our battle with the Crawleys would frighten or depress her. I suggested that she seek medical attention, but she pointed out the likely result if she told a therapist what was actually troubling her. I'm still working for the institute and dodging occasional questions from Jane about what really happened that week, but Alyson has developed an aversion to anything involving the ocean, and she now works in the laboratory of a chemical plant in Cumberland.

The wedding was just a few weeks ago, and we're both very happy. Alyson was in great spirits and I am hopeful that she has finally left the nightmares and other invisible scars behind her. She even caught the bouquet at the reception.

Oh, I forgot to mention that I didn't marry Alyson. We stayed together for almost a year after that terrible night but ultimately realized that we were very good friends but nothing more than that. No, it was Beverly whom I married, and it's probably the smartest thing I've ever done.

FOUR ORIGINAL NOVELLAS BY
BENTLEY LITTLE
DOUGLAS CLEGG
CHRISTOPHER GOLDEN
TOM PICCIRILLI
FOUR DARK NIGHTS

The most horrifying things take place at night, when the moon rises and darkness descends, when fear takes control and terror grips the heart. The four original novellas in this hardcover collection each take place during one chilling night, a night of shadows, a night of mystery—a night of horror. Each is a blood-curdling vision of what waits in the darkness, told by one of horror's modern masters. But as the sun sets and night falls, prepare yourself. Dawn will be a long time coming, and you may not live to see it!

THE HOUR BEFORE DARK

DOUGLAS CLEGG

As children, they played the Dark Game.

When Nemo Raglan's father is murdered in one of the most vicious killings of recent years, Nemo must return to the New England island he thought he had escaped for good and the shadowy farmhouse called Hawthorn. But this murder was no crime of human ferocity. What butchered Nemo's father may in fact be something far more terrifying— something Nemo and his siblings have known since childhood.

"Here comes a candle to light you to bed . . .
And here comes a chopper to chop off your head."

—A SPECIAL HARDCOVER EDITION!—

THE INFINITE
DOUGLAS CLEGG

Harrow is haunted, they say. The mansion is a place of tragedy and nightmares, evil and insanity. First it was a madman's fortress; then it became a school. Now it lies empty. An obsessed woman named Ivy Martin wants to bring the house back to life. And Jack Fleetwood, a ghost hunter, wants to find out what lurks within Harrow. Together they assemble the people who they believe can pierce the mansion's shadows.

A group of strangers, with varying motives and abilities, gather at the house called Harrow in the Hudson Valley to reach another world that exists within the house. . . . A world of wonders . . . A world of desires . . . A world of nightmares.

GERARD HOUARNER
ROAD TO HELL

Max is a man. An assassin, to be exact. But within him lurks the Beast, an unholy demon that drives Max to kill—and to commit acts even more hideous. Throughout the years, the Beast has taught Max well, and Max has become quite proficient in his chosen field. He is an assassin unlike any other. To put it mildly.

But now Max has a son, an unnatural offspring named Angel. Through Angel, the spirits of Max's former victims see a way to make Max suffer, to make him pay for his monstrous crimes. And while Angel battles his father's demons, Max himself must try to escape from the government agents intent on capturing him—dead or alive.

THE BIRDS
AND
THE BEES
SÈPHERA GIRÓN

We barely notice them, though they are all around us, flying overhead, singing . . . or just watching. But lately Gabrielle has been noticing the birds. Especially the mysterious black birds that seem to call to her. They stare at her with their soulless black eyes. Soon incidents with birds begin to appear on the news. People are getting hurt. Then Gabrielle notices that bees, too, are becoming more dangerous. . . .

Birds, bees, hornets, wasps . . . The city is under siege. Death hovers in the sky, then swoops down on the unsuspecting in a swarm. How can mankind fight an enemy that numbers in the billions? Could Gabrielle somehow hold the key?

NIGHT
THE

CLASS
TOM PICCIRILLI

The college winter break is over, and Cal Prentiss faces yet another semester of boring classes. But Cal's boredom is shattered when he discovers evidence of an unspeakable murder that occurred in his dorm room over the break. Obsessed with finding the truth about this gruesome crime, Cal travels further and further down the twisting halls of a university suddenly gone mad. As he gets closer to the heart of the mystery, Cal is surrounded by the supernatural and the grotesque—like the blood that appears on his hands whenever someone close to him dies.
